Some Dogs Do

Jez Alborough

WALKER BOOKS
AND SUBSIDIARIES
LONDON · BOSTON · SYDNEY · AUCKLAND

When Sid set off for school one day,

a happy feeling came his way.

It filled him up so much he found

his paws just lifted off the ground.

Without a how,
without a why,

Sid fell up
towards the sky.

Through swirling puffs of cloud he twirled
above a tiny toy-town world,

in the land
of sun and moon,

like a doggy-shaped
balloon.

At school Sid asked his best friend Ben,
"Did you see me fly just then?"

"Don't be daft," came Ben's reply.
"You're a dog, and *dogs don't fly.*"

"But *I did,*" said Sid.
"*I did ... I did.*"

In the classroom
Sid said, "Hey! Guess what!
I flew to school today!"

His classmates giggled, yelped and yowled.
"Dogs don't fly to school!" they howled.
"But *I did*," said Sid. "*I did*."

Miss Mare the teacher shook her head.
"Now Sid, you shouldn't lie," she said.

"All dogs walk and jump and run,
but *dogs don't fly* — it can't be done."

"But I did," said Sid.

Gus said, "Right! If you can fly,
come outside ... let's see you try!"

Sid's happiness had gone by then.
He tried to get it back again.

He thought about   the clouds up high

and then he jumped towards the sky.

"You see, you're just a dog," said Gus,
"with paws for walking just like us.

That will teach you not to lie.
Now you know that *dogs don't fly.*"

When Sid walked home from school that day,

it seemed a long and lonely way.

And once at home with Mum and Dad,
deep inside he still felt bad.

He did the things he always did,
but something wasn't right with Sid.

His dad came out and asked, "What's up? You seem unhappy, little pup."

Sid sat staring at the sky,
and all he said was, "Dogs don't fly."

Sid's dad slowly raised his head.
"I know a secret, Sid," he said.
"Could you keep it safe inside?"

"What's the secret?"
Sid replied.

He turned around
and then ...
he knew...

Now you know

the secret too!

Sid's happy eyes were open wide.

"I knew it ... DOGS DO FLY!" he cried.

Sid's dad said, "Come, fly then, Sid,"

and that's exactly what Sid did.

Do dogs fly? Is it true?

Some dogs don't, and some dogs do.

Some Dogs Do

for
David

First published 2003 by Walker Books Ltd
87 Vauxhall Walk, London SE11 5HJ

This edition published 2004

20 19 18 17 16 15 14 13

© 2003 Jez Alborough

The right of Jez Alborough to be identified as author/illustrator of this work has
been asserted by him in accordance with the Copyright, Designs and Patents Act 1988

This book has been typeset in Providence Sans Bold Educational

Printed in China

British Library Cataloguing in Publication Data: a catalogue
record for this book is available from the British Library

ISBN 978-1-84428-457-3

www.walker.co.uk

ACKNOWLEDGEMENTS

THE AUTHOR ACKNOWLEDGES THE FOLLOWING CORPORATIONS, MANUFACTURERS, PRODUCTS AND
REGISTERED TRADEMARKS:

Alta Vista
AMD
America Online
Archie
CompuServe
CuteFTP
CYRIX
Digital Equipment Corporation
Excite
Gopher
Hot Bot
IBM
Lycos
Media One Corporation
Microsoft Corporation
Mosaic
Netcom
Netscape Communications
PC Magazine
RAND
Telnet
Usenet
Washington Post
Web Crawler
Windows
Wired Magazine
WordPerfect
WS Gopher
Yahoo

COPYRIGHT NOTICE

TABLE OF CONTENTS

Introduction

The Internet and Change

The Internet has transformed the way many professional activities are conducted. Once considered the province of computer geeks and teenage game players, the Internet is now a dominant force in commerce, government, academics and research. With the advent of the World Wide Web (the portion of the Internet capable of sending and receiving multimedia data), the Internet is considered by many to be a standard business tool.

Indeed, the Web has grown so quickly that many have been caught "asleep at the wheel." Internet bookstores are now the primary method of selling books in several companies. This change occurred while many booksellers were unaware of the Web's potential or dismissed it as an insignificant fad. Traditional catalogue sales of goods and services are now in danger of being overtaken by Web sales. Many major newspapers find that their websites receive many more "hits" and are relatively more profitable than their traditional newspapers. As of January 1999, in excess of 60 percent of adult Americans had an e-mail address. This number is expected to reach 95 percent by 2005. Those who have dismissed the Internet and the Web as not being relevant have done so at their peril.

It is particularly important for the social sciences to take heed of the extent to which the Web is transforming government and social systems. Currently every state government, most major federal agencies, and the majority of all major municipalities in the United States and Canada maintain websites. The great majority of these websites serve as useful administrative tools, not only as advertising vehicles. Here are some examples. The U.S. Internal Revenue Service allows taxpayers to download nearly all IRS forms, as well as filing tax information electronically via personal computers. The Commonwealth of Massachusetts' website allows visitors to search its compiled laws in their entirety, as well as search all active legislation in the current legislative session. The City of Vancouver allows residents to access criminal activity by neighborhood and contact police officials through web forms and e-mail. Government agencies such as the U.S. Census Bureau and the U.S. Department of Justice's Bureau of Justice Statistics have made their databases available online at little or no cost. Many governments and businesses have turned to e-mail and Intranets as their primary mode of internal communication and document transmittal.

While many in academia recognize the sea change occurring as a result of the advent of the Web, there is a concern that many colleagues are being left behind. Without significant and detailed analysis of the Web's impact on social systems and by not using the Web as a legitimate research resource, academia will be left in a reactive, not a proactive, role.

Goals of Survey Research and the World Wide Web

Survey Research and the World Wide Web was written to help bridge the gap between traditional survey research methods and the emerging discipline of web-based survey research. After having read this book the reader should:

- Understand survey research in the context of disciplined inquiry,
- Understand e-mail and web-based surveys and how they differ from conventional surveys,
- Know the strengths and weaknesses of e-mail and web surveys, and
- Be capable of constructing and administering e-mail and web surveys.

Chapter One begins with a discussion of research methods in general and how survey research fits into research methods. Next is a discussion of survey techniques and modalities, including mail, telephone, and interview. Basic survey design regarding each mode is discussed, along with the benefits and potential pitfalls of each. Sampling techniques will be examined, particularly those appropriate for survey research. Finally, the potential impact of web surveys is discussed from the perspective of how they impact the survey research field.

Chapter Two introduces the reader to the Internet and the World Wide Web. A history of the Internet is provided, along with a discussion of how the Web arose from the Internet. The usefulness of the Web for researchers, government officials, students and others is discussed. A prospective look is taken of the Web in terms of its growth and usefulness for researchers.

Chapter Three examines the literature with respect to e-mail and web-based surveys. To the extent that web surveys are so new, other Internet survey tools, such as e-mail surveys and forms-based surveys, are discussed as well. Additionally, Chapter Three discusses the results of three web surveys administered by the author during 1998. These surveys, using various sampling techniques, were administered to state law enforcement agencies, local law enforcement agencies and universities. The findings of these surveys are discussed in the context of other web-based survey research.

Chapter Four is a "how to" guide with respect to constructing web surveys. This chapter will focus primarily on the construction of web, e-mail, and forms-based surveys using Microsoft FrontPage, a standard web development tool. Uploading websites using FrontPage and File Transfer Protocol (FTP) programs will be examined along with notes on how to password protect files and websites.

Chapter Five explores Internet search tools such as AltaVista, Yahoo and Excite. These tools allow the user to find research-oriented information currently on the web helps eliminate the possibility of researchers "recreating the wheel."

Each chapter includes a list of suggested readings along with a series of practice exercises. An interactive website accompanies this textbook as well. The website is located at http://www.nesbary.com/survey/. This website includes examples and learning aids designed to make the process of designing web surveys more practical and enjoyable.

Who Should Read This Book

The study of computers or research methods often strikes fear into the hearts of those navigating their way through higher education or professional training programs. Write a book that discusses both, and some will move as fast as they can in the opposite direction. Fear not! I wish to ally the concerns of those who believe that the topics herein are esoteric or difficult to understand. Regarding computers, this book requires no prior knowledge of programming and no in-depth knowledge of using computer applications. The exercises provided are practical, straightforward and include numerous examples. There are step by step instructions on how to accomplish the task at hand. Screen shots, or actual pictures of the programs used (Microsoft FrontPage, Microsoft Widows) are placed throughout this textbook. Visual examples of what is to be accomplished are included. Basically, anyone capable of turning on a computer and using a mouse can navigate this textbook.

Research methods is the other field of study that elicits apprehension. Chapter One of this book introduces survey research in a non-technical, user-friendly manner. The reader is given:

- The terms of the trade,
- Instructions on the design and administration of surveys,
- Multiple examples of surveys,
- Alternatives for using the Web for conducting survey research, and
- A detailed listing of further readings on survey research.

After reading Chapter One, the reader should be comfortable in designing and administering surveys, as well as using the Web for finding and analyzing information.

Being able to construct a survey or use the Web as a medium for surveying populations is a good skill, but who actually finds this kind of information useful? The answer is anyone who needs to collect representative data from a variety of groups or populations. Here are some examples:

- A state legislator needing public feedback on the expansion of a regional mall in her district.
- A police administrator researching the number and functions of municipal police agencies in Massachusetts.
- A polling organization seeking opinions of the electorate regarding the year 2000 national election.
- A prospective business owner considering moving into a new market.
- A professor seeking detailed information on political science programs offered in Midwestern states.

Anyone seeking data that could be reasonably expected to be collected through a survey should consider reading this book. While web surveys may not necessarily be applicable in all cases, the growth of the Web makes web survey techniques an option for any survey researcher.

What this book is not is a technical manual on how to program in HTML or to become an expert at using Microsoft FrontPage. Nor is this book intended to transform the reader into an expert in research methods and statistics. It is designed to help the reader become proficient at using web survey research tools, probably the most innovative and potentially useful survey research technique of the past ten years.

Acknowledgements

This project is the result of the collaboration of many individuals and several organizations. I will offer my thanks to those who helped me complete this project and hopefully will not omit anyone whose work helped make this project possible. Connie Nesbary, my wife, is, among her many skills, a professional editor who made the completion of this book possible. Thank you, Connie, for your skills, patience and love. At Oakland University, I had the help and support of my colleagues and students. I particularly thank Professor Vincent Khapoya and Professor John Klemanski, both of whom saw the value of this work and allowed me to pursue it with their full support. I would also like to thank Oakland Universities' Teaching and Learning Committee, which provided me with grant funds to purchase software and hardware with which to write this document. Several student assistants, including James Hiller, David Lingholm, Dalia Rasha and Nada Sater were diligent in their work and erudite in their approach in helping construct and administer the survey instruments for Chapter Three of this document. At Allyn & Bacon I thank Sarah Kelbaugh and Karen Hanson for their help and instructive editorial comments and work during this process. Finally, even though I have not had the pleasure of meeting him, I thank Earl Babbie for his lifelong contributions to the study of research methods. Professor Babbie's work transformed at least one researcher from being relatively research phobic to being confident and able enough to attempt a work of this nature.

About the Author

Dale Nesbary is an Assistant Professor in Political Science at Oakland University in Rochester, Michigan, where he teaches courses on World Wide Web Research, Public Budgeting, Quantitative Research Methods, Policy Analysis, State Politics, Police Administration and Program Evaluation. He earned his Ph.D. in Law, Policy and Society at Northeastern University in Boston, Massachusetts. He also holds a Master of Public Administration degree from Western Michigan University and a Bachelor of Arts degree from Michigan State University. He has published in the areas of Internet research, tax policy, state and local finance, commerce, police management and state tax expenditure policy.

He has advised or consulted with many government, private and nonprofit firms including the Archdiocese of Detroit, the Federal Highway Administration, the Michigan Legislature, the Harvard University Police Department, the Boston Police Department, and the National Conference of State Legislatures.

He has held management and analytic positions with Boston Police Department, the City of Boston, the National Conference of State Legislatures in Denver, and the Michigan Senate Fiscal Agency. He is originally from Twin Lake, Michigan, and currently lives in Southfield, Michigan, with his wife, Connie, and children, Nicole and Matthew.

Chapter One: Introducing Survey Research

OVERVIEW

Chapter One introduces the reader to survey research and the potential impact of web surveys on the discipline. The chapter begins with a discussion of research methods in general and how survey research fits into research methods. Next is a discussion of survey techniques and modalities, including mail, telephone, group questionnaire and interview. Basic survey design regarding each mode is discussed, along with the benefits and potential pitfalls of each. Sampling techniques will be examined, particularly those appropriate for survey research. Finally, the potential impact of web surveys is discussed from the perspective of how they impact the survey research field.

INQUIRY AND RESEARCH

Inquiry is an activity fundamental to all human beings. We all wonder about our surroundings, relationships with others, our past, and our futures, among many other things. From this wonder, we embark upon activities that lead to conclusions about ourselves and the world around us. Most fundamentally, we learn that certain activities or events have a causal relationship to other events. That is to say, something that occurs now may affect an event or activity in the future. For example, those of us living in Michigan learn that wearing layers of clothing in mid-December causes us to remain warm when we venture outside. We also learn by observation that if we pour water from a pitcher, it will flow downward. Michigan residents also know that if we take our warm winter clothes with us and wear them on our vacation in Puerta Vallarta, Mexico, the local residents may laugh a little and ask us if we are from somewhere not as warm as Puerta Vallarta.

Humans also learn that many causal relationships are probabilistic in nature. That is to say, effects occur more often when the causes are present, but not always. For example, on December 17, 1997, the high temperature in metropolitan Detroit was 38 degrees (F), just about normal. Warm clothing was definitely a must on that day. However, on the same date in 1998, the high temperature was 62 degrees, well above normal. Many layers of clothing on December 17, 1998 would have *caused* us not to remain warm, but to become overheated. Eventually, people learn that, if they wear warm clothes on warm days, the probability is that they will become overheated.

We also recognize that pouring water from a pitcher almost always causes the water to fall down. If we are subject to a gravitational field, water will always pour down. However if we were in a no gravity environment, the physics of our universe tell us that water would fall from a pitcher in the direction of the pitcher at the time the water was poured.

Whatever the event or activity, humans often attempt to explain why the event occurs or, more simply, why it exists. This inquiry may be conducted in a non-disciplined form or a disciplined form (research). First we will spend a few moments on non-disciplined inquiry.

Two examples of non-disciplined inquiry include tradition and authority. Tradition is the inherited knowledge base about the workings of the world. This can be scientific or unscientific in nature. Traditions may be based on cultural norms, religious beliefs or familial history. Traditions provide relatively consistent belief and behavior systems for individuals and groups.

For example, the acceptance of religious traditions can cause many persons and groups to live and act in ways that enrich their lives. Religions have bound together regions and nations for centuries, in some cases. Many families accept traditional areas of employment, because of the institutional memory of family elders and the familiarity with the vocation. Families of police officers, fisherman, and medical care professionals are prime examples of this.

Authority comprises the acceptance of new knowledge based on the findings of others. Acceptance of authority-based information is usually dependent on the credibility of the authority. Most new car buyers are more likely to accept the evaluation of *Consumer Reports* magazine on the quality of a car, rather than accepting the opinion of a "know-it-all" uncle.

Tradition and authority both have their place in society. Their role in inquiry is more tenuous. Authorities may be given wholly too much credence with respect to issues that may be outside their realm. Religious leaders often offer their opinions on the provision of medical care. When insufficient research is undertaken, the leader depends on his knowledge base rather than tested and provable facts. These activities can lead to poorly crafted public policy. Conversely, political leaders are more than willing to offer opinions and legal remedies on the practice of religion, in some cases in a detrimental manner. This is why the United States Constitution expressly forbids the sponsoring of religious activities by the government.

Research comprises inquiry undertaken on a *systematic* basis intended to add to the general body of knowledge, including the knowledge of society, groups, and individuals. Note that research involves systematic inquiry, including the scientific testing of theories and ideas. This helps preclude the inclusion of non-scientific beliefs, activities and behaviors in the research process. Research is conducted in a number of different modes including:

1. Basic research, designed to identify and examine entirely new fields of knowledge;
2. Applied research, designed to add to existing fields of knowledge; and
3. Experimental research designed to test the validity and/or reliability of new and existing fields of knowledge.

Basic research is conducted commonly in the hard sciences. The development of new treatments to combat heart disease, the study of the effect of zero gravity on cellular growth, and the creation of new storage media for digital information are all examples of basic research. Basic research is also conducted in the social sciences, although traditionally less so than in the hard sciences.

Applied research is conducted routinely in the social sciences. Police agencies and researchers study the effectiveness of ongoing law enforcement strategies, such as community policing. Political scientists examine voting patterns among various demographic, social and economic groups. Social anthropologists often examine the interactions between or within social groups. Whatever the nature of research, a fundamental tenet is the use of experimental research to help answer the questions researchers ask.

According to Nachmias and Nachmias, research comprises a broad range of activities conducted by many individuals and groups, including:

1. The provision of professional, technical, administrative or clerical support and/or assistance to staff directly engaged in research and experimentation;
2. Management of staff who are either directly engaged in research and experimentation or are providing professional, technical or clerical support or assistance to those staff;

3. Activities of students undertaking undergraduate and postgraduate research courses; and
4. Supervision of students undertaking undergraduate and postgraduate research courses.

The following activities are not considered to be research and experimentation, except where they are used primarily for the support of, or as part of, research and experimental development activities. These are, however, legitimate creative, professional, administrative or scientific activities:

1. Preparation for teaching;
2. Literary and artistic activities such as creative writing (However, the preparation of an original report on research and experimental development findings is research and experimental development.);
3. Scientific and technical information services;
4. General purpose or routine data collection;
5. Standardization and routine testing;
6. Feasibility studies (except for research and experimental development projects);
7. Specialized routine medical care; and
8. Routine computer programming, systems work or software maintenance. However, research and experimental development for applications software, new programming languages and new operating systems is included (Nachmias and Nachmias 1996).

The primary objectives of research are to identify and examine entirely new fields of knowledge, add to existing fields of knowledge, and test the validity and/or reliability of new and existing fields of knowledge. To accomplish these objectives, researchers often need to evaluate a broad range of data. Examples of datasets examined include political exit polls conducted during elections, health care group member attitudes about managed health care versus traditional health care, and quality control studies conducted by automobile manufactures. By conducting exit polls, political and media organizations give the public an "educated guess" of the outcome of an election well before the polls close. Obviously, not all voters can be interviewed, so a subset or sample of voters is taken to infer a projected outcome of an election. Blue Cross/Blue Shield regularly surveys its members to assess satisfaction regarding its myriad health care offerings. DaimlerChrysler Corporation regularly tests the quality of its automobiles and components to infer the reliability of its products.

Survey research is the process of collecting representative sample data from a larger population and using the sample to infer attributes of the population. Survey researchers collect information via the administration of a questionnaire (through regular mail, interview, e-mail or the Internet) to a sample of respondents. Public opinion polls, the Nielsen Rating System examining television viewing habits and government census taking are all examples of surveys.

The roots of survey research may be traced back thousands of years. Egyptian rulers conducted a census to account for the number of citizens, workers, animals and facilities. The ancient African kingdom of Ghana regularly surveyed their citizens for purposes of determining wealth and power of the kingdom (Bennet, Jr.1973)

In the United States, survey research may be traced back as far as the early 19th century (Babbie 1991). The presidential election of 1924 signaled a fundamental realignment of political parties in America. Two parties emerged from George Washington's National Unity Coalition. John Adams led the Federalists, and the Democratic-Republicans were led by Thomas Jefferson.

According to Smith (1990), a series of polls were conducted to assess the relative strengths of the presidential candidates. These polls were conducted at public gatherings, such as military musters and town meetings.

SURVEY RESEARCH DESCRIBED

The primary element of any survey is the standardized questionnaire. To ensure appropriate and accurate measurement, a standardized questionnaire ensures that each survey question elicits exactly the same kind of response from each respondent. This is not to say that respondents are expected to provide the same answer. Rather, exactly the same kind of observation technique (question) is employed, leading to consistency in response. If a polling organization wanted to know which political party a respondent belonged to, an appropriate question is:

To which political party do you currently belong? (select one answer):

        ____Democratic
        ____Reform
        ____Republican
        ____None
        ____Other

While there are no absolute assurances that a respondent will answer a question correctly, the respondent is limited to the five choices listed. If any pollster asked the above question differently (for example, leaving out one of the political parties), the question would be rendered useless.

Nearly everyone thinks that they can put together a set of questions designed to gather information useful for any task. However, gathering useful information is not quite so simple. For a survey to be valid, it must:

1. Gather, as precisely as possible, the information the researcher wants;
2. Include questions that mean the same thing to all respondents;
3. Constitute a questionnaire or interview schedule that is pleasing enough to the respondents that they are willing to spend the time to complete it; and
4. Be sufficiently engaging that they will not give superficial or misleading responses (Baker 1999).

Most fundamentally, a researcher must have a clear idea of what information is needed before administering a survey. This clarity must be reflected in the organization and structure of survey questions. The following example illustrates some of the problems faced when attempting to construct a survey without knowing clearly what information is needed. We will use the fictitious case of Captain Arthur Anders, head of the Westlawn Police Department Traffic and Transportation Division. Westlawn is a core city with a population of 100,000 and located in a northern industrial state. Captain Anders wanted to determine if residents of his community were satisfied with traffic flow on a major north-south artery (Empire Avenue) located downtown. To learn more, Captain Anders commissioned a survey of drivers who use the avenue. The survey comprised 1) a count of the number of vehicles using the avenue daily and 2) the random administration of a three-question survey to drivers on the avenue. To administer the survey, police officers stopped vehicles at random and requested that drivers complete and return the survey to police headquarters. The questions asked are as follows:

1. Do you drive through Westlawn daily?
2. Do you drive on Empire Avenue daily?
3. Are you troubled with the amount of traffic that you encounter daily?

Even before examining the nature of the questionnaire, myriad problems are apparent, even to the most novice researcher. If Captain Anders is truly concerned with traffic flow through his community, it is unclear if these questions are clear or concise enough to gather needed information. First, the Captain wants to know what residents think about the amount of traffic on Empire Avenue, not necessarily what those driving on Empire Avenue are thinking. The Captain did not attempt a survey of those living or working on or near Empire Avenue. Contacting these residents may provide the Captain with better information.

Second, a count of cars provides the Captain with an understanding of the number of vehicles using Empire Avenue. It does not, however, provide a sense for whether the number of users is appropriate for that particular stretch of road. In addition to the count, the Captain should refer to city planning documents, highway construction records and past traffic surveys. This provides a much fuller description of the expected and actual use of Empire Avenue over time.

Third, the way the questions are written may be confusing to the reader. Question Three ("Are you troubled with the amount of traffic that you encounter daily?") is particularly vague. Rush hour traffic may not trouble many drivers, while others may have a problem with more than just a few vehicles. A better, alternative question would involve some specific measure of the term "troubled" or a reasonable method of evaluating what comprises a "troubling" level of traffic. Questions regarding level of traffic by time are useful. For example

Are traffic levels on Empire Avenue at 5 p.m.:

____Too high
____About right
____Too low
____I don't drive on Empire Avenue at 5 p.m.

Adding a time parameter to the question allows the traffic department to analyze, with a high level of specificity, concerns about traffic. Rather than simply inquiring about whether or not the respondent is "troubled" by the amount of traffic, this question provides four levels of response at a specific timeframe.

By any measure, "randomly" selecting vehicles for a traffic stop is problematic for several reasons. First, when a police officer stops a vehicle, the reason is almost always bad from the vehicle operator's perspective. Thus, the survey process is off to a psychologically bad start. Second, having police officers distribute citizen surveys is a poor use of police officers' time. Research or administrative staff may provide the service more effectively. Third, because of the first two reasons, the environment in which the survey is being administered is not comfortable, placing the officer and the citizen under stress, with both likely feeling that the process is a waste of their time. This environment would most likely result in a low response rate. Finally, randomizing traffic stops is difficult if not impossible. Even selecting every *nth* vehicle would be problematic given a high traffic volume. Finally, asking drivers to return surveys to a police station would undoubtedly guarantee a low response rate.

SAMPLING TECHNIQUES

To collect good, methodologically rigorous information regarding traffic patterns on Empire Avenue, a "road map" is needed. We need to understand how to identify persons to provide information that is representative of the beliefs of the larger population. Our road map in this case is sample design. Understanding how to design a representative sample can go a long way towards helping a researcher design a valid survey instrument. Only then can we construct a survey that will allow useful information to be collected. This section will examine three commonly used sampling techniques, including random, stratified and cluster sampling. For more information on sampling, please refer to the recommended readings list at the end of this book.

Most fundamentally, a survey describes a group of people. In Westlawn, we want to survey residents of the City and/or users of Empire Avenue. Police administrators attempted to describe the beliefs of the residents of Westlawn by collecting survey data. The survey methodology employed in Westlawn lacked a number of important components. This section will discuss how survey administrators may best construct a survey instrument to collect sample data.

SAMPLING: KEY TERMS

As mentioned earlier, survey research is designed to collect sample data in order to infer attributes to a larger population. The population, defined as the group under study, comprises the residents of the City of Westlawn using Empire Avenue. Clearly, it is not feasible to survey each and every resident of Westlawn, so we must develop a sampling mechanism reliable enough to represent the entire City population. Certain definitions are useful in understanding the underpinnings of a good survey:

Population: The group or phenomenon under study. Example: The 100,000 residents of Westlawn.

Parameter: A characteristic of the entire population. Examples: The number of residents driving on Empire Avenue on a given day, the number of female residents in the population, the number of United States citizens living in Westlawn.

Sampling Frame: The actual list of the individuals comprising the population. The sample is selected from the sampling frame. Example: A database comprising all adults who drive in Westlawn.

Sample: A subset of a population selected to reflect the characteristics of a population. Examples: A subset of residents driving on Empire Avenue on a given day, a subset of female residents in the population, a subset of United States citizens living in Westlawn.

Element: Individuals selected from the sample.

Variable: A set of mutually exclusive attributes. Examples: Gender, age, employment status, level of education. Social researchers describe variables as the distribution of attributes exhibiting variation in a population. Therefore a researcher may describe the gender distribution of a population by presenting a frequency distribution of gender in the population.

Statistic: A characteristic of a sample. Examples: The estimated percent of residents driving on Empire Avenue on a give day, the estimated percent of female residents in the population, the estimated percent of United States citizens living in Westlawn.

Sampling Error: A measure of how much a statistic varies from a parameter. A sampling error of 5 tells us that the actual parameter could fall in a range of 5 percent above or 5 percent below a statistic, yielding a range (confidence interval) of 10 percent.

It is the goal of any survey researcher to generate statistics (characteristics of a sample) that are identical to the parameters of the population from which the sample is drawn. One of the best ways to test the validity of statistics is to conduct your own survey of a relatively small group of individuals. The following exercise demonstrates how a sample may be selected from the population of Westlawn University students.

To compare statistics with population parameters at Westlawn University, it is necessary to have a sampling frame (complete listing) of Westlawn University students along with parameters describing the student population. Most universities maintain detailed descriptive information on their student bodies and activities. You may conduct a similar exercise at your school or organization to determine the accuracy of your survey research skills.

Figure 1.1 provides the distribution of Westlawn University students by gender. Statistics generated from your own survey may be compared with the numbers outlined in Figure 1.1.

Figure 1.1 Distribution of Westlawn University Students By Gender		
Response	**Number (N=1000)**	**Percent**
Female	550	55
Male	450	45

The total population of Westlawn University is 1,000 students, with 55 percent male and 45 percent female students. The sampling frame is a complete list of all Westlawn University students, hopefully including addresses, phone numbers and e-mail addresses. The percentages of males and females in Westlawn University's population are useful parameters for an analysis.

A sample of Westlawn University's population can be used to generate a statistic, which will hopefully match the parameter already available to you. To begin the process, design a simple, one question survey. The only question to be asked is "What is your gender?" The two possible responses are "male" and "female." The elements are the individual students at Westlawn University. We are employing a simple binomial variable (a variable with only two possible attributes) based on gender. Next, administer the survey to a subset of Westlawn students. Most likely, the sample you select will not result in statistics matching exactly the parameters already available. In other words, your sample may not have the exact percentage of male and females, as does the general population.

The following figures represent the results of four hypothetical samples selected from among elements of the same population. Figure 1.2 provides a graphical representation of all

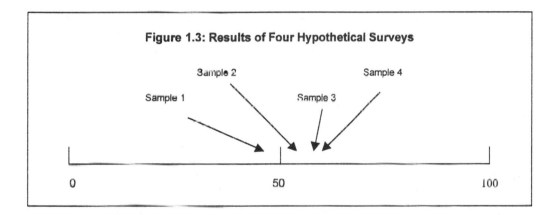

Figure 1.3: Results of Four Hypothetical Surveys

possible values of the parameter in question, that is, the percent of female students in the general university population. The horizontal axis represents the range (0 to 100 percent and outlines the midpoint (50 percent). This kind of table provides us with a simple method of presenting survey results.

Next, we must randomize the sampling frame. To accomplish this, we must obtain a complete listing of students at the university. We then assign a number to each student (from 1-1000 for each student at the university) and settle on the size of our sample.

In selecting a sample, two general rules are important to keep in mind. First, the larger the sample size, the greater the probability the sample will reflect the general population and the greater the probability the statistic will match the parameter. If we selected a sample of ten students out of the thousand at Westlawn University, there is a chance that we will come across a gender specific group of students. For example, we might happen across the women's basketball team or a fraternity. Selecting a larger sample will reduce the possibility that the genders within a specific group will skew (bias) our results.

Also, additional increases in sample size are not as valuable as initial increases with respect to survey accuracy. An increase of our Westlawn student sample from 10 to 30 might result in increasing the level of significance from 90 to 95 percent, while an additional increase in sample size from 30 to 60 might only improve the significance level from 95 to 96 percent. In our sample, we will settle on 100 elements (students).

The next step in the sampling process is to conduct a survey or preferably, a series of surveys. For purposes of this exercise, we will administer our one question survey to four samples comprising 100 elements each.

Figure 1.3 presents four sample statistics representing the results of the four surveys administered. The specific percentage results for samples 1-4 are 47, 52, 57 and 58 respectively. As would be expected, some of the samples (1 and 2) are below the actual percentage of females at the university while the others are above the actual percentage of females. The more samples we draw, the more likely we are to select a group of elements that more accurately reflect the true distribution of students at the university. For example, if we had unlimited resources and were able to administer unlimited surveys, we could generate results that would approximate nearly exactly the actual distribution of male and female students at Westlawn University. If we graphed the results of these many surveys, the resulting graph would look much like a bell shaped curve. Figure 1.4 provides an example of this phenomenon, one of the cardinal rules of probability sampling. Specifically, if many random samples are selected from a population, the resulting statistics will be distributed around the population parameters (in our case, actual percent of female students) in a predictable manner. While some samples will vary, most will fall very close to the actual number. Even without knowing the actual percent of female students, the distribution tells us that the actual percent of female students is between 50 and 60 percent.

Probability sampling also provides us with tools for estimating how much our sample statistics vary from the population parameters. The *standard error* is a statistical tool that explains how closely sample results reflect values of a parameter. The standard error is the standard deviation of a sampling distribution and is calculated as follows:

$$S = \sqrt{\frac{AxB}{n}}$$ where S = the Standard Error, A and B = the population parameters for the

binomial and n = the number of cases in each sample. If the percent of female and male students in our sample = 58 and 42 percent, respectively, and the number of cases in our sample is 100, the formula is calculated in the following manner:

$$S = \sqrt{\frac{.58x.42}{100}}$$ or S = .049 or S = 4.9 percent

The standard error is critical in helping us understand the variation among cases in a sample. It indicates how sample estimates will be distributed around the population parameter. The standard error represents the variability among the results of all samples taken.

Probability theory dictates that specific proportions of a sample estimate will fall within specific increments, with each increment equaling one standard error. Probability theory dictates that 34.13 percent of sample estimates will occur one standard error above the population parameter, while 34.13 percent of sample estimates will occur one standard error below the population parameter. Given a standard error of 5 percent, roughly 68 percent (according to probability theory) of samples taken will fall within 5 percent (plus or minus) of the parameter. Our standard error above of 4.9 percent was within the 5 percent margin of error expected in probability theory.

CONFIDENCE LEVELS AND INTERVALS

Researchers use two primary methods of describing the probability that a sample is an accurate reflection of a population:

- The confidence interval is the range of values within which the actual value falls. For purposes of our example, we might be able to say that the actual percent of females at our university falls within the range of 50 to 60 percent.
- The confidence level outlines the probability (likelihood) that the population parameter falls within the confidence interval. For purposes of our survey, we might be able to say that, based on *n* number of samples, the number of estimated female students will fall within a range of 50 to 60 percent at least 95 percent of the time.

Thus, the confidence interval tells us the range within which the actual value (parameter) may be found, while the level of significance tells us the likelihood that the parameter will be found within the range. For any sample, the more narrow the confidence interval and the higher the significance level the more valid our statistics are. For example, in our school, a confidence interval of 50 to 60 percent is better than a confidence interval of 45 to 65 percent. Similarly, a confidence level (probability) of 95 percent is better than a level of significance of 90 percent.

More on Probability Sampling

As described above, the goal of sampling is to select a set of elements from a population that will accurately reflect the parameters of the population from which the elements were selected. Probability sampling increases the likelihood of accomplishing this goal and provides specific methods for estimating the likelihood of success. Moreover, a probability sample is representative of a sampling frame, if all elements (members) of the sampling frame have an equal chance of being selected.

RANDOM SAMPLING

Random selection is the most important aspect of probability sampling. In random selection, each element has an equal chance of being selected as any other element from the population. Random selection helps remove bias on the part of the researcher and allows the researcher to employ probability sampling techniques.

The classic example of random selection is the flipping of a coin. Assuming a perfectly symmetrical coin, each head or tail has an equal opportunity of being selected each time the coin is flipped. While flipping a coin works well in selecting "sides" in a sporting event (the traditional football coin flip, for example), it does not work as well for the social science researcher. Social science researchers often use random number tables or computer software programs capable of generating random numbers.

Sample accuracy is influenced by the way the individuals or cases are chosen (White 1951). The best method of selecting cases for a sample employs simple random sampling. Here, each member of the population has an equal probability of being included in the sample. To meet this requirement, the survey administrator needs a complete list of the population (sampling frame) being surveyed and a random number generator. The random number list is applied to the population, generating a completely random sample. The latter is easily obtained, usually via any statistics textbook or commonly available statistics programs such as SPSS or SAS. An accurate population list is somewhat more difficult to obtain. Even a complete list of registered university students may not be completely accurate. Late registration and late "drops" may not be accounted for in an official university registration list.

Generating a random sample from the general population is fraught with problems. A census of any jurisdiction is nearly immediately out of date due to in and out migration of residents. Censuses are known to undercount persons living in public housing or densely populated urban areas. Some persons are uncomfortable with government officials and will not respond to census takers or any "official sounding" organization (Brownlee 1975).

Modern technology is helping to overcome some longstanding issues regarding obtaining complete sampling frames. Large and well-funded organizations now maintain very complete lists of individuals and businesses by jurisdiction. Internet "search engines" include virtual telephone lists of every individual and business in the United States and many abroad. These lists are marketed to business and government institutions for marketing purposes, as well as serving as virtual telephone books that are updated on a continual basis. Political organizations are particularly adept at taking advantage of these new technologies. Alan Mann, Director of Public Opinion Research for the Michigan House of Representatives Republican Caucus, manages voting lists that are generated from voting lists and virtual telephone directories. Mr. Mann believes that, by having more complete and accurate population information, he is able to generate better data for his clients (1998).

Computer-generated telephone dialing is a relatively recent innovation in survey research. Based upon a computerized telephone database, phone numbers are randomly selected and dialed a preset number of times. Dialing times may be varied to ensure that persons not home during normal business hours may be contacted.

Many polling organizations, such as Gallup and CNN/USA Today-Gallup, utilize probability sampling techniques in conducting regular polls of U.S. residents. These pollsters have found that to ascertain views of the 270 million U.S. residents, a sample of 1,500 is sufficient to yield a small sampling error of 3 percent. Figure 1.4 reflects sampling errors based upon sample sizes regarding the United States population.

In the 1998 U.S. midterm elections, the CNN/USA Today-Gallup poll reported on the day before the election that there was a 95 percent likelihood that the Republican Party would increase its number of seats in the U.S. House of Representatives. This estimate was provided with a 3 percent margin of error. This means that, given a survey of 1,500 U.S. voters, there is only a three-percent chance that the Republican Party would lose seats in the 1998 midterm election. The Republican Party actually lost five seats in the 1998 midterm election, meaning that the actual vote (parameter) was not within the predicted confidence interval.

It is believed that the estimated outcome of the 1998 midterm election was miscalculated, largely because some respondents provided misleading responses when surveyed. They did this because, while they agreed with the position of the Democratic party on a variety of issues, they did not want to be associated with so-called scandals surrounding President Bill Clinton's Administration. Their way of dealing with this conundrum was to tell survey administrators that they supported Republicans, while they actually intended to vote for Democrats.

For a number of reasons, simple random sampling is not often used. Random sampling can be expensive and time consuming. To conduct a random sample of all residents of the United States requires a sampling frame of approximately 280 million persons. To construct such a sampling frame requires the purchase of a list of every person in the U.S. or the manual development of such a list, neither of which are reasonable alternatives for the researcher of limited means. To manually construct such a list would be very time consuming, as well as very costly. Even a sampling frame of a small community of 25,000 persons would take some doing for the average researcher. This is why other sampling techniques are employed, rather than simple random sampling. The following sections discuss these techniques in some detail.

Figure 1.4 Sample Error Estimates For Various Sample Sizes	
Sample Size	**Sample Error**
1,500	3
1,000	4
750	4
600	5
200	9

SYSTEMATIC SAMPLING

When a sampling frame is readily available, researchers often employ systematic sampling, which requires that every *nth* element from the sampling frame (list) is selected. Of our sampling frame of 1,000 Westlawn University students, we might want to sample every fifth student or every 20th student. The sampling interval is the regular distance between elements selected from the sample. Finally, the sampling ratio is the number of elements selected, divided by the number of elements in the sampling frame.

To avoid human bias, the first student should be selected at random. Initially, human bias may seem to be of little importance when selecting every *nth* element of a sampling frame. However, in some instances, an innocent action taken by a researcher in selecting the first element may inject unintended bias into a study. Following is an example:

In a study of racial attitudes of Westlawn University students, a researcher selects every 10th student and uses student numbers as student identifiers. The researcher begins with student number 7 and therefore selects every 10th student with a student number ending with the number 7. The researcher was unaware that the university codes student numbers by a number of factors, including race. White student numbers end with the numbers 1-5, African American student numbers end with 6-7 and other ethnic groups end with 8-9. The researcher has inadvertently selected only African American students for a study on racial attitudes.

STRATIFIED SAMPLING

Because of the nature of the survey topic or the availability of survey respondents, researchers sometime choose not to use true random sampling. In fact, due to the limitations described above, random sampling may not always be the best choice for choosing cases. Stratified sampling ensures that different groups (strata) are represented in survey responses by administering random samples in each relevant demographic population or other stratum. As an example, when conducting surveys on affirmative action, it is important to ensure that different racial and ethnic groups are included. In this case, a random sample would be administered to White, Black, Hispanic and other strata deemed to be relevant. In another example, a researcher develops a study that examines attitudes of high school students toward use of alcohol. Rather than sampling the entire high school population, the researcher may choose to divide students into strata representing grade, gender, grade point average, or income. While the resulting statistics would not be based upon a random sample of population as a whole, randomly sampling each stratum would ensure that the opinions of each group are represented.

CLUSTER SAMPLING

Cluster sampling may be employed when it is impossible or impractical to construct a complete sampling frame. For example it would be difficult, if not impossible to construct a sampling frame representing widely-distributed populations, such as all university students in the United States, all members of the Presbyterian faith in the United States and Canada, or all Democrats in the State of Michigan. Cluster sampling calls for large groups to be organized into smaller, more manageable groups or clusters. These smaller groups are then sampled randomly. For example, to study the attitudes of Democrats in Michigan, a researcher can obtain member lists from municipal or regional democratic organizations in Michigan. These organizations may then be sampled to answer relevant research questions.

Cluster sampling is commonly used to determine the opinions of residents of a political subdivision, a neighborhood, a region or other geographic subdivision of a larger geographic unit. Professor Luis Garcia of Suffolk University and Research Director of the Boston Police Department recently surveyed the residents of the City of Boston regarding fear of crime (1998). Dr. Garcia employed cluster sampling of the City's neighborhoods to get a clear understanding of the fear of crime by the City's politically and historically important neighborhoods. He drew samples from several of the 800+ neighborhoods in his study.

National polling organizations employ cluster, stratified and random sampling techniques. The country is first divided into geographic clusters and is stratified by region and size of community. From these clusters are selected about 350 sampling locations. Interviewers must conduct surveys within these locations. They are not allowed to survey other locations.

WEIGHTING

Oftentimes, random sampling will not adequately include the opinions or representations of small subpopulations of a larger population. Weighting is a method of ensuring that sufficient elements of under-represented populations are included in an analysis. This can be accomplished in two ways. First, subpopulations may be sampled in a disproportionate manner to ensure sufficient cases for each analysis. Here is an example: CNN/USA Today-Gallup often conducts national opinion surveys on presidential job performance. These surveys are usually conducted by telephone. Telephone surveys are inherently biased against persons who are unable to afford telephone service. To account for this bias, CNN/USA Today-Gallup often selects a disproportionate number of persons to call living in low-income areas. Low-income persons are therefore given a disproportionate opportunity of being selected in the survey.

Second, if the number of elements in each population is known, a specific weight may be applied to each population. Here is an example: A researcher may be interested in examining the views of urban and rural residents of the State of California regarding the siting of maximum-security prisons in the state. A simple random sample of California residents is not likely to provide useful information, since urban Californians outnumber their rural counterparts by a factor of about eight to one. Constructing a survey with two subpopulations, urban and rural would help solve the problem. If the goal is to assess the opinions of urban and rural Californians equally, a specific weight can be applied to rural Californians.

Nonprobability Sampling

When it is not feasible or possible to randomize a sample, other sampling techniques may be appropriate. The next section outlines nonprobability sampling techniques, such as quota, purposive (judgmental) and convenience sampling.

QUOTA SAMPLING

Quota sampling is designed to select a sample that is equivalent to the sampling frame, while using a nonprobability sampling design. In quota sampling, the population is divided into quotas, which represent attributes of variables occurring in the population. For example, if a population is known to have a racial distribution of 50 percent Asian, 15 percent White, 15 percent African American and 20 percent Latino, the researcher will select a sample that includes a racial distribution of the same percentages as the population. Quota sampling differs from stratified sampling, in that the researcher may select any elements from the quota and does not necessarily have to sample the quota randomly.

While quota sampling can be a useful tool, it should not be used when a better sampling design is available. Dividing a population into quotas is substantially similar to dividing a population into strata, thus stratified sampling (a probability sampling design) should be used whenever a comprehensive sampling frame may be constructed or obtained.

PURPOSIVE SAMPLING

Purposive sampling, sometimes called judgmental sampling, occurs when the researcher selects samples in a subjective manner in an attempt to obtain a sample that appears to be representative of the population (Nachmias & Nachmias 1996). Because construction of the sampling frame is dependent on the subjective judgement of the researcher, there is no sure way to determine if the sample is representative of the population being studied. Nonetheless, purposive sampling has proved valuable in predicting the outcome of numerous elections. Quite often, pollsters will sample key congressional districts in an attempt to forecast the outcome of a presidential election. Pollsters also sample key state legislative districts in an attempt to forecast the outcome of a statewide election. More often than not, these techniques are very accurate. For example, in the 1996 presidential election, Michigan's 10th Congressional District held by David Bonior (D-Mt. Clemens) was touted as a key swing district. Many pollsters predicted that as Representative Bonior's district went, the presidential election was sure to follow. Extensive pre-election and exit polling was conducted in an attempt to get a sense of the voters' likelihood of reelecting Bonior. The polls showed that Bonior would win re-election by a margin of 5 to 10 percent. Bonior did win re-election, and the Democrats held onto the White House.

CONVENIENCE SAMPLING

Convenience sampling is arguably the least rigorous of sampling methodologies. In convenience sampling, the researcher selects whatever sample is convenient at the time of the research project. In convenience sampling, the researcher has no method to estimate the representativeness of the selected sample. Therefore, there is no way to use statistics generated from a convenience sample to estimate population parameters. For example, instead of selecting random samples in our research at Westlawn University, a convenience sample would select the first 50 or 100 students available, perhaps a class or a sports team. Instead of using a cluster sample design to survey Boston residents, Professor Garcia might have used a telephone directory of the City of Boston to generate a list of persons to be called. Convenience sampling should be avoided as a method of equating sample statistics to a population parameter.

SURVEY TYPES

After having determined who will be surveyed and the method to be used in collecting data, the next step is to construct the survey instrument. The survey instrument is the tool used to actually gather relevant information. The primary method of gathering survey information is via questionnaire. With a questionnaire, a series of questions are written with the intent of eliciting responses regarding specific issues. Written questionnaires require the respondent to read questions and then to reply in written form. In an interview, 1) questions are asked by the survey administrator, 2) the respondent answers the questions, and 3) the survey administrator writes down the answers. Written questionnaires are nearly always used as the source of questions for an interview.

Traditionally, questionnaires are administered in three forms including mail surveys, telephone interview and personal interview. Questionnaires are administered via mail almost exclusively, while interviews are administered in person or by phone. Mail surveys are the oldest and the most widely used survey instruments. Government institutions, market research firms, politicians, schools and nearly any organization seeking information or data use them. Mail surveys are used when time is not necessarily of the essence, but detail and specificity are.

Prior to discussing the three basic questionnaire types, it is important to set forth certain rules with respect to constructing questions. These rules help ensure that questions are meaningful and maximize the likelihood that respondents will understand each question in the same way.

Question Construction

OPEN VERSUS CLOSED-ENDED QUESTIONS

Researchers have two fundamental choices when asking questions. Open-ended questions ask for the respondent's own answer in a relatively unlimited format. An example of an *open-ended* question is: "What are the major causes of traffic congestion in Westlawn today?" The respondent is given a space in which to draft the answer.

Open-ended questions require the researcher to code answers before they may be interpreted. The coding process requires the researcher to interpret responses, which may lead to inconsistency or misinterpretation of responses. Further, there is the possibility that respondents may provide answers that are off-point, leading to a relatively useless dataset. On the other hand, open-ended questions provide the possibility of rich contextual information being collected in a manner not possible via closed-ended questions.

Alternatively, *closed-ended* questions are designed to elicit uniform and concise responses. Closed-ended questions take many forms including true-false, multiple choice, and fill-in-the-blank, among others. An example of a closed-ended question is:

Empire Avenue needs a center left turn lane:

____True
____False

A strength of closed-ended questions is that they foster uniformity in response due to the limitation in the number of responses. Closed-ended questions are also more easily coded than open-ended questions, because of the specific nature of responses allowed.

Closed-ended questions pose a danger, in that they may be poorly conceived and may lead to invalid responses. To eliminate this possibility, closed-ended questions must incorporate two features. First, any choices from which the respondent chooses must be mutually exclusive. This means that for any set of answers, no two answers may incorporate the same meaning. Second, the choices must be exhaustive. This means that the question must include *all* possible answers.

Finally, open and closed-ended questions may be constructed in question or statement form. Statement form is more likely to be used in true-false questions. In true-false questions, a position or perspective may be summarized in statement form. The response to the statement follows with a true-false option answer.

RELEVANCE OF QUESTION

Most importantly, questions must be relevant to the issue being examined in a questionnaire and relevant to most respondents. While this may appear to be self evident, care must be taken with respect to this issue. For example, Babbie (1991, 150) surveyed a community with respect to their familiarity with 15 local political figures. As a methodological exercise, Babbie included one fictitious name, Tom Sakumoto. In the response, 9 percent indicated that they were familiar with Mr. Sakumoto. Of these 9 percent, half said they saw him on television and in the newspaper. Babbie's point is that some respondents are not familiar with issues or persons. Therefore the researcher must take care that issues included in a questionnaire are as relevant as possible, or else the risk is run of obtaining irrelevant information.

CLARITY OF QUESTIONS

Like relevance, the need for clarity may also appear to be self-evident. However, researchers sometime are too close to an issue to determine objectively whether a particular question is clear or not. Understand that respondents are not likely as familiar with the subject of your questionnaire as you are. For example, as a political science student, you may be familiar with Year 2000 presidential candidates, but not everyone is. The answer to the question: "Which Year 2000 democratic presidential candidate would you choose?" may be obvious to you, but is not necessarily obvious to the general public. A better question is:

Which of the following Year 2000 democratic presidential candidates would you choose? (select one only):

____Richard Gephart
____Al Gore
____Jesse Jackson

DOUBLE-BARRELED QUESTIONS

Double-barreled questions ask for information about two items in one question. An example of a double-barreled question is: "President Bill Clinton should not have been impeached, and the House Republicans should be voted out of Congress as a result." This is not a straight yes and no question. Rational individuals may have differing opinions on President Clinton's impeachment versus the behavior of House Republicans involved in the impeachment process. In fact, four possible responses are available here:

____Impeach Clinton, keep Congressional Republicans
____Impeach Clinton, vote out Congressional Republicans
____Keep Clinton, keep Congressional Republicans
____Keep Clinton, vote out Congressional Republicans

The better way to approach this question is to divide it into two separate statements: "President Clinton should have been impeached - True or False," and "Congressional Republicans should be voted out of Congress as a result of the impeachment process - True or False."

COMPETENCY OF RESPONDENTS TO ANSWER QUESTIONS

Usually the more familiar a respondent is with an issue, the more competent they are to respond to a question about that issue. For the most part, this rule makes sense, but not always. If a researcher is interested in how State of Michigan government employees view civil service promotion policies, the appropriate sampling frame should comprise State of Michigan government employees. It should not comprise non-state employees. State of Michigan government employees are likely to have some familiarity with civil service promotion policies, while non-state employees likely would not. Alternatively, surveying only Michigan Department of Civil Service employees (the department responsible for administering the merit system in Michigan government) would likely give responses skewed toward supporting civil service promotion policies.

MAKE QUESTIONS SHORT

The respondent should be able to read a question, interpret it and select a response with no difficulty. Short and concise questions maximize this possibility. No matter the complexity of an item, simple questions can be devised. If it appears that a simple question cannot be devised, divide the item into two or more questions to facilitate simplicity.

NEGATIVE/BIASED TERMS AND QUESTIONS

Stating questions in the negative can confuse and mislead respondents. When reading the question "The federal government should not spend more federal funds on Social Security," many readers will skip the word "not" and answer as if the federal government *should* spend more money on Social Security. Many others will read the question correctly. By removing the word "not," the question is much clearer.

Biased terms and questions can be even more problematic than those that are negative. If the researcher wanted to lead respondents to a specific answer regarding the question in the above paragraph, the question might be worded as follows: "Don't you believe that the federal government must spend more money on Social Security?" It is clear that the drafter of this question wants the respondent to respond yes to the question. Moreover, something as apparently innocuous as including an institutional name in a question may be a source of bias. The question "Do you support the tax cuts recommended in President Clinton's 2000 budget?" may be perceived as biased, because a person with a high profile is mentioned. Another way to word this question is "Do you support the tax cuts recommended in the United States Executive Budget for 2000?"

Questionnaire Construction

MAIL SURVEYS

Businesses often use mail surveys to update client lists. Each time a person receives a renewal notice for a magazine or journal subscription, that person is being surveyed. The survey may be a simple one-question query asking whether the subscriber wishes to renew to a three-page survey seeking information on personal demographics. When administered in conjunction with follow-up phone calls or interviews, mail surveys can be particularly useful.

The strengths of mail surveys are many. Mail surveys are relatively inexpensive when compared to interviews or telephone surveys. Costs for mail surveys include expenses for staff, paper, copying and postage. Unless a personal interview is to be conducted at or near the office of the survey administrator, transportation costs alone can be prohibitive. Mail surveys are also precise. If properly constructed, there is little ambiguity in a well-written question.

There are a number of potential weaknesses regarding mail surveys, the primary of which is that they are not very flexible. Questions are static, meaning they are limited to what is included on the questionnaire. Once the question is asked, it cannot be changed. Further, it is difficult to ask follow-up questions in more than the most rudimentary fashion. Follow-up questions are limited to the form included on the survey instrument itself. If a question is at all ambiguous, there is no way to clarify other than contacting the survey administrator. Next, and to some most importantly, responses to written surveys can be extremely slow. Weeks and months can pass prior to the receipt of survey responses. Finally, response rate to written surveys is often very low. The survey administrator must hope that the respondent is interested enough to complete the survey and to return it. In addition, both response rate and response time are functions of the accuracy of the mail database being used by the survey administrator. If respondent addresses are accurate, the likelihood of a fast response time and a high response rate increases. If respondent addresses are inaccurate, both response rate and response time are impacted negatively.

TELEPHONE SURVEYS

Telephone surveys can be a very effective method of collecting data. They combine the strengths of written questionnaires with the flexibility of in-person interviews. The survey administrator calls the respondent and reads a series of questions from a written questionnaire sheet. The survey administrator may ask follow-up questions when appropriate and respond to questions from the respondent.

Because the survey administrator must speak personally with each respondent, telephone surveys can be more expensive than other survey types. There is an opportunity cost to each hour spent by a survey administrator asking questions of respondents. Depending on the other responsibilities of staff, these costs can be moderate to very high. At a minimum, personnel costs will equal the salary and benefit costs of each individual conducting telephone interviews.

Another cost associated with telephone surveys are telephone connect charges. Long-distance fees cost from about 5 cents per minute and up. To the extent that each telephone call costs more than the cost to mail each survey, an incremental cost is accrued. In some cases, charges are accrued for local and zone (regional) calls as well. These costs need to be considered when determining how to administer a survey.

INTERVIEWS

Interviews are potentially the most detailed and useful survey techniques. They are also by far the most expensive. Interviews are actually a combination of an in-person interview and a written questionnaire. Because they are conducted in-person, follow-up questions may be asked more easily than in telephone or mail surveys. Personal and anecdotal information may be collected in ways that are not possible when using a mailer or a telephone. Face to face interviewing has existed for centuries and was most commonly used to collect market research data for business and census-related data for government. Businesses use interviews to determine the quality and attractiveness of products, while government collects demographic data and information useful for program and policy evaluation.

The strengths of interviews are clear. Speaking directly to a survey respondent gives the administrator an opportunity to clarify responses in a way that no other technique can offer. For example, if a respondent has a problem interpreting a specific question, the administrator can clarify it immediately. This is particularly useful regarding questions asked concerning personal beliefs and social norms. Asking the yes/no question: "Would you support a woman as a Republican presidential candidate?" might draw a simple response with no additional information. An administrator conducting an in-person interview can "read" the respondents' personal reactions and ask follow-up questions accordingly.

The weaknesses of interviews are also clear. Personal interviews are relatively expensive. They comprise questionnaire construction, respondent identification, travel costs and time. Each year, the U.S. Department of Justice produces a document entitled the National Crime Victimization Surveys. This is an example of a survey most appropriately conducted via regular mail as opposed to interview. This document comprises data collected from thousands of individuals and law enforcement agencies nationwide. Conducting personal interviews would not only be costly, but may also cause respondents to be less forthcoming than they may be if they were responding to a non-personalized paper survey form.

ITEMS TO REMEMBER

Once your survey instrument is complete, there are several housekeeping items to take care of. First, always include return address information on the survey instrument. While this seems obvious, many questionnaires lack this critical piece of information. This information is usually placed at the top of the survey instrument. Return information should include the following:

Your Name
Your Institution
Your Address
Phone Number
Fax Number
An e-mail address
A URL

Second, always request respondent information on the survey instrument, unless you are preparing an anonymous survey. Again, this may seem obvious, but is easily missed. Respondent information is usually placed at the bottom of a survey instrument. Return information should include the following:

Respondent Name
Respondent Institution
Respondent Address
Respondent Phone Number
Respondent Fax Number
Respondent e-mail address
Respondent URL

When we create web surveys, we will create fields in which this information is to be entered.

Of course, ethical guidelines for research need to be followed, based on the type of research that you are undertaking. If disclaimers and/or anonymous responses are required, be sure to include these items with your survey. The study of human subjects and their behavior requires compliance with ethical guidelines of your respective professions.

The final item to remember is to **proof your work**. There is no limit to the number of times needed to reread your work. Remember, the more eyes that view your work the better. After having reread a document many times, the words begin to look the same. Having others read and comment on the questionnaire can provide valuable suggestions.

In summary, when constructing any questionnaire, please follow these general rules:

1. Keep the questionnaire as short as will suffice to elicit the information necessary to analyze the primary research concerns. Be sure, however, to include questions on all the aspects of the research problem that you will need to address.
2. Include only questions which will address your research concerns and which you plan to analyze.
3. Make your questionnaire as appealing as possible to the respondents.

4. If the questionnaire is self administered, keep the instructions brief, but make sure they contain all the information required to complete and return the questionnaire.
5. Consider in advance all the issues a respondent might raise when he or she receives the instrument. Be sure that the questionnaire addresses those issues.
6. Finally, be sure to include return address information on your questionnaire. If the recipient lacks this information, it is very difficult for responses to be returned ;-)

SUMMARY

Survey research comprises both scientific and non-scientific endeavors. With the advent of electronic survey research techniques, such as e-mail, disk based and web-based survey forms, it is important to ensure that correct and appropriate research methods are employed. New technologies can cause excitement; however, one must not lose sight of the fact that new does not always mean better. Thus far, this book has examined briefly some of the ways web-based surveys may assist in conducting survey research. The next chapter will examine the history of e-mail and web-based surveys. This will give the reader a clearer understanding of how and why web-based surveys were developed.

STUDY QUESTIONS AND EXERCISES

1) Research differs from non-disciplined inquiry in several key respects. Please discuss how these methods of inquiry differ from each other.

_____

_____

_____

_____

_____

_____

_____

_____

2) This chapter discusses three basic modes of research. Please list and describe each of these modes.

_____

_____

_____

_____

_____

_____

_____

_____

29

3) This chapter maintains that survey questions should elicit the same kind of response from each respondent. Please draft three examples of standardized questions.

_____

_____

_____

_____

_____

_____

_____

_____

_____

4) According to this chapter, to be valid, a survey must have four primary attributes. Please list them.

_____

_____

_____

_____

_____

_____

_____

5) Please explain the difference between a parameter and a statistic. Provide at least two examples of each.

_____

_____

_____

_____

_____

_____

_____

_____

6) Probability and non-probability sampling techniques are two methods of selecting sample data from a population. Please discuss the strengths and weaknesses of each.

_____

_____

_____

_____

_____

_____

_____

_____

_____

_____

_____

7) Stratified sampling is a commonly used probability sampling technique. Please define stratified sampling. Using the Web, please find and describe three recent political surveys that use stratified sampling. For practice searching the Web, see Chapter 5: Web Search Exercises.

_____

_____

_____

_____

_____

_____

_____

_____

8) Traditional survey administration techniques were discussed in this chapter including mail and telephone surveys, as well as in-person interviews. Please discuss the strengths and weaknesses of each.

_____

_____

_____

_____

_____

_____

_____

_____

SURVEY RESEARCH RESOURCES

The following resource list is an enhanced version of an online bibliography developed by Professor Shelly Carden of the University of Kansas. These books, articles and chapters will provide additional support for anyone wishing to develop a survey instrument.

1. Babbie, E.R. (1990). Survey research methods. Belmont, CA: Wadsworth Publishing Company, Inc. An excellent and comprehensive book that covers everything from issues of validity to question wording to sampling.
2. Baker, Therese L. (1999). Doing social research 3rd edition. Boston, MA: McGraw Hill College.
3. Bradburn, N. & S. Sudman. (1979). Improving interview method and questionnaire design. San Francisco: Jossey-Bass Publishers. Question lengths, open-ended vs. closed-ended questions, etc. are all covered in this volume on constructing better survey questions.
4. Bennett Jr., Lerone (1973). Before the mayflower. Baltimore, MD: Penguin Books.
5. Bradburn, N. & S. Sudman. (1988). Polls and surveys: Understanding what they tell us. San Francisco: Jossey-Bass. This book covers a broad range of issues including sampling, issues of validity, question wording, etc.
6. Brownlee, K.A. (1975). "A note on the effects of non-response on surveys." Journal of the American Statistical Association, 52(227):19-32.
7. Conversation with Luis Garcia, Director of Research, Boston Police Department. October 17, 1998.
8. Converse, J. (1987). Survey research in the united states: roots and emergence 1890-1960. Berkeley, CA: University of California Press. Comprehensive report of the beginnings of survey research in the U.S., with excellent examples and mini-biographies of survey research pioneers.
9. Converse, J. and Presser, J. (1986). Survey questions: Handcrafting the standardized questionnaire. Sage Publications.
10. Fowler, F.J. (1993). Survey research methods. Newbury Park, CA: Sage Publications. Another comprehensive volume covering a wide range of survey research techniques and issues.
11. Fowler, F. (1995). Improving survey questions: Design and evaluation. Newbury Park, CA: Sage Publications. This book has some good suggestions on how to stimulate recall of past behaviors.
12. Gaddis, Susanne E. (1998). How to design online surveys. Training and development.
13. Hoffman, Donna and Novak, Tom (1995). The CommerceNet/Nielsen Internet Demographics Survey: Is it Representative? URL= http://www2000.ogsm.vanderbilt.edu/surveys/cn.questions.html
14. Krewski, D., Platek, R., & Rao, J. (1980). Current topics in survey sampling. New York, NY: Academic Press. Compilation of a series of symposium papers which include: "Survey Sampling Activities at the Survey Research Center," "Survey Research at the Bureau of the Census," and "Should the Census Count Be Adjusted for Allocation Purposes?: Equity Considerations?"
15. Litwin, M.S. (1995). How to measure survey reliability and validity. Sage Publications.
16. Mann, Alan, Director of Public Opinion Research, Michigan House of Representative. Interview, July, 1998.

17. Metha, R. & E. Sivadas. (1995). "Comparing response rates and response content in mail versus electronic mail surveys." <u>Journal of the market research society</u>, 37:429-439.
18. Nachmias, Chava Frankfort, & David Nachmias. (1996). <u>Research methods in the social sciences</u>. New York, NY: St. Martin's Press.
19. Payne, S. (1951). <u>The art of asking questions</u>. Princeton, New Jersey: Princeton University Press. The classic and still cited treatise on wording questions in surveys.
20. Rea, L., & R. Parker. (1992). <u>Designing and conducting survey research: A comprehensive guide</u>. San Francisco: Jossey-Bass Publishers. A good book that is much like others, however it does have excellent computational formulas for determining margin of error for large and small sample sizes, as well as comprehensive formulas for determining sample sizes with differing types of designs.
21. Smith, Tom W. (1990). "The first straw? A study of the origins of elections polls." <u>Public opinion quarterly</u>, 54:21-36.
22. Schuman, Howard, & Stanley Presser. (1981). <u>Questions and answers in attitude surveys: Experiments on question form, wording, and context</u>. New York, NY: Academic Press. Excellent book--the authors conducted at least 100 studies over several years to assess effects of question form, wording, context, and their interactions with each other and respondent background variables. The research is presented in detail, and the authors draw conclusions at the end of each chapter.
23. Steffey, D., & N. Bradburn. (1994). <u>Counting people in the information age</u>. Washington, D.C.: National Academy Press. Detailed discussion of the problems facing the 2000 Census, with explicit recommendations for addressing these problems for the upcoming Census.
24. Sudman, S. (1976). <u>Applied sampling</u>. New York: Academic Press. This book focuses on the costs of surveys, with everything framed in terms of conducting surveys with a limited budget and how to maximize the use of limited resources.
25. Sudman, S., & N. Bradburn. (1974). <u>Response effects in surveys</u>. Chicago: Aldine Publishing Company. This is an older book and one of the first on response effects.
26. Sudman, S., & N.M. Bradburn. (1982). <u>Asking questions</u>. San Francisco: Jossey-Bass Publishers.
27. Sudman, S.; Bradburn, N.; & N. Schwarz. (1996). <u>Thinking about answers: The application of cognitive processes to survey methodology</u>. San Francisco: Jossey-Bass Publishers. This book describes the cognitive processes involved when respondents answer survey questions, applies this knowledge to questionnaire construction, and offers theoretical explanations for the empirical observations of response effects.
28. Survey Research Center. <u>A comparison of mail and e-mail for a survey of employees in federal statistical agencies</u>.
    URL= <u>http://www.bsos.umd.edu/src/statcan.zip</u>
29. Wentland, E., & K. Smith. (1993). <u>Survey responses: An evaluation of their validity</u>. San Diego: Academic Press.
30. White, Ralph. (1951). <u>Value-added analysis: the nature and use of the method</u>. New York: Society for the Psychological Study of Social Issues.

Book Chapters

1. Anderson, A.B.; Basilevsky, A.; & D.P. Hum. (1983). "Measurement: Theory and techniques." In P.H. Rossi, J.D. Wright, and A.B. Anderson (Eds.), <u>Handbook of survey research</u>. New York, NY: Academic Press.
2. Anderson, A.B.; Basilevsky, A.; & D.P. Hum. (1983). "Missing data: A review of the literature." In P.H. Rossi, J.D. Wright, & A.B. Anderson (Eds.), <u>Handbook of survey research</u>. New York, NY: Academic Press.
3. Bradburn, N.M. (1983). "Response effects." In P.H. Rossi, J.D. Wright, & A.B. Anderson (Eds.), <u>Handbook of survey research</u>. New York, NY: Academic Press.
4. Frankel, M. (1983). "Sampling theory." In P.H. Rossi, J.D. Wright, & A.B. Anderson (Eds.), <u>Handbook of survey research</u>. New York, NY: Academic Press.
5. Martin, E. (1983). "Surveys as social indicators: Problems in monitoring trends." In P.H. Rossi, J.D. Wright, & A.B. Anderson (Eds.), <u>Handbook of survey research</u>. New York, NY: Academic Press.
6. Sheatsley, P.B. (1983). "Questionnaire construction and item writing." In P.H. Rossi, J.D. Wright, & A.B. Anderson (Eds.), <u>Handbook of survey research</u>. New York, NY: Academic Press.
7. Sudman, S. (1983). "Applied sampling." In P.H. Rossi, J.D. Wright, & A.B. Anderson (Eds.), <u>Handbook of survey research</u>. New York, NY: Academic Press.

Chapter Two: Introduction to the Internet and the Web

Chapter Two provides a history of e-mail and web-based survey research techniques. The Chapter begins with a history of the Internet, along with a discussion of how the Web arose from the Internet. The usefulness of the Web to researchers, government officials, students and others is discussed. This is followed by a discussion of the development of e-mail and web-based surveys. Finally, an annotated bibliography of Internet and Web resources, evaluative materials and Web directories follows to help broaden the reader's knowledge on this emerging topic.

A Brief History of the Internet

The Internet began in the 1960s as a means of protecting the United States' defense communications infrastructure. Military communications networks have been known to experience reliability problems during wartime. Nuclear war has the potential to destroy a large percentage of the United State's communications capability. Military leaders thought that a post-nuclear military would need an extremely reliable command-and-control system. Most post-nuclear scenarios painted a picture of a weakened military command and control with no effective means of communications. The RAND Corporation was contracted by the U.S. Department of Defense to devise a solution to this problem.

RAND's solution was to implement a computerized command and control system linked by a network with nodes (connecting points) in every state and major metropolitan center in the country. It was hoped that all military installations would eventually become part of the network. The objective was that, no matter how devastating the attack, this network would ensure that surviving military installations would still be able to communicate.

In 1964, RAND released its recommendations. In terms of command and control, these findings were not what the military had in mind. Military organizational structure is based upon a centralized command, broadly based at the lower levels and growing more focused and narrow at the top.

RAND's network had no identifiable central authority. All computers connected to the network (network nodes) were designed to operate independently in case of mass destruction. While this was not the traditional military command model, the plan was accepted and given a chance to succeed. The program, known as the Advanced Research Project Network (ARPA), succeeded. The network grew quickly to include military institutions around the globe and eventually became what we know today as the Internet.

When first developed, ARPA had four network nodes located at universities around the United States. The original installation was located at the University of California at Los Angeles (UCLA). After having proved successful, military institutions were added. Throughout the 1970s, ARPA's network grew. Unlike computer networks preceding it, ARPA could accommodate many different kinds of machines. As long as individual machines could speak the language of the ARPA, the brand and content of the computer was irrelevant.

ARPA's decentralized structure made expansion easy. There existed no one "boss" of ARPA. Nor was there an authority to restrict access to the Internet. Anyone with a compatible system could link into the system. As a result, scientists in non-military institutions linked to

ARPA. It was during this time (the mid 1970s through the mid 1980s) that education, business, and government first made significant inroads into ARPA.

ARPA's original standard for communication was known as NCP (Network Control Protocol). Over time, NCP was superceded by the current, higher-level standard known as TCP/IP. TCP, or "Transmission Control Protocol," converted messages into streams of data at the source, then reassembled them into messages at the destination. IP, or "Internet Protocol," handled the addressing, seeing to it that data were routed across multiple nodes and multiple networks with multiple standards. This is the communication standard that still exists today.

In 1984, the National Science Foundation (NSF) installed a network of computers around the United States. This system, in conjunction with the ARPA network, is now known as the Internet. NSF provided broad access for educational, government, and research institutions. Once the opportunity for profit became clear, many businesses joined the system.

ARPA ceased to exist in 1989. However, its successor, the Internet, thrives. By 1998, nearly 20 million Internet service providers (ISPs) maintained host server computers, with which anyone with a modem could communicate. It is estimated that this number of server computers will increase to approximately 500 million by the year 2000.

Concurrently, the Intent had become the communications mode of choice in many university departments across the country. E-mail has long provided free communications access to anyone on the Internet. While Internet e-mail was not as sophisticated as that provided by emerging on-line services, it worked fairly well and was free. Until recently, on-line services provided proprietary and largely closed systems to their users, making communications beyond their services nearly impossible. The burgeoning growth of e-mail on the Internet created tremendous pressure for on-line services to allow access to Internet e-mail, in addition to their own proprietary systems. By 1996, nearly all online services provided free Internet e-mail, in addition to their own proprietary mail programs.

The use and growth of the Internet is staggering. Consider that:

- In June of 1996, fewer than 40 million people around the world were connected to the Internet. By December 1997, more than 100 million people were connected to the Internet. This number is expected to quintuple by the year 2000.
- Actual users of the Internet are estimated at about four times the number of those connected. Access points include schools, universities, government agencies, businesses and libraries.
- In December of 1996, about 627,000 Internet domain names had been registered. By the end of 1998, that number had tripled.
- Internet traffic doubles approximately every 100 days. This far outstrips the 18 months it takes for computing power to double.
- The Internet's pace of adoption eclipses all major electronic technologies that preceded it. Radio was in existence 36 years before 50 million people tuned in. Television took 13 years to reach the same benchmark. The personal computer took 16 years. The Internet took only four years to reach 50 million users.

It is estimated that half of all users have four-year college degrees and 20 percent have advanced degrees. This information is extremely important to business and is expected to drive the large increase in numbers of servers and subscribers described above.

One of the most powerful features of the Internet is its use of client and server software. Client and server software allows computers to communicate over long distances. Researchers can access a computer database across the country, using the processing power of other computers. Scientists can use powerful supercomputers a continent away. Remote libraries may be searched by anyone with a modem and communications software. Police agencies may access information on offenders across the country or around the world.

Moreover, file transfer protocol (FTP) software allows Internet users to access remote machines and quickly retrieve programs or text. As an example, one megabyte of data, roughly equivalent to a 1,000-page double-spaced document, may be downloaded in about six minutes on standard modems (57,600 bits per second). FTP software was originally available as a stand-alone software package. Today, FTP software is usually bundled (comes packaged) with web-browsing software such as Netscape Communicator or Microsoft Internet Explorer. E-mail (electronic mail) was one of the first Internet services used widely in business, government, and education. The primary advantage of e-mail was transmission speed. As previously described, in the early days of the Internet, transferring files and images was painstakingly slow. It could take up to 10 minutes to transmit a two-page memo, compared with about 3 seconds in the late 1990s. Because sending e-mail messages is much faster than traditional postal service mail, users naturally gravitated toward this more efficient mode of communication. In addition, messages could be sent on the Internet to any location on the globe at little or no cost, no more than the cost of the time to type it. As a result, e-mail became very popular among business and government users.

E-mail is relatively straightforward in the context of a web-browsing program. To send e-mail while using Internet Explorer, the user clicks on the **Mail** button on the toolbar, followed by **New Message** on the Mail submenu. The Mail window opens. At this point, the user types the e-mail address of the recipient in the **To** text box and types the message in the workspace at the bottom of the Mail Window. Clicking the **Send** button will send the e-mail to its destination.

Several other services are available on the Internet. Telnet is a remote log-in service used by many libraries. The Telnet screen is sparse, looking much like a character-based or DOS operating system. If you have searched for a library book using a computer catalogue, you have used Telnet. The USENET is a messaging system, allowing for discussions on a delayed basis. Users post messages to the newsgroup and, later, may read replies. USENET is like e-mail, except the posted information is available for everyone to read. Internet Chat allows for real-time keyboard communication with other users, who all subscribe to the same chat service. Gopher and Archie are hierarchical, text-based, file retrieval and upload systems supported by many universities. All these services may be accessed through a web browser.

Within the context of a web-browsing program, hypertext links that lead to each of these services may be selected. Whether a Gopher or Archie server is being used is not obvious to the user. Prior to the advent of hypertext transfer protocol (http), text-based Gopher and Archie protocols were used extensively to find Internet information. Hypertext transfer protocol has now largely replaced the use of Gopher and Archie protocols.

WHAT IS THE WORLD WIDE WEB?

The most important part of the Internet today is the World Wide Web (the Web or WWW). The Web is a unique part of the Internet in that it utilizes a wide variety of features, such as graphics, photographs, sounds, or video clips. The Web utilizes Hypertext to link this information, so you can travel electronically from one site to another. The Web is the portion of the Internet structured for use with a web browser. In other words, the Web is a subset of the Internet. A web browser is a program that displays text, graphics, audio, and visual information.

This information is accessible by clicking on a hypertext link. Microsoft Internet Explore and Netscape Communicator are examples of web browser programs.

Hypertext

Hypertext is specialized web browser text that transmits the user to another website by means of clicking on the hypertext. It is typically underlined, although it does not have to be. Hypertext provides access to graphics, photographs, sounds, or video clips. Hypertext has revolutionized the way that research is conducted.

With hypertext, one can use a web browser to open a search engine, find a topic, and search the resulting links until the needed information is found. Every day, more hypertext files, research databases, academic journals and business and government resources are made available on the Internet. All state governments, most federal agencies, research organizations, political parties, and law enforcement agencies maintain websites. It is safe to say that, for the most part, researchers need to go no further than the Web to meet their research needs.

The Web comprises all computers on the Internet that may be accessed through web browsers. Web browsers allow the user to access information with little or no training. Links, representing a connection to a webpage at another location, are clearly identifiable on webpages. Clicking on links gives the user access to the information located on a remote computer.

Information on the Web is stored in computers known as web servers at various sites all over the world. When a website is visited, the first page seen is the site's "home page." A home page is like the title page and contents of a book. It describes which site has been accessed and what information is to be found there.

A home page is one type of webpage. A webpage is any page existing on a website. As opposed to the contents, webpages are the actual text of the book. Click on a link (hypertext) on the home page to be transported to a webpage on another website or another webpage on the original website.

Web Content

The most important component of the Web is the information or content retrieved from it. Web content is the vast array of information available on the Internet. Internet content is typically available in the form of webpages and may include graphics, video, audio and text. Without content, there would be no reason for the Internet to exist. The following are examples of what is available on the Web in the criminal justice area alone.

The Justice Information Center website of the National Criminal Justice Reference Service includes a tremendous amount of content for the criminal justice researcher. This website includes data on corrections, the courts, crime prevention, criminal justice statistics, drugs and crime, international issues, juvenile justice, law enforcement, research and evaluation, and victimization. As an example, from this website, a copy of the 1996 National Crime Victimization Preliminary Survey, as well as prior year victimization surveys, may be downloaded. This means that a copy is available of the complete text version of this survey, which covers rape, sexual assault, robbery, assault, theft, household burglary, and motor vehicle theft for U.S. residents aged 12 or older.

The Massachusetts State Police website includes content representative of state/provincial police agencies. Information on contacting police units, pictures of missing and wanted persons, crime statistics, employment, internal organizational structure and police news updates are all a part of this site. Of interest, the Massachusetts site includes a Frequently Asked Questions (FAQ) page. Questions such as "What should I do if I have a motor vehicle accident?" and "Are headphones legal to wear while driving?" are just two of the many questions answered.

The National Archive of Criminal Justice Data is located at the University of Michigan's Inter-University Consortium for Political and Social Research website. The Archives currently hold over 500 data collections relating to criminal justice. This website provides browsing and downloading access to most of this data and documentation. Attitude surveys, community studies, corrections, court case processing, the court system, the criminal justice system, crime and delinquency, official crime statistics, police, victimization, drugs, alcohol, and crime are the categories from which data may be downloaded.

The State University of New York at Albany School of Criminal Justice maintains a website representative of colleges and universities worldwide. Its content includes information on faculty, students, job announcements, and classes offered. Like some other schools (notably, Florida State University and California Lutheran University), SUNY Albany includes an extensive set of criminal justice links.

How Useful is the Web?

The Web has provided access and information to people in a way that was not possible just a few years ago. The following example illustrates the power of the Web on a practical and relevant basis. Catalogue and telephone sales have long been the only reasonable method of purchasing certain products for persons living in rural areas. For example, to purchase an automobile or major appliance meant a very long drive to an urban center or a somewhat less than hands-on evaluation of a product via telephone call or catalogue. Living in rural Michigan, the author's father, A.D. Nesbary, Sr., understands the difficulties of having to drive anywhere from 10 to 40 miles to evaluate goods and services, especially if the item is at all unusual. Last summer, Mr. Nesbary had questions about the possibility of purchasing solar energy products to help ensure a steady and reliable power source for his home. He had no knowledge of solar energy products and asked how he should start his search.

I recommended that he search the Web for solar energy and solar photovoltaic cell products. My father had no idea how to use the Web, so I grabbed my laptop, and we got together for a quick lesson. After logging onto the Web and searching for about a half-hour, we found about 10 companies selling solar photovoltaic cells in and near Michigan. Their websites included detailed information about their products and services. I explained that, without his own computer, he could continue to access the Web by using computers at his local library to search for information about solar energy products.

The most important aspect of this story to me is that a 78-year-old former steel worker living in rural, lower Michigan could find information on solar energy product vendors in about a half hour of learning to access the Web. He did not have to make numerous phone calls to the phone company's information number attempting to find a vendor. He did not have to wait for weeks for a catalogue (possibly outdated) to arrive via regular mail. He did not have to drive up to 40 miles to visit the nearest vender of solar energy products. He could simply access the Web and find several vendors and information on solar products from the comfort of his kitchen table. At worst, the next time he needs information requiring some level of research, he can visit his local library (one mile away) and access the Web.

THE INTERNET AND WEB SURVEYS

With the advent of the Internet, interpersonal communications have changed dramatically. E-mail, websites, Internet chat, newsgroups and listserves have provided the ability for researchers to communicate with their peers nearly instantly. The Internet has also provided powerful new methods of conducting survey research.

Internet surveys are available in three basic flavors, including e-mail, disk-based and web- or forms-based. Examples of each may be found in Chapters Three and Four. The oldest form of Internet survey is the e-mail survey. E-mail surveys are nearly identical to regular mail surveys in that they both employ written questionnaires. E-mail and regular mail differ in that e-mail surveys are transmitted and returned via e-mail rather than regular mail. E-mail surveys employ the following methodology:

- Potential respondents are identified,
- An e-mail survey is sent to the respondents,
- The respondent answers the e-mail survey and returns the survey form via e-mail, and
- The survey administrator codes and analyzes data received.

A second form of Internet survey is the disk-based survey. Disk-based surveys comprise questionnaires placed on computer diskette in word-processing format or executable (.exe) format. In word-processing format, the respondent opens the questionnaire in a word processing program (Microsoft Word, WordPerfect, WordPro and others) and fills in the blanks just like a paper questionnaire. In executable format, the questionnaire is stored in database format, giving the survey administrator and respondent tremendous flexibility in developing and answering questions. The executable file is actually an application written in a database (Paradox, Access, etc.). Disk-based surveys employ the following methodology:

- Potential respondents are identified,
- A survey is sent to the respondents via computer diskette or e-mail attachment,
- The respondent answers the survey and returns it via e-mail attachment or computer diskette, and
- The survey administrator codes and analyzes data received.

Disk-based surveys are unique in that they may be transmitted via regular mail or by e-mail. Transmitting surveys via diskette is useful in cases where e-mail is not feasible and/or the survey administrator prefers to automate the survey process. Transmitting disks via e-mail attachment is useful in cases where not all respondents have Web access. The respondent may still complete and return an automated survey in a fashion similar to a web survey. The survey administrator may collect and automatically code disk-based data in a fashion similar to a web survey, although the process can take longer.

Forms-based web surveys comprise a hypertext document (webpage) placed on the survey administrator's website. Web surveys are often found on websites oriented to politics and the media.

The survey administrator has two methods of contacting potential respondents. First, based on e-mail instructions, the respondent locates the survey website and completes the questionnaire. Second, the survey administrator can survey regular users of the website on which the survey instrument is located.

Web surveys combine the accuracy of a written survey with the flexibility of an interview. The interviewee must enter data in the correct location ensuring increased accuracy. Web surveys provide the added flexibility and power of database entry and analysis. Structured properly, web survey responses may be entered and stored in database format. The data may be automatically coded and analyzed, saving a tremendous amount of time and effort on the part of the survey administrator.

Moreover, web-surveys employ the following methodology:

- Potential respondents are identified,
- An initial e-mail is sent to potential respondents notifying them of the web location of the survey. A hyperlink to the survey form may be included in the e-mail,
- The respondent answers the survey and returns it by clicking a "submit" or "return" button, and
- The survey administrator codes and analyzes data received.

Web surveys can also be relatively inexpensive. With web surveys and e-mail surveys, there are no mailing or long distance telephone costs. Further, coding and analysis costs may be kept to a minimum, if database tools are used to retrieve survey responses.

Early studies demonstrate the strengths and weaknesses of e-mail surveys. Metha and Sivadas (1995) found that e-mail surveys could be equally or more effective than regular mail surveys, both in response rate and response time. They found that the bulk of e-mail responses arrived within three days of administration, as opposed to about three weeks for regular mail surveys. They also found that e-mail responses were much less costly than regular mail surveys.

Comely (1998) also found that e-mail surveys were much quicker than regular mail surveys. He found that the average e-mail response arrived in 4.2 days, while regular mail responses took 10.8 days. Most e-mail responses (87%) arrived in 7 days or less, while most regular mail responses (63%) arrived in 8 days or more. Comely found a slightly higher response rate among regular mail respondents (17%) than e-mail respondents (13.5%).

Web surveys have many important limitations. First, only those persons and organizations with Web access may complete web surveys. In 1999, nearly half of households do not have Web access in the home, meaning all of these households without Web access are precluded from responding to web surveys. Second, it is argued that web surveys are likely not to capture responses from minorities and the poor. This is because minorities and the poor have fewer computers in the home, as compared to the general population. Another weakness of web surveys is security. Without password protection or other security scheme, any person happening across the web survey may respond to it. This means that there may be no way of identifying the survey respondent.

SUMMARY

The Internet has grown from a tool of military strategists to a vehicle for commerce, communication, and education. Although the need for military communications reliability was the primary reason the Internet was developed, its decentralized structure and standard communications protocols allowed for fast growth. Improving technologies (software, hardware, and network), along with grant money from the National Science Foundation, allowed the Internet to move from a primarily military application to other uses.

STUDY QUESTIONS AND EXERCISES

1) Use of the Internet grew dramatically with the advent of the Web. Why do you think that this is so? Has government use of the Internet expanded, along with growth in other areas?

_____

_____

_____

_____

_____

_____

_____

_____

2) What are the primary differences between the Internet and the World Wide Web?

_____

_____

_____

_____

_____

_____

_____

3) Several ways were discussed about how the Web is useful as a research resource. Please describe three limitations of the Web as a research resource.

_____

_____

_____

_____

_____

_____

4) Web surveys are said to have a number of inherent methodological weaknesses, not the least of which is a tendency toward selection bias. How must the Web change before selection bias issues are eliminated? Draw upon what you learned in Chapter One for your answer.

_____

_____

_____

_____

_____

_____

_____

_____

INTERNET AND WEB RESOURCES

The following resource list outlines a wide variety of Internet and Web evaluation resources. You will be able to access information on web searching, evaluate Web resources and find links to numerous web directories. This resource list was developed by Laura Gayle Green of the University of Missouri-Kansas City and is available online at: http://cctr.umkc.edu/user/lggreen/crtthk.htm. Ms. Green provides many useful annotations to her notes, and her website is replete with Internet and Web resources.

All links herein were verified as of February 1999. If a link does not work, visit the Survey Research companion website at http://www.nesbary.com/survey. There you will find updates to pages included in this book.

1. The Argus Clearinghouse. URL=http://www.clearinghouse.net/
2. Bryn Mawr-Haverford research guide 1: Library research. (1997). Bryn Mawr, PA: Bryn Mawr College.
   URL=http://www.brynmawr.edu/Library/Docs/resguide1.html
3. Recommended readings in critical thinking. (1997). Rohnert Park, CA: Center for Critical Thinking.
   URL=http://www.sonoma.edu/cthink/K12/k12library/recommend.nclk
4. Alexander, Janet E., & Marsha A. Tate. (1997). Evaluating web resources. Chester, PA: Widener University.
   URL=http://www.science.widener.edu/~withers/webeval.htm
5. University of Washington. (1997). Evaluation criteria. Seattle, WA: University of Washington.
   URL=http://weber.u.washington.edu/~libr560/NETEVAL/criteria.html
6. University of Washington. (1997). Evaluation criteria, continued. Seattle, WA: University of Washington.
   URL=http://weber.u.washington.edu/~libr560/NETEVAL/criteria2.html
7. Widener University. (1996). Web evaluation techniques: Bibliography. Chester, PA: Widener University.
   URL=http://www.science.widener.edu/~withers/wbstrbib.htm
8. Widener University. (1997). Web evaluation techniques: Bibliography. Chester, PA: Widener University.
   URL=http://www.science.widener.edu/~withers/wbstrbib.htm
9. Alexander, Janet E., Tate, Marsha A., & Mike Powell. (1997). Modular web teaching pyramid. Chester, PA: Widener University.
   URL=http://www.science.widener.edu/~withers/pyramid.htm
10. Auer, Nicole. (1997). Bibliography on evaluating internet resources. Blacksburg, VA: Virginia Polytechnic Institute and State University.
    URL=http://refserver.lib.vt.edu/libinst/critTHINK.HTM
11. Bartelstein, Andrea, & Anne Zald. (1997). "Teaching students to think critically about internet resources." Seattle, WA: University of Washington Libraries.
    URL=http://weber.u.washington.edu/~libr560/NETEVAL/
12. Bates, Mary Ellen. (1997). "The internet: Part of a professional searcher's toolkit." Online, 21(1):47.

13. Brandt, D. Scott. (1996). "Evaluating information on the internet." <u>Computers in libraries</u>, 16(5):44-46.
14. _____. (1996). "Relevancy and searching the internet." <u>Computers in Libraries</u>, 16(8):35.
15. _____. (1997). <u>Why we need to evaluate what we find on the internet</u>. W. Lafayette, IN: Purdue University.
    Also cited as "Anyone can (and probably will) put anything up on the internet."
    URL=<u>http://thorplus.lib.purdue.edu/~techman/eval.html</u>
16. Caplan, Priscilla. (1997). "Will the real internet please stand up?" <u>The Public-Access Computer Systems Review</u>, 8(2).
    URL=<u>http://lib-04.lib.uh.edu/pacsrev/1997/capl8n2.htm</u>
17. Caywood, Carolyn. (1997). "Library selection criteria for WWW resources." [N.p.]. An early version appeared on p. 169 of the May/June, 1996 issue of <u>Public Libraries</u>.
    URL=<u>http://www6.pilot.infi.net/~carolyn/criteria.html</u>
18. Courtois, Martin P. (1996). "Cool tools for web searching: An update." <u>Online</u>, 20(3):29.
19. Courtois, Martin P., Baer, William M., & Marcella Stark. (1995). "Cool tools for searching the web." <u>Online</u>, 19(6):14.
20. Craigmile, Bob. (1995). "Will librarians hack it on the highway?" <u>Computers in Libraries</u>, 15(1):24.
21. Deardorff, Thom. (1997). <u>Finding and evaluating information on the web</u>. Seattle, WA: University of Washington.
    URL=<u>http://weber.u.washington.edu/~tdeardor/Webtour/Finding.html</u>
22. _____. (1997). <u>Web world tour: A handbook for travelers</u>. Seattle, WA: University of Washington.
    URL=<u>http://weber.u.washington.edu/~tdeardor/Webtour/webtour.html</u>
23. DiMaggio, Tanya. (1997). <u>Evaluating online information</u>. Austin, TX: University of Texas. From <u>The Kid's Internet Gateway</u>.
    URL=<u>http://volvo.gslis.utexas.edu/~kidnet/kidgate.html</u>.
    URL=<u>http://volvo.gslis.utexas.edu/~kidnet/evalinfo.html</u>
24. Engle, Michael. (1997). <u>The seven steps of the research process</u>. Ithaca, NY: Cornell University Library.
    URL=<u>http://www.library.cornell.edu/okuref/research/skill1.htm</u>
25. Engle, Michael, Ormondroyd, Joan, & Tony Cosgrave. (1996). <u>Critically analyzing information</u>. Ithaca, NY: Cornell University Library.
    URL=<u>http://www.library.cornell.edu/okuref/research/skill26.htm</u>
26. Gordon, Mark W. _____. "Sorting it out: Habits of mind." <u>Electronic Learning</u>, 15(6):S10.
27. Grassian, Esther. (1997). <u>Thinking critically about WWW resources</u>. Los Angeles, CA: UCLA College Library.
    URL=<u>http://www.library.ucla.edu/libraries/college/instruct/critical.htm</u>
28. Jacobson, Trudi, & Laura Cohen. (1996). <u>Evaluating internet resources</u>. Albany, NY: State University of New York at Albany.
    URL=<u>http://www.albany.edu/library/internet/evaluate.html</u>
29. Janicke Hinchliffe, Lisa. (1997). <u>Evaluation of information</u>. Urbana, IL: University of Illinois.
    URL=<u>http://alexia.lis.uiuc.edu/~janicke/Eval.html</u>

30. _____. (1997). <u>Resource selection and information evaluation</u>. Urbana, IL: University of Illinois.
    URL=<u>http://alexia.lis.uiuc.edu/~janicke/Evaluate.html</u>
31. Kimmel, Stacey. (1996). "Robot-generated databases on the World Wide Web: These robots retrieve WWW documents and index data, and then store it in a database." <u>Database</u>, 19(1):40.
32. Kirk, Elizabeth E. (1997). <u>Evaluating information found on the internet</u>. [N.p.]
    URL=<u>http://milton.mse.jhu.edu:8001/research/education/net.html</u>
33. McGann, Jerome. (1996). "Radiant textuality." <u>Victorian Studies</u>, 39(3):379.
34. Micco, Mary. (September 1996). "Part 1: Subject authority control in the world of the internet." <u>Library and Information Science Research Electronic Journal</u>, 6(3).
    URL=<u>http://www.lib.ncsu.edu/stacks/l/libres/libres-v6n03-micco-part_1.txt</u>
35. Micco, Mary. (September 1996). "Part 2: Subject authority control in the world of the internet." <u>Library and Information Science Research Electronic Journal</u>, 6(3).
    URL=<u>http://www.lib.ncsu.edu/stacks/l/libres/libres-v6n03-micco-part_2.txt</u>
36. Munson, Kurt. (1996). "World wide web indexes and hierarchical lists: Finding tools for the internet." <u>Computers in Libraries</u>, 16(6):54.
37. Notess, Greg R. (1996). "Catch the lightning: Keeping current with the net." <u>Online</u>, 20(3):86.
38. O'Malley, Chris. (1995). "Drowning in the net." <u>Popular Science</u>, 246(6):78.
39. Pagell, Ruth A. (1995). "Quality and the internet: An open letter." <u>Online</u>, 19(4):7.
40. Scholz, Ann. (1996). <u>Evaluating world wide web information</u>. W. Lafayette, IN: Purdue University Libraries.
    URL=<u>http://thorplus.lib.purdue.edu/research/classes/gs175/3gs175/evaluation.html</u>
41. _____. (1996). <u>Evaluating world wide web information</u>. W. Lafayette, IN: Purdue University Libraries.
    URL=
    <u>http://thorplus.lib.purdue.edu/library_info/instruction/gs175/3gs175/evaluation.html</u>
42. Schrock, Kathy. (1997). <u>Kathy Schrock's guide for educators: Critical evaluation surveys</u>. With the advent of the World Wide Web and the huge amount of information that is contained there, students need to be able to critically evaluate a Web page for authenticity, applicability, authorship, bias, and usability. The ability to critically evaluate information is an important skill in this information age.
    URL=<u>http://www.capecod.net/schrockguide/eval.htm</u>
43. Sipe, Jeffrey R. (1997). "Although the net runneth over, info seekers had best beware." <u>Insight on the News</u>, 13(23):40.
44. Smith, Alastair. (1997). <u>Criteria for evaluation of internet information resources</u>. Wellington, New Zealand: Victoria University of Wellington.
    URL=<u>http://www.vuw.ac.nz/~agsmith/evaln/evaln.htm</u> >
    URL=<u>http://www.vuw.ac.nz/~agsmith/evaln/index.htm</u>
45. _____. (1997). "Evaluation of information sources." [N.p.]
    URL=<u>http://www.vuw.ac.nz/~agsmith/evaln/evaln.htm</u>
46. Tate, Marsha A., & Janet E. Alexander. (1996). "Teaching critical evaluation skills for world wide web resources." <u>Computers in Libraries</u>, 16(10):49-55.
47. Taubes, Gary. (1995). "Indexing the Internet." <u>Science</u>, 269:1354-56.

48. Tillman, Hope N. (1997). <u>Evaluating quality on the net</u>. Babson Park, MA: Babson College.
URL=<u>http://www.tiac.net/users/hope/findqual.html</u>
49. Tomaiuolo, Nicholas G., & Joan G. Parker. (1996). "An analysis of internet search engines: Assessment of over 200 search queries." <u>Computers in Libraries</u>, 16(6):58.
50. Wittman, Sandra. (1997). <u>Evaluating web sites</u>. Des Plaines, Illinois: Oakton Community College.
URL=<u>http://www.oakton.edu/~wittman/find/eval.htm</u>

Chapter Three: Introduction to Web-Based Surveys

Chapter Three examines the history of web-based surveys. To the extent that web surveys are so new, other Internet survey tools, such as e-mail surveys, executable file surveys, and Internet search engines are discussed as well. The strengths and weaknesses of survey research are examined, along with the results of three web surveys administered by the author during 1998. These surveys were administered to state law enforcement agencies, local law enforcement agencies and major universities in the United States. The intent of these surveys is to compare response rate and response time of web surveys versus traditional surveys.

THE LITERATURE

The literature on Internet-based survey research in the social sciences is only now beginning to appear in mainstream academic journals. Prior to 1995, the bulk of the published work on Internet-based surveys appeared in market research and business-oriented publications. Most of these studies examine the utility of regular mail surveys and e-mail surveys. Very few useful studies exist regarding the utility of web-based surveys versus regular mail surveys.

Most notably Kelly-Milburn & Milburn, 1995; Landis, 1995; Rosen & Petty, 1995; McGlade, Milot, & Scales, 1996; and Stanton, 1998; have reported on the potential of email, listservers, and newsgroups as research tools. Some organizations have applied these new technologies in the areas of personnel retention and selection (Berner, 1994; Schmitt, 1997). Moreover, an application of these technologies that appears to have tremendous practical application is the use of the Internet for organizational surveys. Kuhnert and McCauley (1996) examined and discussed a variety of new technologies, including email, as viable resources for organizational data collection. They argued that these new technologies were potentially so effective that paper surveys would, in the relatively near future, fade into the background. Stanton (1998) found that the amount of missing data will be lower for data records collected using the WWW than for data records collected using traditional paper and pencil surveys. To test the validity of his work, Stanton used a square root and an ANOVA test. ANOVA results indicated that the Internet data had significantly fewer missing datapoints.

Thus far, the data on Internet-based surveys is mixed when compared to regular mail surveys. On the positive side, a series of studies have been conducted that support the limited use of e-mail surveys. SGA Market Research conducted an e-mail survey as part of a project for the Henley Centre on Media Futures. Their surveys included 1,000 regular mail surveys, 1,769 regular mail surveys with the option to answer the survey via a website, and 795 e-mail surveys. The response rate for regular mail surveys was 15.4 percent, 13.5 percent for e-mail surveys, and 17 percent for regular mail with a website option. Only one percent of regular mail respondents took advantage of the website option when offered. SGA found e-mail surveys to be much more cost effective than regular mail surveys, saving approximately $3,000 or 20 percent when compared to regular mail surveys.

CommerceNet and NielsenMedia conducted one of the first comprehensive examinations of the utility of Internet surveys in December 1995. The study examined the demographic makeup of Internet users, as well as the value of the Internet as a research tool. The study comprised two separate Internet use surveys:

1. A random telephone survey of 4,200 United States and Canadian residents,
2. An online survey of 32,000 self-selecting respondents.

CommerceNet and NielsenMedia suggested that the results of the online survey could be used, with minor modifications, as a means of assessing television viewership, much in the manner as the popular Nielsen Ratings systems. This claim came under severe scrutiny. Hoffman and Novak (1995) suggested that Internet respondents are younger, better educated and wealthier than the average United States and Canadian resident, and, therefore, the online surveys did not provide a valid measure of television viewership. Vanderbilt recommended a weighting system to render the Internet survey more valid. These criticisms clearly show the strengths and potential pitfalls of Internet surveys, if they are not constructed in a methodologically rigorous manner.

Advertising Age Magazine (1997, p. 36) reports that marketers in search of quick, inexpensive research data within narrowly targeted audiences are turning increasingly to the Web. Several market research companies, including ASI Market Research, Custom Research, Inc., M/A/R/C Research and Roeper Starch Worldwide partnered with Digital Marketing Services to conduct custom research on America Online. ASI, in a separate partnership, is conducting online research for several Fortune 500 firms including General Motors Corporation, Kodak, IBM, Levi Strauss & Co., Proctor Gamble Co., Sprint Corporation and Visa. While no definitive results are available as of December 1998, to the extent that the partnerships are ongoing bodes well for the utility of Internet-based survey research.

Not every study deems Internet-based survey research ready for prime time. The Georgia Institute of Technology Graphics, Visualization and Usability Center found that the Internet was not yet appropriate for survey research (GVUC 1997). Their studies showed that Internet users were predominately male and predominately college-educated, very dissimilar from the norm in the population of the United States. The Customer Service Group, a research and consulting firm, agreed with GVUC, but for different reasons. They found that the Internet makes finding specific research targets relative simple, but that many companies are very skeptical (Customer Service Group 1997). Companies believe that the Internet will allow competitors access to trade secrets. Further they believe that expensive mistakes may be made in the rush to take advantage of the Internet "gold mine."

John Chisholm, President of CustomerSat.com, argues that certain web-based surveys lack security, and that steps must be taken to ensure that survey results are valid. Chisholm recommends first that any web survey include an access password. Passwords may be e-mailed to potential respondents to ensure that they alone respond to the intended survey. Chisholm also recommends that web surveys be posted to a hidden directory known only to the survey administrator and respondent. This would further ensure that only intended respondents answer the survey.

Greguras and Stanton (1996) were among the first to develop a methodologically rigorous e-mail survey tool. Their study of academic qualifications used a listserver to publicize the availability and contents of a brief, open-ended questionnaire. This listserver broadcast an identical e-mail message to approximately 1,000 potential participants in a special interest discussion group. A very limited (N < 20) sample of individuals returned acceptable responses, and their results were coded and reported.

The University of Maryland's Survey Research Center and Joint Center in Survey Methodology also found problems with e-mail surveys (Maryland 1997). They administered a survey intended to determine response rate and response quality of e-mail surveys versus regular mail surveys. Their survey was intended to measure the organizational climate within many statistical agencies in the U.S. government. Approximately 8,200 surveys were sent, half via regular mail and half via e-mail. Of the regular mail surveys, 70.7 percent were returned; while only 42.6 percent of e-mail surveys were returned.

The reasons for the disparity in response rate are many. First, agencies provided a list of e-mail addresses and regular mail addresses for their employees. The e-mail lists proved to be fairly inaccurate, while the employee lists proved to be much more accurate. Second, different e-mail programs caused survey responses to be read differently. Many older e-mail programs are incapable of reading advanced text formatting or handling e-mail attachments. As a result, some information transmitted by researchers did not reach respondents. Third, e-mail attachments were sent without sufficient instructions regarding how to handle them. E-mail attachments 1) require the recipient to copy the attachment to a different location on the computer to enable it to be read, or 2) may require the attachment to be opened in a manner different than opening standard e-mail. As opposed to determining how to handle the attachments, some respondents chose not to respond at all.

The Maryland survey revealed other problems that made e-mail surveys less cost effective than expected. Nearly 40 percent of all e-mail responses required clerical action to render them readable, including converting answers received as attachments, messages that needed decoding and responses that were edited on a word processor prior to being returned. In all, 1,724 of the 4,066 e-mail responses required some type of corrective action before the data could be entered into a database.

1998 WEB SURVEY RESULTS

Web surveys are almost non-existent in the public sector. To help "fill in the gap," I developed a series of surveys designed to compare response rate and response time of web surveys and regular mail surveys. Specifically, surveys were sent to 50 state law enforcement agencies, 30 major city police agencies and 26 major, research, university political science departments. The entire universe of state law enforcement agencies was surveyed, while samples of local law enforcement and university political science departments were taken.

The three sets of surveys were designed to determine how the organizations use the Web in their day to day activities. For example, law enforcement agencies were asked if they use the Web to transmit scanned images of wanted criminals or missing persons. Universities were asked whether their professors place syllabi or department scheduling information on the Web. The detailed results of these surveys are being prepared under separate title and will be submitted for publication in mainstream peer-reviewed publications.

While methodology will be discussed in each of the following subsections, I will make note of some issues at this point. The specific sampling methodology for each survey will be discussed later in this Chapter. In summary, half of the surveys were administered via web survey, while the other half were administered via regular mail. Follow-up calls and e-mails were sent to all non-respondents approximately one month after initial mailing of the surveys.

Web surveys are often criticized, because it is argued that it is difficult to determine the identity of the respondent. As the argument goes, anyone reading e-mail or happening across a website may respond to it. I will respond to these arguments on several fronts.

First, e-mails often offer *more* security and more likelihood of response than regular mail surveys. Most e-mails are sent to or received from private, individual e-mail accounts. While this is no absolute proof that the named respondent will respond, there is security in knowing that the respondent nearly always has password access to the account. Unless someone else knows the respondent's e-mail password, that account cannot be accessed. With regular mail, there is no security, only the hope that the respondent will receive and respond to the survey.

Second, web surveys may be placed in secure directories (located on a fixed disk drive), offering an additional layer of security. To access the directory, the respondent must have a password or must be notified of the location of the secure directory by the researcher. Thus, only those intended to respond to a survey may respond.

Third, if a web survey is located in a hidden directory, that survey will not be available to the casual web browser. Moreover, it is very difficult to locate hidden directories on remote computers. A hacker would have to guess the name of the hidden directory and the name of the file in which the survey is stored in order to access it. Even if the survey is placed in the root (main) directory of a remote computer, the file is still relatively difficult to find by the casual web surfer.

The only possible way a file could be found through web surfing is if the file is located and catalogued by a "web spider" program. Web spiders are programs that search all accessible (non-hidden or non-secure) directories on computers linked to the World Wide Web. HotBot, WebCrawler and Alta Vista are programs that use web spiders to locate and catalogue files for placement on their search engines. Web spider programs will not find any file located on a secure Intranet (business or government website) or in a hidden directory. Even files that are found by web spiders are usually not listed on search engines for at least a month if not longer. If the researcher does not create hidden or secure directories, he or she may want to require responses within a short period of time. This minimizes the likelihood of a casual web searcher finding a web survey by accident.

The short story here is that web-based surveys can be made to be very secure by placing them in hidden directories or by providing password protection. The only reasonable way for anyone to find a survey placed in a hidden directory or a password-protected file is for a survey administrator to provide instructions on the location of the survey. Instructions on creating hidden directories and password-protected survey files are described later in this book.

STATE LAW ENFORCEMENT SURVEY

On January 27, 1998, the author distributed a survey instrument to state law enforcement agencies in each of the 50 states. The survey had two purposes:

- To determine what law enforcement-related information was available on websites maintained by state law enforcement agencies, and
- To determine the response rate and response time of web-based surveys versus regular mail surveys.

The complete results of this survey detailing law enforcement-related materials that are available on websites maintained by state law enforcement agencies can be found online at http://www.nesbary.com/survey.

METHODOLOGY

A survey was administered to the 50 state law enforcement agencies. Since the entire universe of state law enforcement agencies was selected, there was no need to construct a sample. Half of the surveys were administered via regular mail, while the other half were administered via web-based form. The following section describes how the survey was administered.

SURVEY DESIGN AND ADMINISTRATION

In December 1997, a pretest phone and Internet survey was conducted to determine the accuracy of contact information. Pretesting is an important part of any survey and is particularly important when planning to contact respondents by e-mail (Gaddis 1998). During January 1998, state government and related websites were examined to determine which state law enforcement agencies maintain websites. Upon developing a preliminary list of websites, each agency was called by phone to confirm the location and existence of a website. While it was time consuming to search the Web and phone every agency, it was necessary to identify, with a high level of certainty, state law enforcement agencies with websites. Thirty-eight agencies were found to have websites.

Second, agencies with working e-mail addresses were identified. Each of the 38 agencies with websites was found to maintain functional e-mail accounts. In January 1998, test e-mails were sent to the persons identified as being associated with the accounts, to ensure that the accounts were valid. Responses were received in each case. It was important to identify working e-mail accounts, because e-mail communication was the vehicle through which respondents were to be notified of the location of the web survey. Of the 38 agencies with working e-mail accounts and web addresses, 25 were selected to participate in the e-mail portion of the survey, while the remainder participated in the regular mail portion of the survey.

Next, the web survey was constructed and uploaded to the Web. The survey forms were constructed using Microsoft FrontPage. The survey instrument may be found in Figure 3.1. A non-working version of the survey is located online at http://www.nesbary.com/survey. The survey instrument included full instructions on completing and submitting the document to the survey administrator. The survey instruments sent via e-mail and regular mail were substantially the same. The only differences were 1) responses were made via web form (web survey) versus handwritten form (regular mail survey), and 2) the web form was returned via "submit" button, while the regular mail form was returned via letter (postage and return envelope included). E-mails were sent notifying the respondents of the location of the survey instrument on the Web. Respondents were initially given one month from January 27, 1998 to complete the survey.

Once e-mail responses were received, confirming e-mails were sent to the responding agencies to ensure the validity of the respondent and to thank the respondent for participating in the survey. A follow-up telephone call (and e-mail for those agencies with e-mail accounts) was made on February 27, 1998, as a reminder to agencies that had not yet responded.

State Law Enforcement and the Web

Dear Law Enforcement Official:

This survey is designed to learn how you use the world-wide-web in your daily activities. Please take a few minutes to complete it. Once you have completed the survey, click the submit button at the bottom of the page. You will receive a copy of the survey results (around May 1998). If you have any questions, please contact Dale Nesbary, James Hiller or Nada Sater at 248-370-2375. Thank you in advance for your cooperation.

Dale Nesbary, Assistant Professor
James Hiller, Research Assistant
Nada Sater, Research Assistant
Department of Political Science
Oakland University

1) Please enter the following information regarding your law enforcement agency:

Name	
Title	
Organization	
Street Address	
Address (cont.)	
City	
State/Province	
Zip/Postal Code	
Work Phone	
FAX	
E-mail	
URL	

2) Please indicate whether you transfer the following law enforcement information over the World Wide Web. Check all that apply:

☐ Ballistics Information

☐ Crime Statistics (UCR or related data)

☐ Fingerprint Information

☐ Mug Shots

☐ On-Line Crime Reports

☐ Wanted Persons

☐ Missing or Unidentified Persons

☐ Workload Data (daily, hourly crime activity)

3) Please indicate whether you transfer the following administrative information over the World Wide Web. Check all that apply:

☐ Personnel Data
☐ Budgetary Data
☐ Traffic Reports (road conditions, etc.)
☐ Contact Information
☐ Data on Organization Structure

4) Enter the number of sworn staff in your agency

[　　　　　　　]

5) Enter the number of total employees in your agency

[　　　　　　　]

6) Enter the number of citizens (population) in your jurisdiction

[　　　　　　　]

7) Enter the number of total offenses committed in your jurisdiction in 1996

[　　　　　　　]

8) Enter the number of UCR Part One offenses committed in your jurisdiction in 1996

[　　　　　　　]

9) Please click the following button if you prefer completing World Wide Web based forms as opposed to regular mail (U.S. Mail) forms.

☐ Check here if you prefer completing Web based forms

10) Please list other ways that your organization uses the World Wide Web

[　　　　　　　　　　　　　　　　　　　　　　　]

Thanks again for your help. Click the "Submit Form" button to send me your responses. Click the "Reset Form" button to clear your responses and start over.

SURVEY RESPONSE

Figure 3.2 presents the results of the state law enforcement survey as it relates to web survey and regular mail response.

Figure 3.2 State Law Enforcement Survey Web Versus Regular Mail Response			
Surveys Sent	Web (25)	Regular Mail (25)	Total (50)
Response Rate	9 (36%)	1 (4%)	10 (20%)
Responses Received < 3 days	3 (12%)	0 (0%)	3 (6%)
Responses Received < 10 days	8 (32%)	0 (0%)	8 (16%)
Responses Received < 40 days	9 (36%)	1 (4%)	10 (20%)
No Response	16 (64%)	25 (96%)	40 (80 %)

Figure 3.2 reports actual and percentage responses and may be read in the following manner: For *Response Rate*, nine of the 25 web responses were received, equaling 36 percent of all web surveys administered. Of the 50 surveys administered (both web and regular mail) 10 (20 percent) were received. Similarly, for *Responses Received* in less than 10 days, eight (36 percent) web responses were received, no regular mail responses were received, meaning a total of eight of the 50 surveys were received in less than eight days.

The overall response rate for all surveys was 20 percent. The most striking dimension is found in response rates for web versus regular mail surveys. Responses were received from nine (36 percent) of the 25 web surveys administered, while only one (four percent) regular mail survey was received. Response time results were similar to response rate in that web responses were received much more quickly than regular mail responses. Three web surveys were actually received within three days of notification, two of which were received on the same day of notification. The one regular mail response took in excess of 40 days to receive.

Respondents were asked to provide feedback on their preferences regarding web and regular mail surveys. First, Question Nine asked respondents to indicate if they preferred to respond to web surveys or regular mail surveys. All 10 respondents indicated that, if given a choice, they would respond via the Web, as opposed to regular mail.

Several respondents were interviewed by telephone to elaborate on this preference. The consensus was that web surveys were less expensive and faster than regular mail surveys. Two respondents indicated that just not having to "push paper" was reason enough to prefer web surveys. Others indicated that they appreciated not having to spend money on a phone call to clear up misunderstandings regarding questions. They could send e-mail for that purpose at no cost.

LOCAL LAW ENFORCEMENT SURVEY

The second of the three surveys was distributed to selected local law enforcement agencies. Administered on January 20, 1998, the survey had two purposes:

- To determine what law enforcement related information was available on websites maintained by local law enforcement agencies, and
- To determine the response rate and response time of web-based surveys versus regular mail surveys.

As was the case with state law enforcement agencies, this section focuses on the response rate and response time of web-based surveys versus regular mail surveys. The complete results of this survey regarding law enforcement-related materials available on websites maintained by local law enforcement agencies is available online at http://www.nesbary.com/nesbary.

METHODOLOGY

A survey was administered to 32 local law enforcement agencies. Thirty-two is clearly a much smaller number of agencies than the thousands of local law enforcement agencies in the United States. The decision was made to distribute a small number of surveys to large local law enforcement agencies. Typical sources of law enforcement contact information (Jeffers Manual, for example) are very comprehensive, but at least 6 months old by the time they are published. These data sources rarely include e-mail or website information on listed agencies; and, therefore, they would be of little use regarding the web survey component of this study. The decision was made to select local law enforcement agencies with a research staff capable of responding to surveys (regular mail or web surveys) in a relatively timely manner. This limited the number of potential respondents to a relatively small percentage of the total.

Moreover, local law enforcement agencies are not represented on the Internet, as well as state law enforcement agencies. To help ensure that a broad range of competent respondents were identified, the decision was made to use a non-probability sampling technique, judgmental sampling. The sample selected included large police agencies with at least 500 sworn staff (police officers) and internal research capacity. For local law enforcement agencies to be included in this study, they must have had the following attributes:

1. Have at least 500 sworn staff (as of 1997),
2. Be located in a municipality with a population of at least 300,000 (1990 Census),
3. Have a departmental research office, and
4. As a group they were distributed fairly evenly among the States.

The following cities met these criteria and are listed in Figure 3.3.

| Figure 3.3 ||
| **Local Law Enforcement Survey Sampling Frame** ||
Municipality	**Website Maintained**
Atlanta	Yes
Austin	Yes
Baltimore	Yes
Boston	Yes
Chicago	Yes
Cincinnati	Yes
Cleveland	Yes
Columbus	No
Dallas	No
Detroit	No
El Paso	Yes
Ft. Worth	No
Honolulu	No
Houston	Yes
Indianapolis	No
Jacksonville	No
Kansas City	Yes
Las Vegas	No
Memphis	No
Miami - Dade County	Yes
Milwaukee	No
Nashville	No
New York	Yes
Oklahoma City	No
Philadelphia	No
Phoenix	No
San Antonio	Yes
San Diego	No
San Francisco	No
San Jose	Yes
Seattle	No
St. Louis	No

SURVEY DESIGN AND ADMINISTRATION

The survey design and administration process for local law enforcement was substantially similar to the survey design and administration process for state law enforcement. In December 1998, a pretest phone and e-mail survey was conducted to determine the accuracy of contacts. Upon developing a preliminary list of websites, each local agency was called by phone to confirm the location and existence of their website. Fourteen municipal law enforcement agencies were found to have websites.

Second, local law enforcement agencies with working e-mail addresses were identified. Of local law enforcement agencies with websites, all had functional e-mail accounts. Again, test e-mails were sent to the persons identified as being associated with the accounts to ensure that the accounts were valid. Responses were received in each case. It was important to identify working e-mail accounts, because e-mail communication was the vehicle through which respondents were to be notified of the location of the web survey. Each of the local law enforcement agencies with working e-mail accounts and websites were selected to participate in the Web portion of the survey, while the remainder participated in the regular mail portion of the survey.

Third, the web survey was constructed and uploaded to the Web. The survey instrument may be found in this document as Figure 3.4 and online at http://www.nesbary.com/survey. The survey instrument included full instructions on completing and submitting the document to the survey administrator. The survey instruments sent via web survey and regular mail were substantially the same. Again, the only differences were 1) responses were made via the web form (web survey) versus handwritten form (regular mail survey) and 2) the web form was returned via "submit" button, while the regular mail form was returned via letter (postage and return envelope included).

E-mails were sent notifying the respondents of the location of the survey instrument on the Web and how to respond to the survey Respondents were initially given one month from January 20, 1998 to complete the survey.

As was the case with state law enforcement agencies, confirming e-mails were sent to the responding local law enforcement agencies to ensure the validity of the respondent and to thank the respondent for participating in the survey. A follow-up telephone call (and e-mail for those agencies with e-mail accounts) was made on February 20, 1998 as a reminder to agencies who had not yet responded to the initial survey.

Local Law Enforcement and the Web

Dear Law Enforcement Official:

This survey is designed to learn how you use the world-wide-web in your daily activities. Please take a few minutes to complete it. Once you have completed the survey, click the submit button at the bottom of the page. You will receive a copy of the survey results (around May, 1998). If you have any questions, please contact Dale Nesbary or Dalia Rasha at 248-370-2375. Thank you in advance for your cooperation.

Dale Nesbary, Assistant Professor
Dalia Rasha Research Assistant
Department of Political Science
Oakland University

1) Please enter the following information regarding your law enforcement agency:

Name	
Title	
Organization	
Street Address	
Address (cont.)	
City	
State/Province	
Zip/Postal Code	
Work Phone	
FAX	
E-mail	
URL	

2) Please indicate whether you transfer the following law enforcement information over the World Wide Web. Check all that apply:

☐ Ballistics Information

☐ Crime Statistics (UCR or related data)

☐ Fingerprint Information

☐ Mug Shots

☐ On-Line Crime Reports

☐ Wanted Persons

☐ Missing or Unidentified Persons

☐ Workload Data (daily, hourly crime activity)

3) Please indicate whether you transfer the following administrative information over the World Wide Web. Check all that apply:

☐ Personnel Data
☐ Budgetary Data
☐ Traffic Reports (road conditions, etc.)
☐ Contact Information
☐ Data on Organization Structure

4) Enter the number of sworn staff in your agency

[ ]

5) Enter the number of total employees in your agency

[ ]

6) Enter the number of citizens (population) in your jurisdiction

[ ]

7) Enter the number of total offenses committed in your jurisdiction in 1996

[ ]

8) Enter the number of UCR Part One offenses committed in your jurisdiction in 1996

[ ]

9) Please click the following button if you prefer completing World Wide Web based forms as opposed to regular mail (U.S. Mail) forms.

☐ Check here if you prefer completing Web based forms

10) Please list other ways that your organization uses the World Wide Web

[ ]

Thanks again for your help. Click the "Submit Form" button to send me your responses. Click the "Reset Form" button to clear your responses and start over.

SURVEY RESPONSE

Figure 3.5 presents the results of the local law enforcement survey as it relates to Web and regular mail response.

Figure 3.5 Local Law Enforcement Survey Web Versus Regular Mail Response			
Surveys Sent	Web (14)	Regular Mail (18)	Total (32)
Response Rate	4 (29%)	7 (39%)	11 (34%)
Responses received < 3 days	2 (14%)	0 (0%)	2 (6%)
Responses received < 10 days	4 (29%)	1 (6%)	5 (16%)
Responses received < 40 days	4 (29%)	7 (39%)	11 (34%)
No response	10 (71%)	11 (61%)	21 (66%)

Figure 3.5 reports actual and percentage responses and may be read in the following manner: For *Response Rate*, 4 of the 14 web responses were received, equaling 29 percent of all web surveys administered. Of the 32 surveys administered (both web and regular mail), 11 (34 percent) were received. Similarly, for *Responses* received in less than 10 days, 4 (29 percent) web responses were received, and one (six percent) regular mail response was received, giving a total of five out of 32 surveys received in less than eight days.

The overall response rate for local law enforcement surveys was 34 percent, slightly higher than the 20 percent response rate for state law enforcement. Responses were received from four (29 percent) of the web respondents. This did not differ much from the 36 percent response rate for state law enforcement web surveys. Response time results were similar to response rate in that web responses were received quicker than regular mail responses. All web responses were received within 10 days, two being received within three days.

With respect to regular mail, local law enforcement response rates were much different than for state law enforcement. While only one state law enforcement agency responded by regular mail, seven, or 39 percent, of local agencies responded in that manner. This is much higher than the 4 percent regular mail response rate for state agencies and higher than the 36 percent web response rate for state agencies.

Again, respondents were asked to provide feedback on their preferences regarding web and regular mail surveys. First, Question Nine asked respondents to indicate whether or not they preferred to respond to web-based surveys. Each of the four web respondents indicated that they prefer web surveys, while five of the seven regular mail respondents indicated that they would prefer regular mail, if given the option.

Respondents were again interviewed by telephone to elaborate on this preference. Local law enforcement officials generally felt that web surveys were less expensive and faster than regular mail surveys. They liked the ease of use of web surveys and recognized the potential of using existing computer equipment for multiple purposes. Those without Web capacity argued that they would have to incur the expense of going online, just for the opportunity to send surveys and similar documents via the Web. They also identified increased training costs, as well as dedicating computer equipment to meet online needs.

UNIVERSITY SURVEY

The final survey was distributed to selected universities. Administered on January 24, 1998, the survey had two purposes:

- To determine the extent to which selected university political science departments use the Web for internal department administrative purposes, and
- To determine the response rate and response time of web-based surveys versus regular mail surveys among selected research universities with websites.

As was the case with state and local law enforcement agencies, this section focuses on the response rate and response time of web-based surveys versus regular mail surveys. The complete results of this survey regarding university political science use of the Web for internal, departmental administrative purposes are available online at http://www.nesbary.com/survey.

SURVEY DESIGN AND ADMINISTRATION

A survey was administered to 21 university political science departments (see Figure 3.6).

Figure 3.6 University Political Science Department Survey Sampling Frame	
Indiana University	University of California Berkeley
University of Iowa	University of California Los Angeles
Michigan State University	Stanford University
University of Michigan	Arizona State University
Northwestern University	University of Arizona
Ohio State University	University of Southern California
Penn State University	University of Oregon
Purdue University	Oregon State University
Indiana University	University of Washington
University of Wisconsin	Washington State University
University of Minnesota	

The universities were selected for a number of reasons. First, all of the universities chosen had formal organizational relationships, belonging to the Big 10 and Pacific 10 athletic and academic conferences. These conferences have specific admission standards, including the academic reputation and curriculum of member universities, minimum student admission standards, and longstanding conference relationships on a number of levels. These relationships and standards have lead to a number of similarities among the universities that remain to this day. Second, each school maintains comprehensive undergraduate and graduate political science and/or public policy programs. This ensures that the specific departments to which the surveys were sent have some consistency in mission and scope. Third, each political science department maintains an e-mail address and website. A primary intent of this study was to determine whether political science departments, with the capacity to respond to a web survey, would do so, given the options of responding via regular mail or by web survey.

Serious consideration was given to randomizing the survey. Randomizing the study was rejected for several reasons. First, it was important to assess the willingness of political science departments to respond to the survey via web form, if they had the capacity to respond. While many departments have e-mail and a website, some use the websites solely as an advertising or marketing tool. By selecting departments with comprehensive websites, the respondents were more likely to have thought through the utility of websites or the lack thereof. This is not to say that a randomized study of this topic would not be meaningful. In some ways, (methodological rigor and replication of results) a randomized study would be more beneficial, than the judgmental process used in this study

SURVEY RESPONSE

Figure 3.7 presents the results of the university survey as it relates to web and regular mail response.

Figure 3.7 University Political Science Department Survey Web Versus Regular Mail Response			
Surveys Sent	Web (11)	Regular Mail (10)	Total (21)
Response Rate	8 (73%)	2 (20%)	10 (40%)
Responses received < 3 days	1 (8%)	0 (0%)	1 (5%)
Responses received < 10 days	5 (42%)	1 (9%)	6 (29%)
Responses received < 40 days	8 (67%)	2 (20%)	11 (34%)
No response	4 (33%)	8 (80%)	21 (52%)

Figure 3.7 reports actual and percentage responses and may be read in a manner similar to the law enforcement surveys. To summarize, regarding *Response Rate*, 8 of the 11 Web responses were received, equaling 73 percent of all web surveys administered. Of the 21 surveys administered (both web and regular mail), 10 (48 percent) were received. Similarly, for *Responses Received* in less than 10 days, five (42 percent) web responses were received, and one (nine percent) regular mail response was received. A total of six of the 21 surveys were received in less than eight days.

Moreover, the overall response rate for university surveys was 48 percent, much higher than the response rates for state and local law enforcement agencies. Web responses were received from eight (67 percent) of the web respondents. This is much higher than the 36 percent response rate for state law enforcement web surveys. Web responses were received more quickly than regular mail responses. Five web responses were received within 10 days; one being received within three days.

With respect to regular mail, universities responded in a manner similar to state law enforcement and at a lower rate than local law enforcement. Two (20 percent) regular mail responses were received; one of which was returned within 10 days and the other received within 40 days.

Respondents were asked to provide feedback on their preferences regarding web and regular mail surveys. In Question Nine, all respondents, both web and regular mail, indicated that they prefer web surveys.

University respondents were also interviewed by telephone to elaborate on this preference. Here again, there was a strong preference for use of technology. The resistance to adding technology in the form of Web connections did not exist, since all universities were already connected to the Web. Since many universities have had e-mail access for over a decade, they were very willing to take advantage of technologies that exploit speed and convenience. Alternatively, several respondents mentioned the danger of selection bias. Familiarity with technology can lead to a bias toward that technology and a bias against other forms of communication and data analysis.

SUMMARY

This examination of the literature and test of e-mail surveys produced many interesting outcomes and contradictions. Web and e-mail surveys have been used quite extensively in market research and customer service. The results of these surveys have provided useful data for businesses in planning marketing strategies. Web and e-mail surveys have also made inroads into academic and government research. Because of the limited penetration of the Internet, however, it is still difficult, if not impossible, to construct randomized samples of general populations. This severely limits the application of web and e-mail surveys.

Moreover, it is predicted that, by 2002, nearly all businesses and most households will have some level of Web access. This will improve the likelihood that methodologically sound random samples will be able to be constructed. By then, researchers will be able to accurately compare large scale web surveys against telephone and regular mail surveys.

STUDY QUESTIONS AND EXERCISES

1) Please list three strengths and three weaknesses of e-mail surveys.

_____

_____

_____

_____

_____

_____

_____

_____

_____

_____

2) Search the literature for three examples of e-mail surveys. Critique the surveys on the following dimensions: a. selection bias, b. response time, and c. response rate.

_____

_____

_____

_____

_____

_____

_____

_____

3) Search the literature for three examples of web surveys. Critique the surveys on the following dimensions: a. response time and b. response rate. Do respondents return web surveys more quickly than regular mail surveys? Are response rates higher for web surveys than regular mail surveys? What can be done to improve response rate and response time for web surveys?

_____

_____

_____

_____

_____

_____

_____

_____

_____

_____

_____

INTERNET DATA COLLECTION RESOURCES

These resources examine many of the new Internet-based, data collection resources. They were drawn from "An Empirical Assessment of Data Collection Using the Internet," arguably the most comprehensive examination to date of Internet-based research tools: Stanton, Jeffrey M. (1998). An empirical assessment of data collection using the Internet. Personnel Psychology, 51(3):709-725.

1) Bailey, E.K., & M. Cotlar. (1994). Teaching via the internet. Communication Education, 43(2):184-193.
2) Berner, R. (1994, August 6). An update for resumes: Software lets computer do the choosing. Patriot Ledger, p. 25. (From SIRS Researcher on the Web, Boca Raton, FL: SIRS, Inc. Producer and Distributor.) URL=http://researcher.sirs.com/cgi-bin/rcs-article-display?4WR117A
3) Commercenet. (1995, October). The Commercenet/Nielsen internet demographics survey. Palo Alto, CA: Author.
4) Greguras, G.J., & J.M. Stanton. (1996). Three considerations for I/O graduate students seeking academic positions: Publish, publish, publish. The Industrial/Organizational Psychologist, 33(3):92-98.
5) Harris, J.B. (1994). Electronic impersonations: Changing the context of teacher-student interaction. Journal of Computing in Childhood Education, 5.241-255.
6) Igbaria, M., & S. Parasuraman. (1989). A path analytic study of individual characteristics, computer anxiety and attitudes toward microcomputers. Journal of Management, 15:373-388.
7) Kantor, J. (1991). The effects of computer administration and identification on the job. Descriptive Index (JDI). Journal of Business & Psychology, 5:309-323.
8) Kelly-Milburn, D., & M.A. Milburn. (1995). Cyberpsych: Resources for psychologists on the Internet. Psychological Science, 6:203-211.
9) King, W.C., & E.W. Miles. (1995). A quasi-experimental assessment of the effect of computerizing noncognitive paper-and-pencil measurements: A test of measurement equivalence. Journal of Applied Psychology, 80:643-651.
10) Kraut, A.I. (1996). An overview of organizational surveys. In Kraut, A.I. (Ed.), Organizational Surveys, pp. 1-17. San Francisco: Jossey-Bass.
11) Kuhnert, K., & D.P. McCauley. (1996). Applying alternative survey methods. In Kraut, A.I. (Ed.), Organizational Surveys, pp. 233-254. San Francisco: Jossey-Bass.
12) Landis, C. (1995). An exploratory study of science educators' use of the Internet. Journal of Science Education and Technology, 4(3):181-190.
13) McGlade, L.T., Milot, B.A., & J. Scales. (1996). "The world wide web: A new research and writing tool. The American Journal of Clinical Nutrition, 63:981-982.
14) Mead, A.D., & F. Drasgow. (1993). Equivalence of computerized and paper-and-pencil cognitive ability tests: A meta-analysis. Psychological Bulletin, 114:449-458.
15) Mehta, R., & E. Sivadas. (1995). Comparing response rates and response content in mail versus electronic mail surveys. Journal of the Market Research Society, 37:429-439.
16) Niehoff, B.P., & R.H. Moorman. (1993). Justice as a mediator of the relationship between methods of monitoring and organizational citizenship behavior. Academy of Management Journal, 36:527-556.

17) Rosen, E.F., & L.C. Petty. (1995). The Internet and sexuality education: Tapping into the wild side. <u>Behavior Research Methods, Instruments and Computers,</u> 27:281-284.

18) Rosenfield, P., Giacolone, R.A., Knouse, S.B., & L.M. Doherty. (1991). Impression management, candor, and microcomputer-based organizational surveys: An individual differences approach. <u>Computers in Human Behavior,</u> 7:23-32.

19) Schmitt, C.H. (1997, March 2). Behind the wave: Consequences of the digital age. San Jose Mercury News, pp. 1S-5S. (From SIRS Researcher on the Web, Boca Raton, FL: SIRS, Inc. Producer and Distributor.)
URL=<u>http://researcher.sirs.com/cgi-bin/res-article-display?7TC085A</u>

20) Stanton, J.M. (1997). Traditional and electronic monitoring from an organizational justice perspective. Manuscript under review.

21) Sussman, V. (1995, November 13). Gold rush in cyberspace. <u>U.S. News & World Report</u>, p. 72. (From SIRS Researcher on the Web, Boca Raton, FL: SIRS, Inc. Producer and Distributor.)
URL=<u>http://researcher.sirs.com/cgi-bin/res-article-display?5TC060A</u>

Chapter Four: Survey Design in Microsoft FrontPage

Chapter Four is a "how to" guide to construct web surveys. This chapter focuses on the construction of web and e-mail surveys using Microsoft FrontPage, a standard web development tool. Specifically, the reader will gain knowledge in all of the following by completing this chapter:

- Create a Microsoft FrontPage website (necessary to take full advantage of FrontPage forms development features);
- Assign creative and advanced formatting features to the website;
- Create multiple form fields including text boxes, scrolling text boxes (large capacity text box capable of accepting approximately 64 pages of text), drop down fields and lists;
- Assign password protection to fields, webpages, and directories;
- Test your website;
- Publish (upload) your website using Microsoft FrontPage;
- Upload a survey using File Transfer Protocol;
- Send a survey via e-mail.

Chapter Four comprises multiple exercises and uses the following conventions:

- **Times New Roman Bold** text denotes the beginning of an exercise.
- **Arial Bold** text denotes text to be entered, mouse movements or keystrokes.
- Two actions separated by a slash (e.g., **File/SaveAs**) denote that you are to take two steps in succession. In this case, first click on **File** on the Menu Bar, then **Save As**.

WEB DESIGN – HARDWARE AND SOFTWARE REQUIREMENTS

To design a web-based survey form and publish it to the Web, it is necessary to have certain minimal tools at your disposal.

1. Pentium-based personal computer or equivalent,
2. Sufficiently fast (56K or better) modem,
3. Internet Service Provider (ISP) that hosts FrontPage websites,
4. Microsoft FrontPage or equivalent web development software.

Details on each of these items follow. For more information on how to buy a personal computer and ISP connections, visit the Survey Research Companion Website at http://www.nesbary.com/survey.

PENTIUM-BASED PERSONAL COMPUTER

While a 486 computer can run most software packages, today's graphics-intensive software requires significant processing power. Nearly all university, government and business personal computers are Pentium or better (including AMD and Cyrix processors) computers with sufficient processing power to handle programs like FrontPage. If you are in the market to purchase a personal computer, here is the minimal configuration I would recommend:

1. Pentium II or better processor running at 333 MHz (megahertz) or faster
2. 64 MB of random access memory (RAM)
3. 6 GB (gigabytes) of hard disk space
4. 56K V.90 standard internal modem or faster
5. CD ROM (or better) disk drive
6. 15 inch monitor

A computer with these features costs between $600 and $1,000 in 1999 dollars. While you can easily spend more than twice that amount, I do not recommend it. A low to mid-level personal computer should not cost more than $1,000 with monitor and printer, independent of when you buy it.

The computer described above is a relatively low-end model that is capable of multitasking or capable of running several programs at once. This is important for website developers, because you are likely to run a word processor, a web browser and a website development program at the same time.

MODEM/ISP

Currently, Internet connections at most institutional sites (government agencies, universities and businesses) are more than sufficient to access the Web for browsing or uploading websites. The typical institutional connection is extremely fast, running in the multiple megabyte per second range assuming a network connection directly to the Internet. The only times these connection speeds slow down are when many users (usually hundreds) access the Web at the same time.

Home users face different problems. The fastest common connection at home is a high speed 56K V.90 analog modem, costing from $30 to $100 in 1999 dollars. 56K modems are fine for home connections and, in fact, may seem to run faster than an institutional connection with many users connected at once. Analog modems connect directly to home telephone lines, making configuration relatively easy.

Cable modems, becoming more widely available, run at speeds equal to institutional network connections (1-5 megabytes per second) and are slightly more expensive ($100 - $200) than analog modems. However, the connection cost with cable modems can run up to three times that of analog connections. This is because cable modems connect to coaxial television cable lines, and often require the purchase of cable television service prior to gaining access to cable internet service.

Most Internet service providers provide Web access for as little as $10 per month ranging up to about $40 per month. $10 per month provides basic access, usually with a limited number of hours per month. $40 per month provides unlimited access with full FrontPage capability. Usually $20 per month provides unlimited access time and some FrontPage capability. Fortunately, many institutions now support Microsoft FrontPage or at least allow employees and/or students to upload files to corporate webspace. If this is true with your institution, you will not have to spend your hard-earned money on an external ISP.

Whether you use your institution or an external ISP, be sure to tell your Internet service provider that you want to publish a FrontPage website. Your ISP will a) tell you if they support

FrontPage websites and 2) if so, they will provide you with a URL (Internet location) to which you may publish your website. Usually your website will look something like this: **http://www.youruniversity/~yourwebsite**, where **youruniversity** = the name of your Internet service provider and **yourwebsite** = the username assigned to you by your Internet service provider. For example, the author's website at Oakland University is http://www.oakland.edu/~nesbary. When using Microsoft FrontPage, you will need to enter your URL the first time you publish a FrontPage website. After that, FrontPage automatically enters your URL for you.

INTRODUCTION TO MICROSOFT FRONTPAGE

Microsoft FrontPage is one of many website development tools available on the market today. Macromedia DreamWeaver, Netscape Composer, and HotMetal are other website development tools that are commonly used. What these programs have in common is that you need little or no html (hypertext markup language) experience to use them. They all employ what is called WYSIWIG (What You See Is What You Get) interfaces. This means that what you type or edit on screen is roughly equivalent to what you will see when your website is published. This does not mean that if you are an html expert you cannot employ html in developing your website. To the contrary, these programs allow you to use WYSIWIG and html editing side by side. WYSIWIG allows the user to develop a website as easily as using a program such as Microsoft Word or WordPerfect. Even survey forms like the ones we will construct are very easily designed. WYSIWIG allows the user to concentrate more on methodological issues in designing surveys, rather than the difficulty of using an unfamiliar software program.

Microsoft FrontPage is a particularly useful website development tool because it automates many functions that formerly required in-depth programming knowledge. FrontPage utilizes web form technology to enter data and several file formats, including text, database, and html to store survey results.

Web forms are more easily created using FrontPage than programming in html. Here are some examples. Figure 4.1 is a copy of the Nesbary Consulting Group feedback form, a document substantially similar to a web survey. The document includes text and tables, both of which may be edited in a manner similar to a word-processing or spreadsheet program. The database and html functionality of the form is transparent to the user. Figure 4.2 represents the same document in html language. Clearly, editing a document in WYSIWIG format is a more pleasant experience than editing the same document in html.

Figure 4.1: Webpage in WYISWIG View

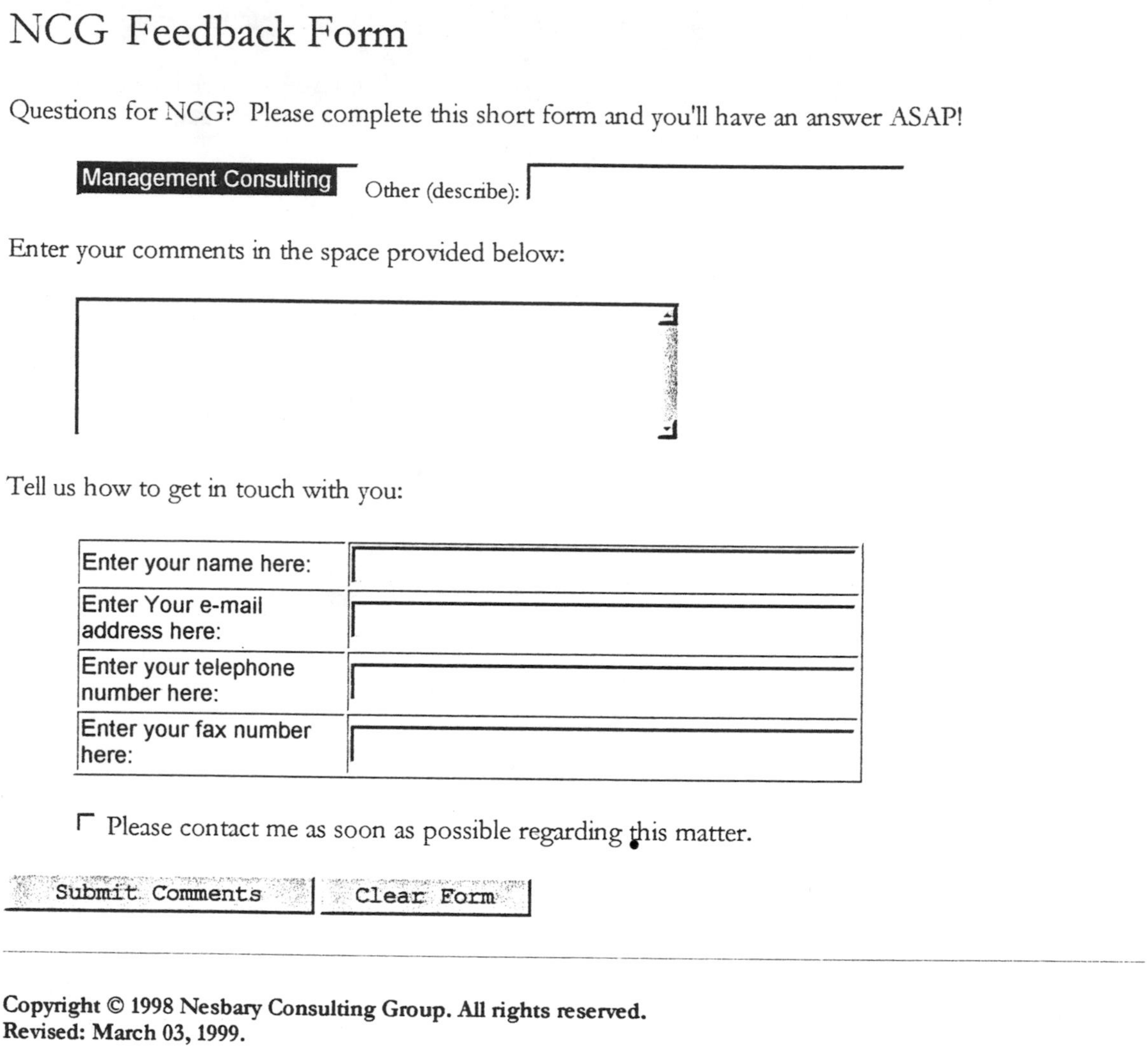

NCG Feedback Form

Questions for NCG? Please complete this short form and you'll have an answer ASAP!

Management Consulting   Other (describe): |

Enter your comments in the space provided below:

Tell us how to get in touch with you:

Enter your name here:	
Enter Your e-mail address here:	
Enter your telephone number here:	
Enter your fax number here:	

⌐ Please contact me as soon as possible regarding this matter.

| Submit Comments | Clear Form |

Figure 4.2: Webpage in HTML View

```
<html>

<head>
<title>Nesbary Consulting Group Feedback Form</title>
<meta name="GENERATOR" content="Microsoft FrontPage 3.0">
<meta http-equiv="Page-Enter" content="revealTrans(Duration=2.0,Transition=8)">
</head>

<body bgcolor="#FFFFFF" text="#000080" link="#000080" vlink="#000080">

<p><font face="Garamond" color="#004080"><!--webbot bot="PurpleText"
PREVIEW="Feedback Form" --> </font></p>

<p><font face="Garamond" color="#004080"><big><big><big>NCG<big> </big>Feedback
Form</big></big></big></font></p>

<form method="POST" action="--WEBBOT-SELF--">
  <!--webbot bot="SaveResults" startspan U-File="_private/feedback.txt" S-Format="TEXT/TSV"
  S-Label-Fields="TRUE" S-Builtin-Fields="Date Time REMOTE_NAME REMOTE_USER HTTP_USER_AGENT"
  S-Form-Fields --><input TYPE="hidden" NAME="VTI-GROUP" VALUE="0"><!--webbot bot="SaveResults"
endspan --><p><font face="Garamond"
color="#004080"><big>Questions for NCG?  Please complete this short form and you'll
have an answer ASAP!</big></font><dl>
    <dd><font face="Garamond" color="#004080"><select name="Subject" size="1" multiple>
        <option selected value="Management Consulting">Management Consulting</option>
        <option value="Classroom Issues">Classroom Issues</option>
        <option value="Database Development">Database Development</option>
        <option value="Speaking">Guest Speaking</option>
        <option value="This Website">This Website</option>
        <option value="Website Development">Website Development</option>
        <option>(Other)</option>
      </select> Other (describe): <input type="text" size="26" maxlength="256"
    name="SubjectOther"></font></dd>
  </dl>
  <p><font face="Garamond" color="#004080"><big>Enter your comments in the space provided
below:</big></font><dl>
    <dd><font face="Garamond" color="#004080"><textarea name="Comments" rows="5"
cols="42"></textarea></font></dd>
  </dl>
  <p><font face="Garamond" color="#004080"><big>Tell us how to get in touch with you:
</big></font><dl>
    <dd><table border="1" width="566">
        <tr>
          <td width="226"><font color="#004080">Enter your name here:</font></td>
          <td width="328"><font face="Garamond" color="#004080"><input type="text" size="35"
          maxlength="256" name="Username"></font></td>
        </tr>
        <tr>
          <td width="226"><font color="#004080">Enter Your e-mail address here:</font></td>
          <td width="328"><font face="Garamond" color="#004080"><input type="text" size="35"
          maxlength="256" name="UserEmail"></font></td>
        </tr>
        <tr>
          <td width="226"><font color="#004080">Enter your telephone number here:</font></td>
          <td width="328"><font face="Garamond" color="#004080"><input type="text" size="35"
          maxlength="256" name="UserTel"></font></td>
        </tr>
        <tr>
          <td width="226"><font color="#004080">Enter your fax number here:</font></td>
          <td width="328"><font face="Garamond" color="#004080"><input type="text" size="35"
          maxlength="256" name="UserFAX"></font></td>
        </tr>
      </table>
    </dd>
  </dl>
  <dl>
    <dd><font face="Garamond" color="#004080"><input type="checkbox" name="ContactRequested"
```

Installing Microsoft FrontPage

To use FrontPage, you must have the program installed on your personal computer or available through your institution's network. If FrontPage is available on your computer, you may skip to the next section. If not, here is how you install FrontPage.

Step One: Insert the Microsoft FrontPage CD ROM into your CD Drive. The FrontPage setup program should start automatically.

Step Two: Setup will search your computer for required **networking** components. If these components are not installed (Windows 95 or 98), you will be prompted to install them. Click **Yes** at the prompt to install and follow the instructions. If the programs are already installed, you will not be prompted. If the Microsoft Personal Web Server Software is not found on your computer, you will be prompted to install it. Click the **Yes** prompt and follow the instructions. After installing these components, you may be prompted to restart your computer. If so, restart the computer and wait for Setup to continue. Then move on to Step Three.

Step Three: Setup displays the Select Language dialog box. American English is the default setting. If you wish to select a language other than American English, select the language and click **OK**.

Step Four: Setup next asks you to start the installation of FrontPage. Click **Install FrontPage 98**, or the version you are using, to start the Microsoft FrontPage Installation.

Step Five: Setup offers two options, **Typical** and **Custom**. The Typical option allows you to begin using all FrontPage options immediately. FrontPage and the Microsoft Personal Web Server are required to run FrontPage and upload websites to your ISP. By selecting **Custom**, you may choose to install only those FrontPage components not already installed. For example, the Microsoft Personal Web Server may already be installed; thus, there would be no need to reinstall it. Unless you lack hard disk space, I suggest that choose **Typical** and click **Next**.

Step Six: After Setup installs the Personal Web Server, Setup may prompt you to restart your computer. After your computer restarts, Setup continues.

Step Seven: Setup prompts you to start FrontPage Explorer, the program in which the structure and layout of websites are created.

Step Eight: At this point, Setup allows you to install other FrontPage components including Microsoft Image Composer and Microsoft Internet Explorer. Image Composer is an image-editing program, especially suited for creating images for use with websites. Microsoft Internet Explorer is one of the two primary web browsers available currently, the other being Netscape Communicator by America Online. If your computer has sufficient hard disk space, I suggest installing Image Composer, if you plan on doing serious website development. Install Internet Explorer only if another browser is not installed.

The FrontPage Environment

FrontPage includes several programs, FrontPage Explorer, FrontPage Editor and the FrontPage Server Extensions, which run on the Microsoft web server. FrontPage Explorer (an example is displayed in Figure 4.3) is used to construct your website (known as a FrontPage Web), including creating and organizing files, importing and exporting files, and testing and repairing hyperlinks. You may also use FrontPage Explorer to open FrontPage Editor and to publish your website when you have completed it.

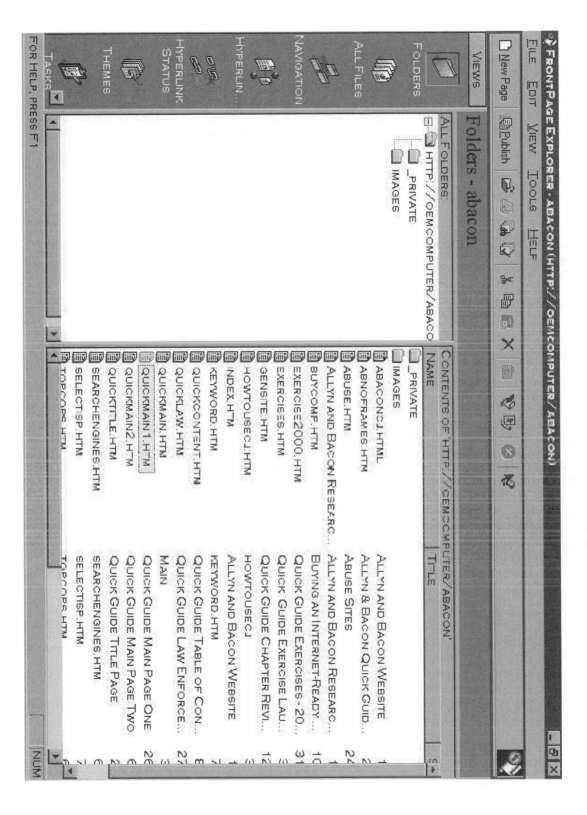

Figure 4.3: FrontPage Explorer

FrontPage Editor (an example is displayed in Figure 4.6) is used to create, design and edit webpages. You will use the editor to create web surveys and any other documents you so choose. As indicated earlier in this book, FrontPage uses WYSIWIG editing, so you will not need to learn html to create and edit webpages. If you so desire, FrontPage provides an html view, allowing advanced web designers the ability to edit webpages with a high level of specificity. However, all the tools you need to create a website and survey form are available in WYSIWIG view.

FrontPage Server Extensions are a set of programs that are installed on the web server computer on which FrontPage websites are stored. When the Microsoft Personal Web Server is installed on your computer, the Server Extensions are installed as well. The Server Extensions allow you to process forms, administer websites, create discussion groups and allow users to access and edit your webpages based upon the extent desired. The form creation feature of the Server Extensions is very important for purposes of creating web surveys. Web design software without these features nearly always require users to have extensive html and database programming experience.

Creating a FrontPage Web

Before creating a web survey form, it is necessary to create a website in which the form will be located. Again, FrontPage uses the term "Web" rather than website, so don't let this confuse you. To create a new FrontPage Web, follow these steps:

Step One: Click the **Start** button on the Taskbar, point to **Programs** and then click **Microsoft FrontPage**. FrontPage Explorer opens and the **Getting Started** dialog box is displayed. The Getting Started dialog box allows you to create a new FrontPage Web (remember, this means "website" for purposes of this chapter) or open existing webs (again, websites) (see Figure 4.4).
Step Two: Choose **Create a New FrontPage Web** in the Getting Started dialog box, then click **OK**. The **New FrontPage Web** dialog box opens. You now have the option of creating an unlimited variety of websites.
Step Three: In the New FrontPage Web dialog box, select the **One Page Web** radio button at the top of the dialog box. This choice creates a simple website comprising only a homepage. We will add the survey form later.
Step Four: Next to the number "2" at the bottom of the dialog box, type **Survey Research Web** as the title of your new web. You will label each web with a personalized title as each one is created. Click **OK**. FrontPage creates a new FrontPage Web titled "Survey Research Web." You may be prompted to enter a username and password at this point. If so, enter the username and password assigned to you by your system administrator.

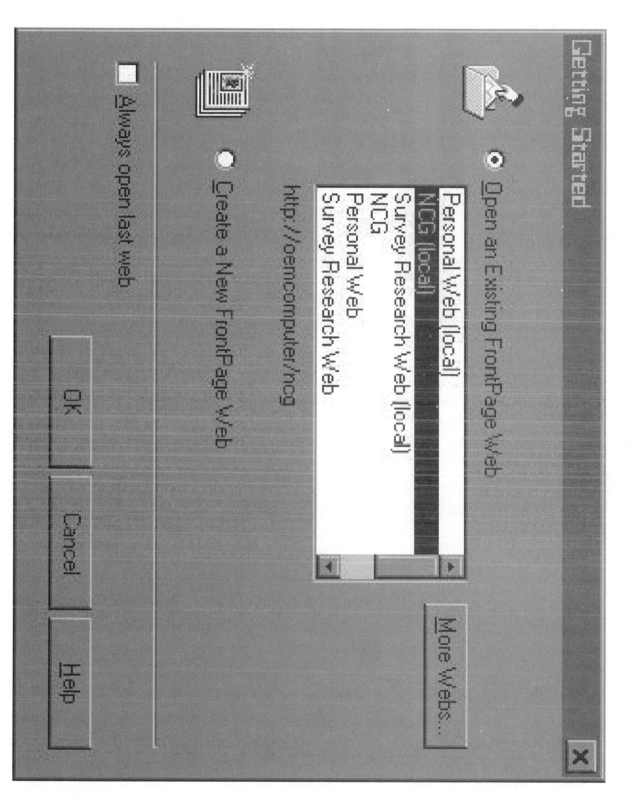

Figure 4.4: Getting Started Dialog Box

Figure 4.5: Survey Research Website in Navigation View

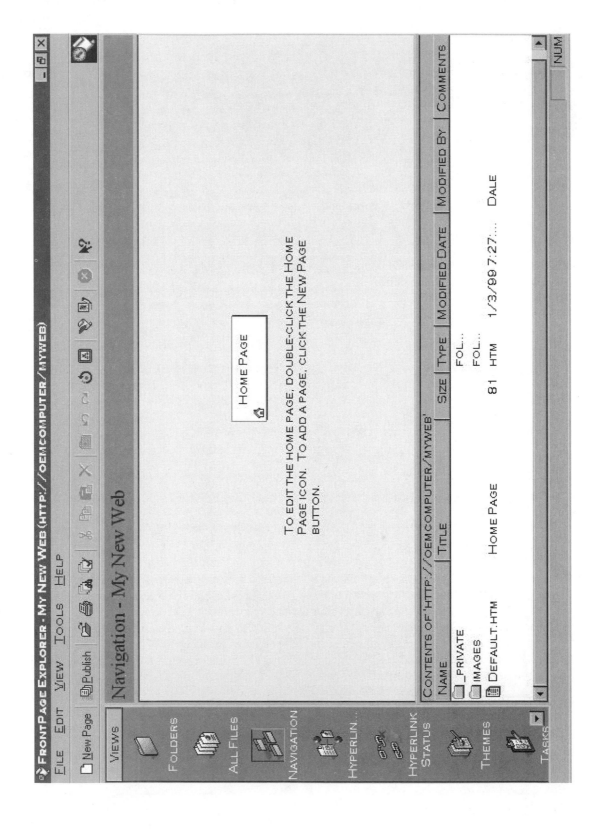

FrontPage Explorer changes in appearance to display the Survey Research Web in **Navigation View**. Navigation View allows you to view your web from a graphical perspective. Your homepage is displayed, along with any other webpages you have added to your web. Since this web has only one page (default.htm), no links are visible. At this point, I will take a few moments to discuss the function of the file default.htm.

Default.htm, automatically created by FrontPage when you create a web, is your homepage. Default.htm is the automatic name given to the homepage of any website. Index.htm is the other name recognized by html language as a homepage. If your website has a page named default.htm or index.htm, visitors to your site will be directed to that page automatically. Unless there are links from your homepage, there is no easy way for visitors to view other webpages on your website. It is therefore very important to ensure that your homepage is well designed. It must include links to your other webpages and other websites on the Web to which you want to link. Later in this book, we will discuss how linking and page design is done in detail.

At the bottom of FrontPage Explorer is a window with a different representation of your web. You see your homepage (named Default.htm) along with two folders, named **Private** and **Images**. Any images added to your web will be placed automatically in the Images folder, while files used for website administration are placed in the Private folder. You have the option of creating survey forms that automatically store and code responses to your survey. If you choose to take advantage of these features, the files that store the coded responses will be automatically created and located in the Private folder.

FrontPage Explorer provides three other views, along with three utility functions (refer to Figures 4.3-4.5 for screen shots). These are located in the left window of FrontPage Explorer and are accessible via a series of icons. Here is a short synopsis of what they do:

- **Folder View** lists all folders and files in alphabetical order. Folder view is useful if your website has numerous webpages. From an organizational perspective, it is often easier to search for webpages by folder rather than to scroll through a long list of files.
- **All Files View** lists all files, sortable by buttons appearing at the top of the FrontPage Explorer window. You may sort by filename, page title, folder, orphan status, file size, date and time created, and file author.
- **Hyperlink View** lists all webpages and any links to the currently selected webpage. If you select a webpage in the left window, that page and any page linked to it will appear in the right window.
- **Hyperlink Status** lists all links to pages in and external to the current web. If a link is broken (e.g., a link is "broken" if it is connected to a missing or unavailable webpage), the broken link is listed, along with the page in which the link is located.
- **Themes View** are design elements that may be applied to any web. To give a web a consistent look and feel, apply a theme, and all webpages in the web will have a similar look. Over 40 themes are available. Webpage colors, graphics, background, foreground, headings, buttons and lines may all be modified via Themes View.
- **Tasks View** may be assigned to any component of a web. Using Tasks is a good way to remind yourself of what needs to be done to complete your web.

Modifying Your Home Page

Your homepage is the entry to your web and is the most important page from the perspective of visitors to your website. A poorly designed homepage can spell disaster, if you want regular visitors to your website. If you want survey respondents to find your survey form, a poorly designed homepage may confuse them and cause your response rate to be lower than you would wish. To be well-designed, your homepage (and any other webpage on your website for that matter) must be clean, simple and easy to navigate. During this next exercise, we will modify your homepage for ease of use.

To modify your homepage, double-click on the **Homepage** icon in Navigation View. The FrontPage Editor window opens with a blank page available for editing. This blank page is your homepage. As you can see, there is not much to see or do on it thus far (see Figure 4.6). It needs functionality and a little sprucing up before it is ready for prime time.

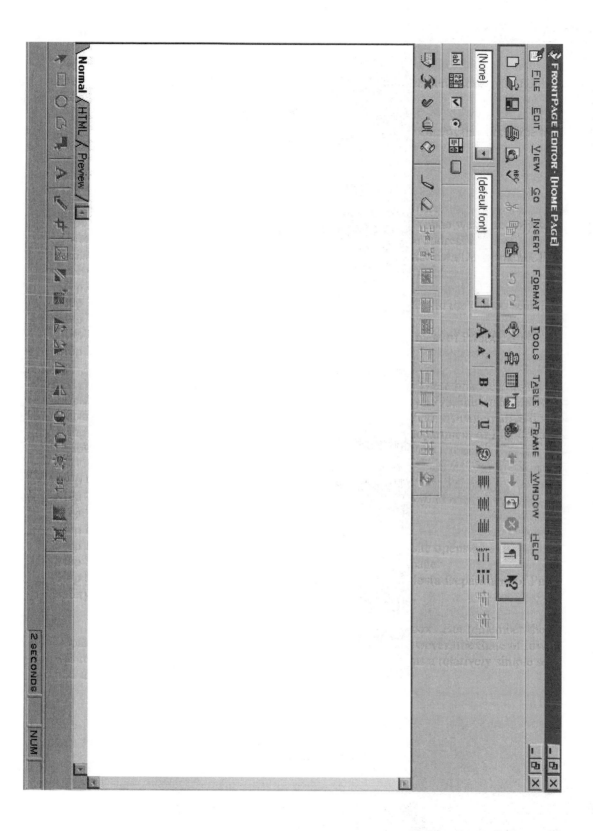

Figure 4.6: Homepage in FrontPage Editor

To apply a consistent look and feel to all webpages in the Survey Research website, we will apply a theme to the web. To apply a theme to a web:

Step One: Click the **FrontPage Explorer** button on the Taskbar. This displays the FrontPage Explorer in Navigation View.

Step Two: Click the **Themes** button in the Views window on the left side of the screen. This displays the Themes window on the right side of the screen.

Step Three: Currently the Survey Research Web does not use themes. To apply a theme, click the **Use Selected Theme** radio button in the upper left corner of the Views window. This displays the first Theme (Arcs) among the more than 40 listed. Use the scroll arrow at the bottom of the Themes list to find the **Postmodern Theme** and select it.

Step Four: Click the FrontPage Editor button on the Taskbar. This displays our homepage with the Postmodern Theme applied. An example of FrontPage Editor displaying a page with the Postmodern Theme applied may be seen in Figure 4.7.

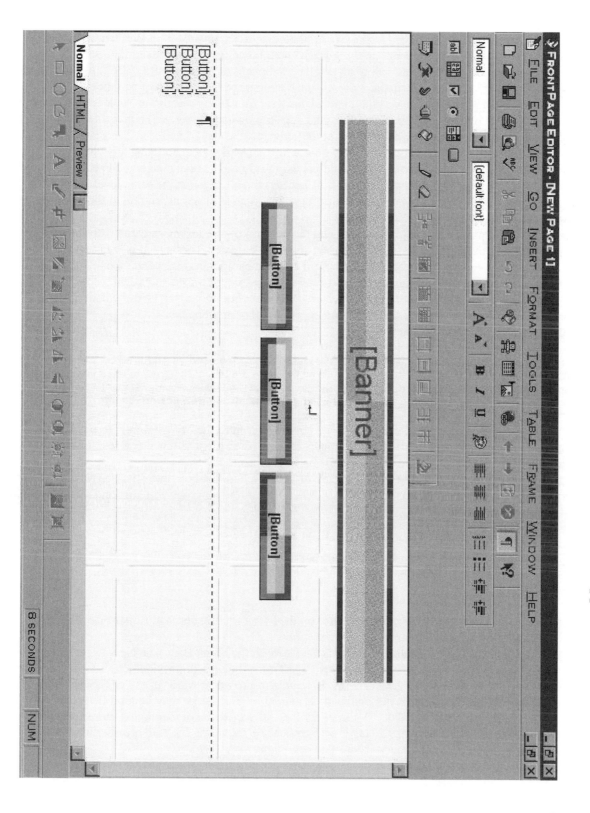

Figure 4.7: Homepage with Postmodern Theme Applied

Note that the Postmodern Theme, like all themes, placed a Navigation Bar beneath the page title and placed a Link Bar on the right side of your homepage. The Navigation Bar comprises a series of buttons that link to all primary webpages in your website. The Link Bar links to all other pages that link to the current page ("child pages" in Microsoft parlance).

When you preview your website in a web browser or actually publish or "upload" your website to the Web, navigation bars and link bars appear only as necessary. To give you an example, there are no pages in your website at the same level as the homepage. Therefore, no navigation bar will appear on your homepage, but a link bar will appear showing any child pages. Similarly, when you preview any child pages (the Opinion Survey page and Feedback Form to be created below), a navigation bar will appear with all pages at the same level. No link bar will appear in browser preview mode since there are no child pages in relation to the Opinion Survey and Feedback Form.

We will now add a paragraph describing the purpose of our survey research website.

Step One: Click the **Show/Hide** (Paragraph) button on the Standard Toolbar. It is the second to last button on the toolbar. The Show/Hide button displays paragraph marks and other nonprinting characters. Paragraph marks and returns are displayed on the webpage.

Step Two: Click your mouse in the lower center portion of your homepage. Your cursor appears next to the paragraph mark near the lower center portion of your webpage.

Step Three: Enter the following text:

Welcome to the Survey Research Website. This website includes surveys prepared by (list your name and organization here). The Opinion Survey listed on the left is designed to elicit your opinions regarding the President, Congress and the state of the U.S. economy. If you have any questions about this website, contact us by clicking the Feedback Form link on the left.

Step Four: In this step, we will change the text color of our introductory paragraph to navy and increase the size of the text to 12 pt. Select the paragraph of text that you just entered. Click **Format/Font** on the Menu Bar. The Format dialog box opens.

Step Five: Click **12 pt** in the Size list box, click **Arial** in the Font list box, and click the **Navy** color choice from the Color drop-down menu. Click the **OK** button when you are done.

Adding Additional Pages to the Survey Research Web

Your web will consist initially of three pages: a homepage, a web survey and a contact page (feedback form). The contact page will be added first. To add this page to the Survey Research Web:

Step One: Click **Tools/Show Front/Page Editor** on the Menu Bar. FrontPage Editor opens with a preformatted page with the Postmodern Theme applied.

Step Two: To create a new contact page, click **File/New** on the Menu Bar. The New Page/Frame dialog box is displayed (Figure 4.8). The New Page/Frame dialog box provides about 50 choices of templates and 10 choices for frames. The 50 templates provide a wide variety of choices. Nearly every kind of business or personal page is available. Each page may be modified to meet the needs of the web designer. The 10 frames choices offer methods of displaying more than one webpage in the same web browser. This is accomplished by dividing the web browser into distinct frames, which operate independently of each other.

Step Three: Select **Feedback Form** from the page list and click **OK**. A new Feedback Form with the Postmodern Theme applied is displayed in the FrontPage Editor (Figure 4.9). At this point, the Navigation Bar at the top of the page and the link bar at the left side of the page are placeholders only. The placeholders will be replaced by real links after we link the Feedback Form to the homepage. We will do this a little later in this exercise. The Feedback Form also includes a comment (purple text) describing what the Feedback Form does. This text is intended to help you understand how to use the Feedback Form and will not appear in the web browser view.

Step Four: Now we will modify the Feedback form so that it fits with the rest of the website. Let's modify the introductory text first. Delete the paragraph beginning with **Tell us what you think** and replace it with the following text:

We want your help to improve this website. Please give us comments on the surveys included herein, as well as on the overall appearance of the website. Please click the Submit Comments button at the bottom of the page when you are done.

Use the Format menu on the Menu bar to change the font of the text to Arial 12 pt with navy text.

Step Five: Next we will modify the form fields included on our Feedback Form. For the question **"What about us do you want to comment on?"**, we will modify the choices that appear in the Website drop down menu. Right-click the **Website** drop-down box. Select **Form Field Properties** from the shortcut menu

Step Six: Select and remove, by clicking the **Remove** button, the following menu items: **Company, Products, Store** and **Employee**.

Step Seven: We will add an item to the drop-down menu. Click the **Add** button. The Add Choice dialog box appears. Type **Survey Form** in the Choice text box. Click **OK** when you are done. Finally, click **Move Up** to move up our Survey Choice item so it appears between "Website" and "Other" on our drop-down menu.

Step Eight: Because we created the Feedback Form in FrontPage Editor, it is not automatically linked to the rest of the website. To create the link, first switch to FrontPage Explorer and select **Navigation View**. Click the **Feedback** icon in the bottom pane and drag it into the top pane just below the homepage. A blue link line appears from the homepage to the Feedback icon.

Step Nine: It is also useful to enter a title for each webpage created. The title appears on the Title Bar of the window in which the webpage is displayed. The Title Bar is just above the Menu Bar and lists the name of the program running (Microsoft Internet Explorer or Netscape usually), as well as the open webpage (file). Enter **Feedback Form for Survey Research Website** in the title text box.

Figure 4.8: Feedback Form

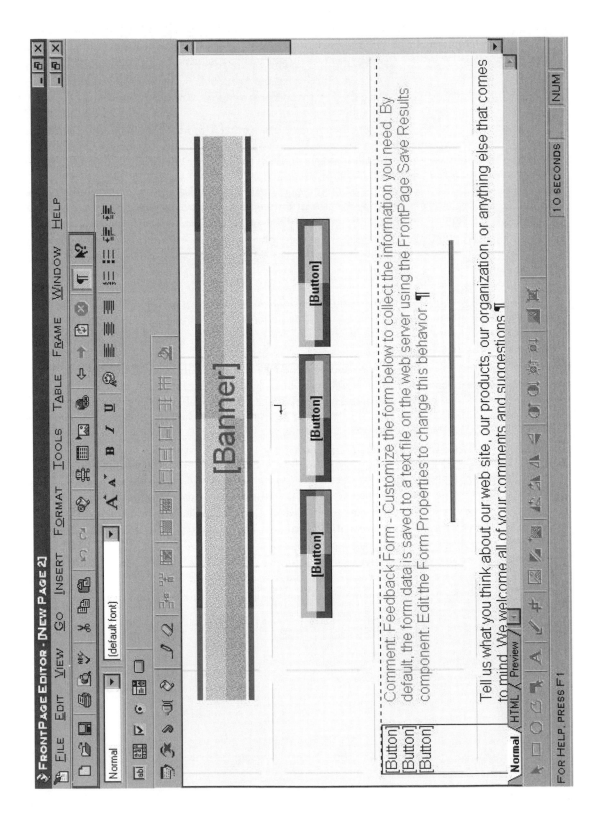

Titles are important since they give the person visiting a website an idea of the purpose of the website. To see titles of other webpages, visit various websites to check for titles. You will note that most webpages list titles on the Title Bar. If the web designer did not enter a title for the webpage, "untitled" will appear on the Title Bar after the name of the web browser. "Untitled" is not useful information, thus it is important to take the time and add a title to each webpage that you create.

Step Ten: The final step in creating our feedback form is to save the webpage. Click **File/Save As** on the Menu Bar. The Save As dialog box is displayed. We will enter the file name in the URL text box at the bottom of the Save As dialog box. The URL doubles as a file name and an Internet location. Enter **Feedback** as the URL.

The Feedback Form webpage was constructed from a template. We did not have to know the underlying features of each element of the feedback form to create it. During the next exercise, we will create a survey instrument in FrontPage Editor. We will add the basic form fields needed to construct a survey. Each field used reflects components of the Feedback Form that we created earlier.

First, though, we will provide a user-friendly title for our homepage and then provide a name for the blank webpage created when we opened the FrontPage Editor. As you recall, our homepage was given the name Default.htm when we created our website.

Step One: Click the FrontPage Explorer button on the taskbar. This displays FrontPage Explorer. If FrontPage Explorer is not in Navigation View, click the **Navigation View** button in the Views window.

Step Two: Right-click the **Home Page** icon. A shortcut menu appears. Select **Rename** from among the options.

Step Three: Type **Survey Research Website**. This is the title we have selected for our homepage. The name of the webpage remains Default.htm.

CONSTRUCTING AN OPINION POLL WEB SURVEY

The next three sections of Chapter Four guide us through the construction of three kinds of Internet surveys. First we will create a two-page web survey based upon a 1998 Washington Post public opinion survey regarding President Bill Clinton and the major political parties (Figure 4.9). We will take the same survey and construct an e-mail survey.

Figure 4.9: Washington Post Survey

Washington Post-ABC News Political Poll
Questions 1-6
Wednesday, September 30, 1998

This document is partial questionnaire derived from an ABC News-Washington Post poll is based on random telephone interviews with 1,505 adults from September 25-28. The margin of error is plus or minus 2.52 percentage points. It may be found in its entirety on the web at:
http://www.washingtonpost.org/wp-srv/politics/polls/vault/stories/data093098.htm

1. Do you approve or disapprove of the way Bill Clinton is handling his job as president?

Strongly Approve_____   Somewhat Approve_____
Strongly Disapprove _____   Somewhat Disapprove_____
No Opinion_____

2. Do you approve or disapprove of the way Clinton is handling the nation's economy

Strongly Approve_____   Somewhat Approve_____
Strongly Disapprove _____   Somewhat Disapprove_____
No Opinion_____

3. Do you approve or disapprove of the way the U.S. Congress is doing its job?

Strongly Approve_____   Somewhat Approve_____
Strongly Disapprove _____   Somewhat Disapprove_____
No Opinion_____

4. Who do you trust to do a better job coping with the main problems the nation faces over the next few years - Clinton or the Republicans in Congress?

Clinton
Republicans
Both equally
Neither
No Opinion

5. Right now, are you inclined to vote to re-elect your representative in Congress in the next election or are you inclined to look around for someone else to vote for?

Re-elect
Look Around
Depends

6. Overall, which party, the Democrats or the Republicans, do you trust to do a better job in coping with the main problems the nation faces over the next few years?

Democrats
Republicans
Both equally
Neither

Constructing a web survey involves a process similar to creating any other FrontPage document. We will create the survey using the Form Page Wizard available in FrontPage Editor. The Form Page Wizard is a FrontPage function designed to help users create surveys, feedback forms and other forms-based documents. Our survey will be based upon the Washington Post survey outlined in Figure 4.9, so have Figure 4.9 available for review. We will copy questions from the survey into the Form Page Wizard. This process involves several steps so be patient ;-).

Step One: Click the **FrontPage Explorer** button on the taskbar. This displays FrontPage Explorer. If FrontPage Explorer is not in Navigation View, click the **Navigation View** button in the Views window.

Step Two: Double-click the **Home Page** icon. The Survey Research homepage opens in FrontPage Explorer. The New dialog box opens with the Page Tab selected. Here we may select from among several types of new pages.

Step Three: Double-click **Form Page Wizard** from the list of available. The Form Page Wizard entry dialog box opens. It describes the purpose of the Form Page Wizard and gives tips on how to navigate it successfully.

Step Four: Click the **Next** button. You are asked to name your page and provide a page URL for it. Name your page **Opinion Survey**. Name the page URL **opinion.htm**. This provides a specific Web location and name for the survey.

Step Five: Click the **Next** Button again. At this point you are asked to edit or enter new questions in the form. Since we have none, we will have to add questions.

Step Six: Click the **Add** button at the top of the dialog box. Here you may choose the type of question from a predefined list at the top of the dialog box. Scroll down the list and choose **one of several options**. When we have finished our survey, Question One will allow the user to select from a series of options to answer the question. To create the actual question to be asked, we will enter information in a text box the bottom of the dialog box. The text box includes the following text: "Edit the prompt for this question" (see Figure 4.10). We use Question One drawn from the Washington Post survey. Therefore, delete the text: "Choose one of the following options" and replace it with the following text:

Do you approve or disapprove of the way Bill Clinton is handling his job as President?

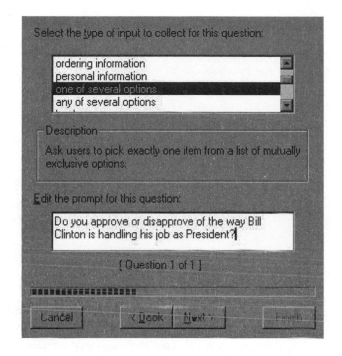

**Figure 4.10
Input Options Dialog Box**

Step Seven: Click the **Next** button. The **Input Type** dialog box opens (see Figure 4.10). In this box you enter the specific choices from which a respondent will answer. For Question One, enter the following text, pressing the **Enter** key after each entry:

**Strongly Approve
Somewhat Approve
Somewhat Disapprove
Strongly Disapprove
No Opinion**

Note that in the middle of the dialog box, you are asked: "How should the user choose an answer?" Click the **Radio Buttons** option in the middle of the dialog box. A Radio Button looks like this: ☺ After we have finished our survey, Question One will look like this:

Figure 4.11: Question One Radio Buttons

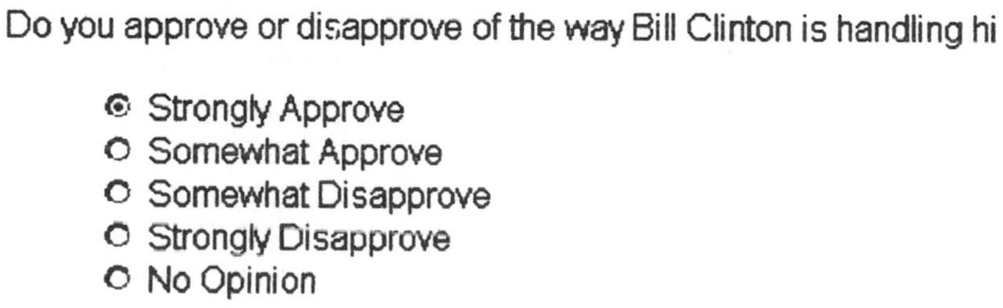

Do you approve or disapprove of the way Bill Clinton is handling hi

    ⦿ Strongly Approve
    ○ Somewhat Approve
    ○ Somewhat Disapprove
    ○ Strongly Disapprove
    ○ No Opinion

In the bottom of the Input Type dialog box is a text box in which we will enter the variable name for Question One. The variable name allows the Form Page Wizard to associate Question One options (Somewhat Approve, etc.) with a webpage on which the responses will be stored. Not surprisingly, we will name Question One "QuestionOne" (with no space between words and no quote marks).

Step Eight: Click the **Next** button. We have now completed one of the questions in our survey. There are six questions from the Washington Post survey to enter. Enter the other five using the same technique you employed in steps 5-7 of the exercise above. The only differences in Questions 2-6 are the question names and input variable names. Question names will be Question Two etc., and input variables will be the respective choices for each question. Input variables for Questions 2-3 will be the same as for Question One. Input variables for Question Four are:

Clinton
Republicans
Both Equally
Neither
No Opinion

There is one other difference. For questions 4-6, choose the drop-down menu when asked: "How should the user choose an answer?" This choice allows the user to click a drop-down arrow which reveals the answer options. The answers will be stored in the same manner as are radio buttons. Ordinarily, for consistency, you will create radio buttons, drop-down menus or lists. We are selecting different options, so that you will have experience creating both. Figure 4.12 shows the Input Type dialog box as it appears for Question Four:

Figure 4.12
Input Type Dialog Box

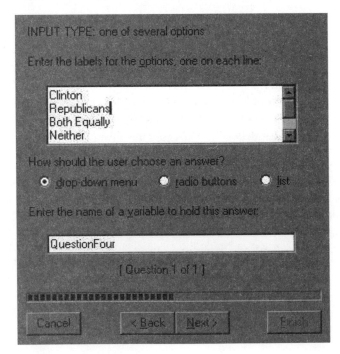

Step Nine: Once you have entered all six questions, click the **Next** button. Here you are given a series of presentation options for your six questions in radio button format. Keep the default (automatic) selection **As a numbered list**. We will not create a table of contents nor will we use tables.

**Figure 4.13
Presentation Options
Dialog Box**

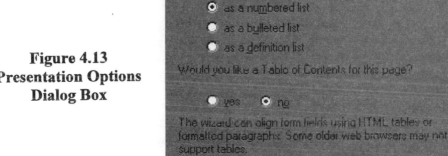

Step Ten: Click the **Next** button. In the Output Options dialog box, you are asked to name the document in which survey results will be stored. The options available are **web page, text file** or **custom CGI script**. Web page and text file results are stored on your website and are available only to you. This is because they are stored in a non-viewable directory (folder) named **Private**. Only you, the webmaster, may access the Private directory. Web page format is an html-formatted document that may be viewed through a web browser. Text file format is plain ASCII text and is best viewed in a word processor. CGI formatting allows the user to dictate customized features for the web page such as returning results through e-mail. Use the CGI option **only** if you do not have a FrontPage capable Internet service provider.

 Step Eleven: The Output Options dialog box also asks you to name the document in which survey results will be stored. Name the document "opinionresults" (no quotes). In this case, do not enter the .htm file extension, as FrontPage will do this automatically.

Step Twelve: Click the **Next** button and see the Finished dialog box. Click **Finish** and your survey is completed. Switch to Navigation view for a moment. Note that two documents appear in the bottom pane, those being **opinionsurvey.htm** and **opinionresults.htm**. Opinionsurvey.htm is the survey document in which respondents will enter their opinions and responses. Opinionresults.htm is the webpage in which responses will be collected. Later in this chapter, we will submit a few responses to see how the opinionresults.htm file works.

Step Thirteen: Now that the form is created, we must save it to our FrontPage Web. Click the **File/Save** menu option. This opens the File/Save dialog box. Save the file as "opinionsurvey" (no quotes).

Step Fourteen: The Opinion Survey page needs to be linked to other pages in the Survey Research web. Click the **FrontPage Explorer** button on the Taskbar. This opens FrontPage Explorer in Navigation View. If FrontPage Explorer is not in Navigation View, click the **Navigation View** Button on the left border of FrontPage Explorer. Find the Opinion Survey file in the bottom pane of FrontPage Explorer. Drag the Opinion Survey to the top pane of FrontPage Explorer, just to the right of the Feedback Form. An Opinion Survey icon is created with a blue link line to the Survey Research home page.

Our survey form is relatively complete, but it lacks two critical pieces of information. Remember in Chapter One, we identified two items that are fairly obvious parts of a survey instrument, but easily forgotten. Those items are return address information and respondent information. In this next exercise we will enter these items. First, let's enter the return address information.

Step One: While in FrontPage Explorer, make sure that you are in Navigation View. Next, Double-click the **Opinion Survey** button in the top pane. This displays the Opinion Survey document in FrontPage Editor.

Step Two: Just under the Opinion Survey title is a line of placeholder text reading: "This is an explanation of the purpose of the form." We will replace this text with the following text.

This is a web survey designed to elicit your opinion regarding the President, Congress and the state of the U.S. economy. Please take a few minutes and respond to these six questions. To complete the questions, click on the appropriate button, select an item from a drop down list or fill in the blank. Click the "Submit" button at the bottom of the survey once you have finished, or click the "Reset Form" button to clear your response and start over. If you have any questions regarding this survey, you may contact us at:

- **Your Name**
- **Your Institution**
- **Your Address**
- **Your Phone Number**
- **Your Fax Number**
- **Your e-mail address**
- **Your URL**

Of course, replace the generic text bulleted above with your actual address information.

Next we will add respondent information. To do this, we will use the Formatting and Forms Toolbars in FrontPage Editor.

Step One: Scroll down to the bottom of the Opinion Survey. Click your mouse after the Question Six text box (Democrats is displayed in the box) and above the Submit button. Press the **Enter** key twice to give yourself some working space in which to enter the respondent information.

Step Two: There are three paragraph marks after the Question Six text box. These spaces are not aligned to the left margin. Click the middle paragraph mark and click the **Decrease Indent**

button on the Formatting Toolbar (second toolbar down). The Decrease Indent button is the fifth button from the right.

Step Three: Enter the following text, spaces included. After entering the text, we will insert a series of text boxes adjacent to each line of text in which respondents will place their organizational information.

Please enter the following information to allow us to send you the results of this study:

Your Name:
Your Organization:
Your Address:
Your City, State and Zip:
Your e-mail Address:
Your Phone Number:

Thank you again for responding to our survey. Please click the submit button to send us your responses.

Step Four: If the Formatting Toolbar is not displayed, Click **View/Toolbars** on the Menu Bar, then select **Forms**. The first button on the formatting toolbar is the **One-Line Text Box** button.
Step Five: Click your mouse immediately after the **Your Name** text. Press the **space bar** once. Click the **One-Line Text Box** button. A text box appears after "Your Name."
Step Six: Repeat Step Five for each of the remaining organizational items.

Some of the text boxes may not be wide enough to accommodate the text to be entered. This needs to be corrected. Also, all text boxes need to be assigned names. These are the names that we will see in the webpage in which our survey results will be stored. If we do not change the default (automatic) names of the text boxes, we will end up with cryptic names like T1 or T2. This will become clear when we test our survey form later in this chapter. Let's go through the text boxes one by one.

Step One: First we will widen the Organization text box. Right-click on the Organization text box. A shortcut menu appears. Select **Form Field Properties**. Here is what the Form Field Properties dialog box looks like:

Figure 4.14: Form Field Properties Dialog Box

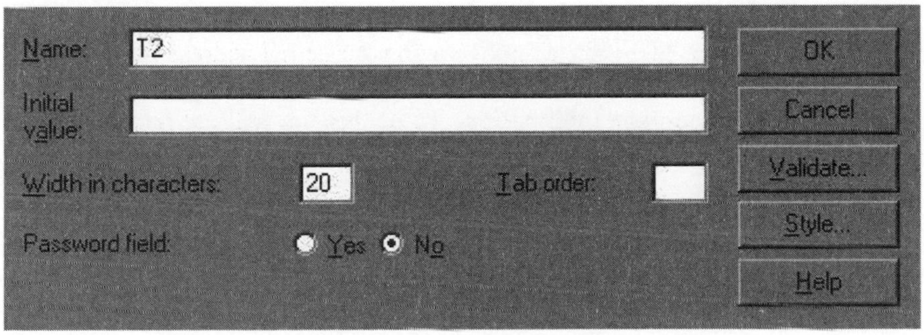

Step Two: Since the Organization text box is the second one that we entered, it is named "T2". Delete "T2" and type **Organization** in the Name text box. Note that the Name text box will not accept spaces as valid characters. Next, delete **20** in the Width in Characters text box and replace it with **30**. When you are done, click **OK**.

Step Three: Repeat Steps One and Two. Type the following information into the remaining Form Field Properties dialog boxes as indicated below:

Field	Name	Width
Your Name	**RespondentName**	**20**
Your Address	**Address**	**30**
Your City, State and Zip	**CSZ**	**30**
Your e-mail Address	**Email**	**30**
Your Phone Number	**Phone**	**20**

Note that FrontPage gives you the option to password protect any field. We will not take advantage of this option. However, this option is useful for those of you who want to restrict access to a portion of a survey. (See "An Additional Note on Password Protection" later in this chapter for more information.)

We will enter and edit two more text boxes to our survey. In this text box, we will ask the respondent an open-ended question designed to get his/her opinion on the work that Congress and the President are doing.

Step One: In the Opinion Survey, scroll down until you are just above the Respondent Information section. Click your mouse between Question Six and the Respondent Information section, then press the **Enter** key two times.

Step Two: Type the following text: **7. What is your opinion of the job that Congress is doing?** Press the **Enter** key once after you have entered the text.

Step Three: Type the following text: **8. What is your opinion of the job that President Clinton is doing?** Press the **Enter** key once after you have entered the text. If your text is incorrectly aligned or is not the correct font size, use the Format menu, Formatting Toolbar or appropriate keystrokes (e.g., **Backspace** or **Delete**) to correct any problems.

Step Four: Click your mouse one space below Question 7, then click the **Scrolling Text Box** button. It is the second button on the Forms Toolbar. This places a scrolling text box after the text. Repeat the process for Question 8. You now have scrolling text boxes after both questions.

Step Five: Rename and resize both text boxes. To do this, Right Click on the boxes and complete the appropriate lines as follows:

Question	Name	Width	Lines
7	**Congress**	**40**	**7**
8	**President**	**40**	**7**

The Width text box defines the width of the scrolling text box while the lines text box defines the number of lines displayed in the text box. Limiting the number of lines displayed does not limit the number of characters that may be entered in the text box. A scrolling text box may accept up to 64,000 characters, well over 100 pages of typed text.

Test the Survey Research Website

Microsoft FrontPage allows you to test the functionality of your website prior to uploading it to the Web. Testing your website is important, particularly for forms-based webpages. You may enter test data into your form, submit the data and examine the results on your personal computer, prior to putting your work out for the world to see. In the next exercise, we will test our website, survey and survey results webpages.

Step One: Switch to Navigation View. Double-click the **Survey Research Website** icon. Your homepage opens in FrontPage Editor.

Step Two: Click the **Preview in Browser** button on the Standard Toolbar. Microsoft Internet Explorer or Netscape Navigator opens with your homepage displayed. FrontPage Editor also includes a Preview Tab that, when clicked, displays a webpage in preview mode. Preview in Browser is the preferred method, however, because it allows for full graphic and web functionality, while the FrontPage Preview Tab does not.

Step Three: Click the **Feedback Form** link on the left side of the homepage. The Feedback Form opens. Note that three navigation buttons appear at the top of the page. The Home and Opinion Survey buttons are working buttons leading to each respective page. The Feedback button is a placeholder, only to recognize the currently open page.

Step Four: Click the **Opinion Survey** button. The Opinion Survey opens.

Test the Opinion Survey

Next we will enter information into our form and examine the results page to make sure that information was recorded there. We will then submit the data we entered and check the "optionresults" webpage to ensure that our results were recorded there.

Step One: The Opinion Survey should still be open in your web browser. Enter or select the following information for each of the eight questions. You may, of course, select answers that fit your actual position on the issues ;-)

Question Number	Response
1.	Somewhat Approve
2.	Strongly Approve
3.	No Opinion
4.	Clinton
5.	Look Around
6.	Democrats
7.	Congress could do a better job of focusing on bread and butter issues.
8.	The President is doing an excellent job of handling the economy, but needs to manage his personal life better.
Your Name:	Enter your real name here
Your Organization:	Enter your real organization here
Your Address:	Enter your real address here
Your City, State and Zip:	Enter your real city, state, and zip here
Your e-mail Address:	Enter your real e-mail address here
Your Phone Number:	Enter your real phone number here

Step Two: Click the **Submit** button at the bottom of the form. Depending on your Web browser settings, you may receive a message indicating that you are submitting information over the Internet or your local Intranet. This is a security message and may be ignored unless you want your information to be transmitted via more secure method. See your system administrator if you require more security.

Step Three: The Form Confirmation Page opens. Your page should look something like this:

Figure 4.15: Form Confirmation Page

> **QuestionOne:** Somewhat Approve
> **QuestionTwo:** Somewhat Approve
> **QuestionThree:** No Opinion
> **QuestionFour:** Clinton
> **QuestionFive:** Look Around
> **QuestionSix:** Democrats
> **RespondentName:** John Q. Public
> **RespondentOrganization:** Back Bay Marketing, Inc.
> **Address:** 1111 Marlborough
> **CSZ:** Boston, MA 02135
> **email:** backbay@isp.com
> **Phone:** 617-555-5555
>
> **Congress**
>
> Congress could do a better job of focusing on bread and butter issues.
>
> **President**
>
> The President is doing an excellent job of handling the economy, but needs to manage his personal life better.

Your responses will appear in the order that you created form fields. For example, if you create your base form and add additional fields later, those additional fields will appear at the bottom of your confirmation page. To resolve this problem, you must edit each form field and enter a **Tab Order** number. This is accomplished by right-clicking each form field, selecting **Form Field Properties** from the shortcut menu and adding a sequential **Tab Order** number for each Form Field.

Each time someone responds to your survey, an additional set of responses will be placed below responses already received. To clear the optionresults page, open it in FrontPage Editor and delete responses received. Then you may receive additional responses on a clean slate.

Publishing (Uploading) the Website

Now that you have a working website and survey form, the only thing left to do is to upload your website to your Web host or Internet Service Provider (ISP). Microsoft FrontPage uses the Publish command to upload files. Publishing your website transfers files from your personal computer to the server computer maintained by your ISP. If your ISP supports (has installed) Microsoft FrontPage Server Extensions, **always** use the Publish command. If your ISP does not have Microsoft FrontPage Server Extensions installed, **always** use the File Transfer Protocol (FTP) process outlined later in this chapter. If you do not follow these instructions, you can render your website unusable.

Here's how you publish a website:

Step One: Switch to FrontPage Explorer. Locate the **Publish** button. It is the second button on the Standard Toolbar.

Step Two: Click the **Publish** Button. After a few seconds, you will be asked for authorization information, including a **username** and a **password**. This is information that you obtained from your Web host or ISP.

Step Three: Enter your **username** and **password**. After a few seconds, the upload of your website will begin. You will see several messages on the Status Bar (just above the Taskbar at the bottom of your screen), including **Listing Pages** and **Publishing**. When the upload process is complete, you will see a **Published** message. Your web survey is now available and accessible on the World Wide Web. Congratulations!

To summarize, the most time consuming part of creating a FrontPage survey is deciding what questions you want to include in your survey instrument. This is a process that you would go through whether or not you used FrontPage. As you have seen from these exercises, building the survey in FrontPage is somewhat similar to creating a document in any personal computer software application. Just remember that these are the basic steps involved:

- Create your survey instrument
- Create a FrontPage Web
- Create a Survey using the Form Page Wizard
- Add and/or modify the questions that you want to use
- Save your work
- Upload your survey

Once you have created an initial FrontPage Web, there is no need to create other webs. You may store all of your surveys in your main (root) web.

An Additional Note on Password Protection

Microsoft FrontPage offers three methods of password protection. As mentioned earlier, certain form fields (one-line text boxes) may be set to require a password. This is accomplished by selecting the **Password Field** button in the Form Filed Properties dialog box. Password protection on a single document or an entire website must be created while your page is "live" (already published) on the Web.

All ISP and web hosting services are different, but generally the website administrator (you) will have some ability to provide or restrict access to certain webpages. The following process works if your ISP allows you to administer your website from a remote location via FrontPage. If your ISP does not allow you to use FrontPage to administer your website from a remote location, they probably offer their own site administration program for their users. **Check with your ISP or web hosting service first before going through this process.** If you attempt to use FrontPage permissions or password functions without knowing (from your ISP) what you may or may not do regarding remote website administration, you may cause problems with the functionality of your website.

WEBSITE PASSWORD PROTECTION/REMOTE WEBSITE ADMINISTRATION

To password protect an entire FrontPage Website, you must open your website while you are connected to the Web. Here is the process:

Step One: Connect to your Internet Service Provider.
Step Two: Open the website needing password protection. In FrontPage Explorer, click **File/Open FrontPage Web** on the Menu Bar. The Getting Started dialog box opens (see Figure 4.16).

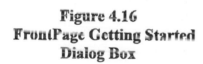

**Figure 4.16
FrontPage Getting Started
Dialog Box**

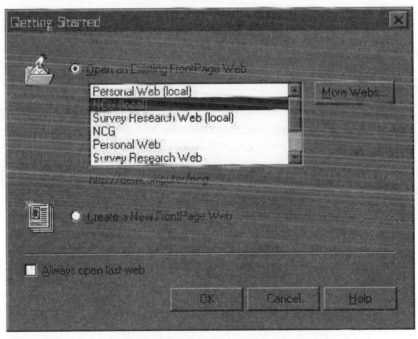

Step Three: Click the **More Webs** button and the Open FrontPage Web window opens (see Figure 4.17). Initially a list of webs appears in the **Select a Web Server or disk location** text box. Enter your Internet Protocol (IP) address in the **Select a Web Server or disk location** text box. Your IP address is a number ranging from 8-12 digits and was provided to you when you registered with your ISP. Click the **List Webs** button, then click the **OK** button when you are done.

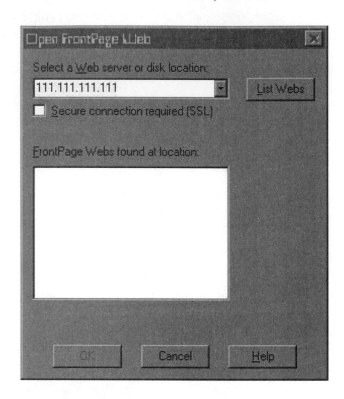

Figure 4.17
FrontPage Getting Started
Dialog Box

Step Four: Enter your username and password. Your website opens. You are now able to manage your web files located on your ISP's computer.

Step Five: Now we will password protect the entire website. **Click Tools/Permissions** from the Menu Bar in FrontPage Explorer. The Permissions dialog box opens. In the Settings tab, select **Use Unique Permissions** for this Web and click **Apply**. In the Users tab, two radio buttons at the bottom of the dialog box allow you to determine who has access to your website. Currently, everyone has access to browse your website. If you wish to restrict access to your website, click the **only registered users have browse access** button, then click **OK**. (Figure 4.18 shows the default.)

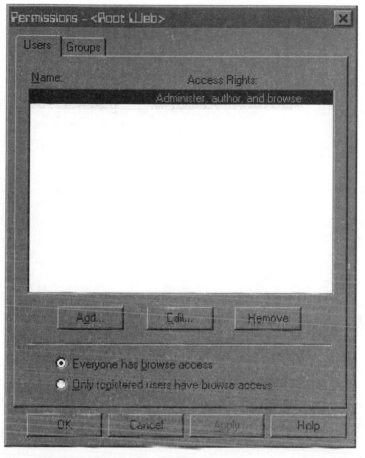

**Figure 4.18
FrontPage Permissions
Dialog Box**

Step Six: Click on the FrontPage Explorer button on the Taskbar. You are now viewing your website (known as the "root web" after it is uploaded to your ISP).

Step Seven: From the root web, open FrontPage Editor by clicking **Show FrontPage Editor** button.

Step Eight: On the FrontPage Editor File menu select **New**.

Step Nine: In the New Page dialog box, select **User Registration**, and click **OK**. FrontPage Editor creates a new page containing a user registration form and explanatory text. You can copy the form to any page in the FrontPage root web or leave it on the current page and edit the text. The form is labeled "Form Submission" by default. You can change its label. The user registration form also supplies a page that confirms the user's user name.

Step Ten: Right-click anywhere in the user registration form.

Step Eleven: From the shortcut menu, select **Form Properties**.

Step Twelve: In the Form Properties dialog box, select **Options**. The Setting for Registration Form Handler dialog box opens.

Step Thirteen: In the Web Name field of the dialog box, enter the name of the FrontPage website for which you are registering users with password access for your site and click **OK**. If you are registering users for a page located in your root web, the name of the web is "root". If you are registering users for a page located in a "child" web (a website located in a subfolder of the root web), enter the name assigned to the website. If you have questions about this, check with your ISP to determine if your web is a root or child web.

Step Fourteen: Make sure that the registration form is accessible to users of the root web. The best way to ensure user accessibility to a registration page is to create a hyperlink from your homepage to the user registration page. The next steps describe how to create a hyperlink to your homepage.

Step Fifteen: Open your homepage in the FrontPage Editor.

Step Sixteen: Place a link to the user registration form on your homepage. We will place the link in the welcome paragraph. After the word "economy" in the second to last sentence of the welcome paragraph, add the following text: **You must have a password to gain access to the opinion survey. <u>Click Here</u> to gain access**.

Step Seventeen: Select the words <u>Click Here</u>. Click the 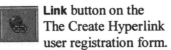 **Link** button on the Standard Toolbar at the top of your screen. It looks like this: The Create Hyperlink dialog box opens. In the URL text box, enter the URL of the user registration form. You may also click the URL down arrow to select the form. If you created a user registration form, it will be listed among the webpages in your FrontPage website. After entering the URL, click **OK** and then save your work. The link from your homepage to your registration is completed.

Step Eighteen: Publish your website. Now any users wanting access to your website beyond the homepage must enter a password.

PUBLISHING A SURVEY WITHOUT FRONTPAGE SERVER EXTENSIONS

While many FrontPage users will have access to an ISP supporting FrontPage server extensions, other users will not have this advantage. FrontPage provides several ways to modify your web survey so that it is functional, even without the advantage of FrontPage server extensions.

The easiest way to use a FrontPage form without access to FrontPage server extensions is to require your form to e-mail the form results to you. This may sound somewhat complicated, but it is actually a relatively simple process. Here is the short story:

- Create your survey instrument
- Create a Survey using the Form Page Wizard
- Insert a **mailto** html tag to your survey
- Add and/or modify the questions that you want to use
- Save your work
- Upload your survey using a File Transfer Protocol (FTP) Program

It bears repeating that if you use an ISP that supports FrontPage server extensions **do not** use the FTP process to upload files. This may corrupt your files and cause you to lose your work. Use an FTP program, **only** if your ISP does not support FrontPage server extensions.

Creating the e-mail Survey

In the following exercises, we will not create a survey from scratch, rather we will copy the Opinion Survey, save it under a different name and modify it, so that we can have responses e-mailed to us. Here's the process:

Step One: Switch to FrontPage Explorer. Click the **Folders View** button. A list of all files and folders appears in the upper pane on the right side of FrontPage Explorer.

Step Two: Double-click the **opinionsurvey.html** file. The Opinion Survey File opens in FrontPage Editor. Save the Opinion Survey file under the name **emailsurvey**. Do this by selecting **File/Save As** on the **Menu Bar**. Type **emailsurvey.html** in the URL text box and type **e-mail version of opinion survey** in the Title text box.

Step Three: Some FrontPage options will not function correctly without access to FrontPage server extensions. Navigation Bars are among the non-working functions. Select the **banner** and the **navigation bar** at the top of the Opinion Survey by holding down your right mouse button and dragging across them. Press the **delete** key to delete them. Change the heading from "Opinion Survey" to **E-Mail Survey**. Also, select the seven contact items at the top of the form. The existing bullets will not function, since they also require FrontPage server extensions. Replace these buttons with a numbered list using the **Format/Bullets and Numbering** commands from the **Menu Bar**. Finally, delete the bars at the top and bottom of the survey. They also will not work without FrontPage server extensions. You may insert your own images to replace the bullets and bars if you like.

Step Four: Now we will add the "mailto" tag to our survey form. We will use the Form Field Properties dialog box to accomplish this. Scroll down to the survey form. The survey form is surrounded by dashes. Right-click the survey form and select **Form Properties** from the shortcut menu. The Form Properties dialog box opens. It looks like this:

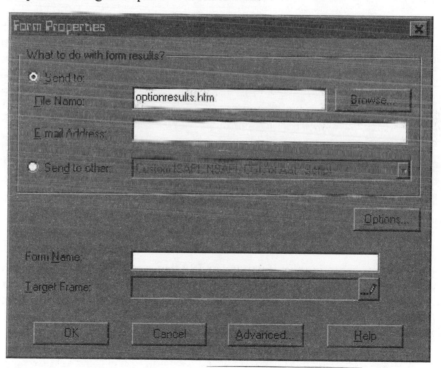

**Figure 4.19
Form Properties
Dialog Box**

You might confuse the Form Properties dialog box with the *Form Field Properties* dialog box. These are two different dialog boxes. The Form Properties dialog box acts on the entire form, while the Form Field Properties dialog box acts on fields individually.

Step Five: The Form Properties dialog box gives you two options for sending form results. First, you may send the results to a file (**Send to File** option). This is the default (automatic) option for FrontPage. With this option, FrontPage creates a file (optionresults.htm in the case of the Opinion Survey) in which to store any responses. To access responses, you open the results file on the Web. Second, you may choose to set FrontPage to send all of your web forms via e-mail. If you know absolutely that you will not use FrontPage server extensions, select this choice and enter the e-mail address (e.g., **yourname@isp.com**). To take advantage of this option, you must have your ISP configure your website to send all forms via e-mail. I do not recommend this, because you will lose much in the way of FrontPage web form functionality.

In our case, we are going to select the **Send to Other** option. This option allows you to write programs (CGI script and others) to store your results in, or you may enter an e-mail address to which the results may be sent. To continue, select the **Send to Other** radio button, then click the Options button.

Step Six: The **Options for Custom Forms Handler** dialog box opens. It looks like this:

Figure 4.20: Options for Custom Forms Handler Dialog Box

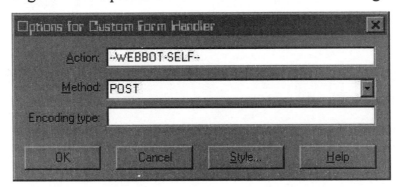

Step Seven: Delete the text "--WEBBOT SELF --" in the Action text box. Enter the html tag **mailto:** (including the colon) followed by your e-mail address (**mailto:username@isp.com**, for example) in the Action text box. The **mailto:** html tag tells FrontPage to e-mail any responses to the e-mail address indicated in the Action text box. Leave the other text boxes as they are. You have the option of formatting your results through the Style button, but we will not format our results in this exercise. When you are done, click **OK** twice, then save your work.

Uploading the e-mail Survey

To test the e-mail survey, we must upload it to the Web. Since, in this case, our ISP does not support FrontPage server extensions, we cannot use the Publish command to upload our file. Thus, we must upload our file via other means.

File Transfer Protocol (FTP) software is the best method of uploading a file to the Web. There are many popular FTP software packages, including CuteFTP, WSFTP and Reflection FTP. All of these packages cost less than $40 (1999 dollars), function in a similar manner, and are relatively straightforward to use. In the next exercise, we will use CuteFTP to upload our survey file.

Step One: Open your FTP package. In our case we will open CuteFTP. The FTP Site Manager dialog box opens. At this point, select the ISP to which you will upload your survey file. If you have not added an ISP, click the **Add Site** button. The Add Host dialog box opens. Here you enter information provided to you by your ISP. Add information using the following format:

Text Box	What to Enter
Site Label	A user-friendly name for your site, e.g., My Survey Website
Host Address	The Internet Protocol (IP) address for your ISP, e.g., 222.222.22.2
User ID	The User ID that you use to access your ISP and website
Password	The Password that you use to access your ISP and website
Remote Directory Filter	Your ISP may designate a directory (e.g., html) in which your place your uploaded files. Enter that information here.
Initial Local Directory	You may designate a directory on your personal computer to open automatically. Usually, this is the directory in which your website files are located.

If you have already added an ISP, select the ISP and then click the **Connect** button at the bottom of the Site Manager. Examples of the FTP Site Manager dialog box and the Add Host dialog box may be reviewed in Figures 4.21 and 4.22:

Figure 4.21: CuteFTP Site Manager Dialog Box

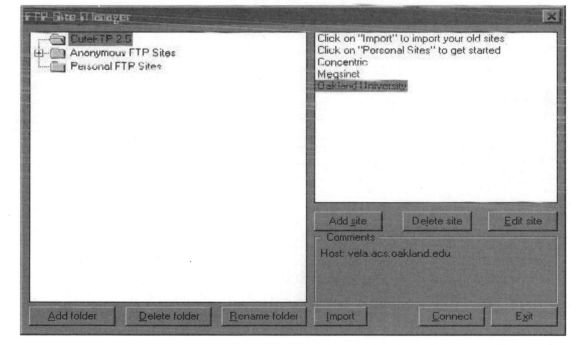

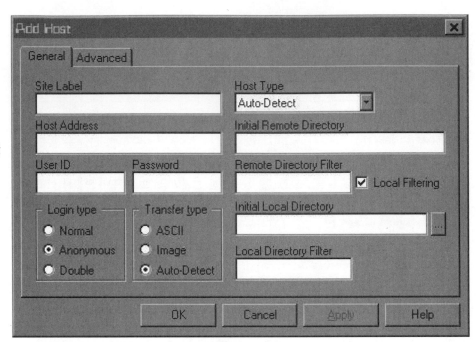

**Figure 4.22
CuteFTP Add Host
Dialog Box**

When CuteFTP opens, you will see a Login dialog box with a few messages from the system administrator. Click **OK** to see the main FTP Screen. An example may be seen in Figure 4.23. **Step Two**: Next, we will upload our e-mail survey. CuteFTP, like other FTP programs, uses an Explorer-like interface. Your computer's files are located on the left side of the screen, while your ISP's files, including your website is located on the right side of the screen. To upload a file, you must locate the file to be uploaded on your personal computer (left side of screen), then drag the file to your website on your ISP's computer. Locate the **emailsurvey.html** file on your computer and drag the file to your ISP's computer (right side of screen). A small dialog box opens, asking you if you want to upload a file. Click **Yes** to confirm.

All ISPs are different. Many ISPs create a special directory in which you are to place your files. This directory is usually named **html**. If this is the case, make sure that you drag your files to that directory. If a special directory is not designated, simply drag files to be uploaded to the right side of your screen.

Many ISPs also allow users to create directories in their personal websites. This is what I have done in my Oakland University website, outlined in Figure 4.23. Figure 4.23 shows several directories in which I place files for various purposes including Forms (actual surveys that I have administered), PA653 (a class that I teach) and Survey (sample survey forms supporting this book). Creating subdirectories for your website helps organize remote files in a sensible manner. If you use an ISP that supports Microsoft FrontPage server extensions, this process takes place automatically.

Figure 4.23: CuteFTP Main Screen

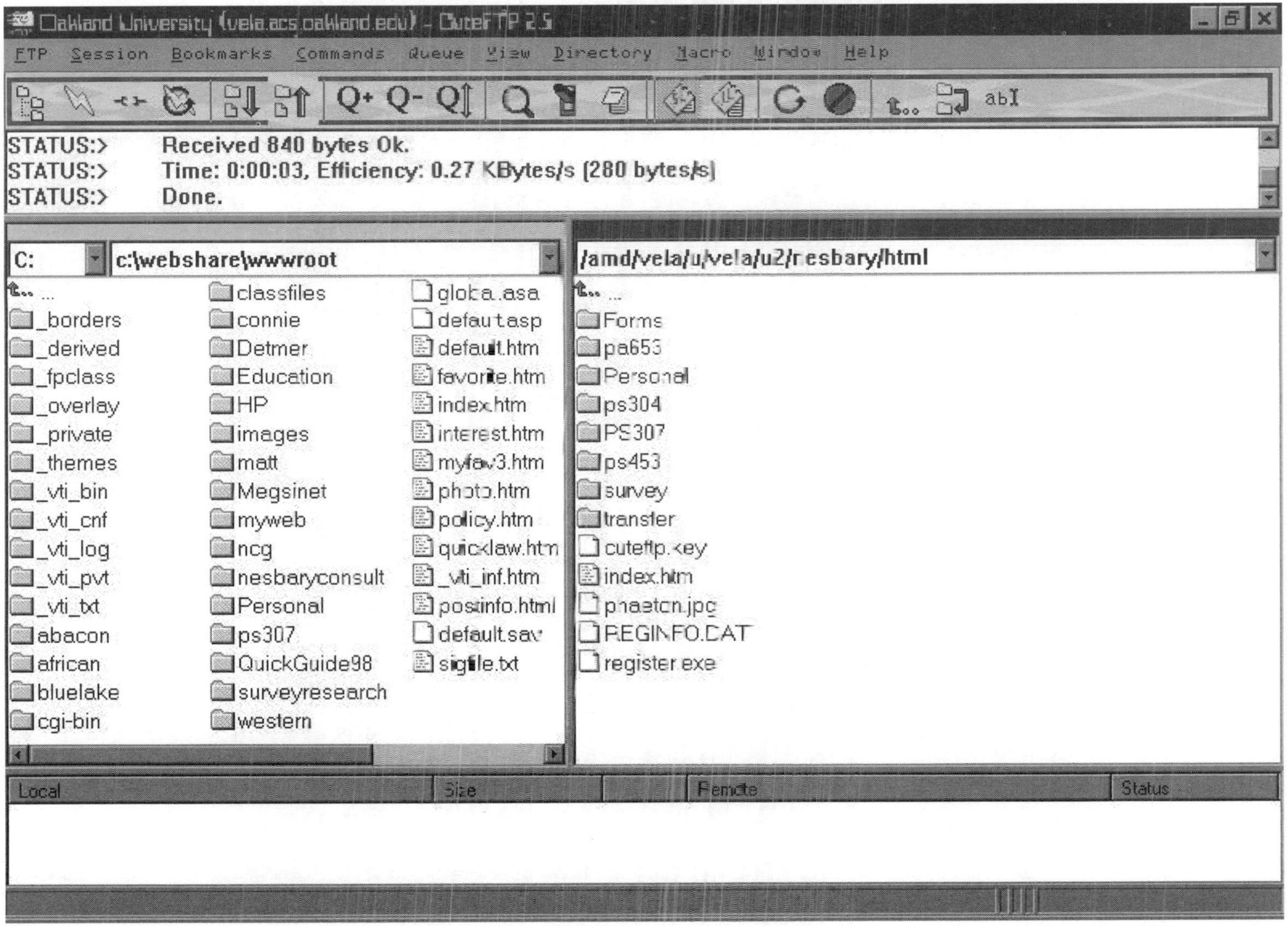

Testing the e-mail Survey

Once uploaded, we must test the e-mail survey form to ensure that it works properly. We will use Microsoft Outlook Express, an e-mail program that comes bundled with Microsoft Internet Explorer. Here is the process:

Step One: Open your Web Browser and enter the URL of your survey
(e.g., http://www.isp.com/~survey).
Step Two: Complete the survey, entering information of your choice for each question.
Step Three: Click the **Submit** button at the bottom of the survey. This action sends the results to the e-mail address that you entered.
Step Four: To view the results, open your e-mail program. It usually takes a few minutes for the form to be transmitted to an e-mail account. Your e-mail account may be accessed via your web browser or dedicated e-mail program (e.g., Eudora, Pine). To open your e-mail program, use one of these techniques:

- **Double-click your e-mail program icon.**
- **Click the e-mail button on the Microsoft Internet Explorer Toolbar (upper right corner). Select Read Mail from the menu.**
- **Click the e-mail button on the Netscape Navigator Status Bar (lower left corner).**
- **Click the appropriate e-mail button in other web browsers (E.G., AOL, Prodigy).**

Step Five: Microsoft Outlook Express opens in Inbox View (see Figure 4.24). All e-mails recently received are listed in the upper-right corner of the Outlook Express window. This window displays the source and subject of the e-mail, as well as the date the e-mail was received. Unread e-mails are displayed in **bold** text, while read e-mails are displayed in normal text. Form results may be identified by the subject indicated. Any e-mail received from a FrontPage form will have a subject listed as **Form Posted From Microsoft Internet Explorer**.

I (Dale Nesbary) sent the second e-mail from the top with a subject line reading **Form Posted From Microsoft Internet Explorer**. Note that, just to the right of this e-mail, is a small paperclip icon. This icon represents an **e-mail attachment**, which is a file that is sent along with the e-mail. This file represents the results of the form I e-mailed to myself. Of course, your form results were sent to the e-mail address that you indicated in FrontPage.

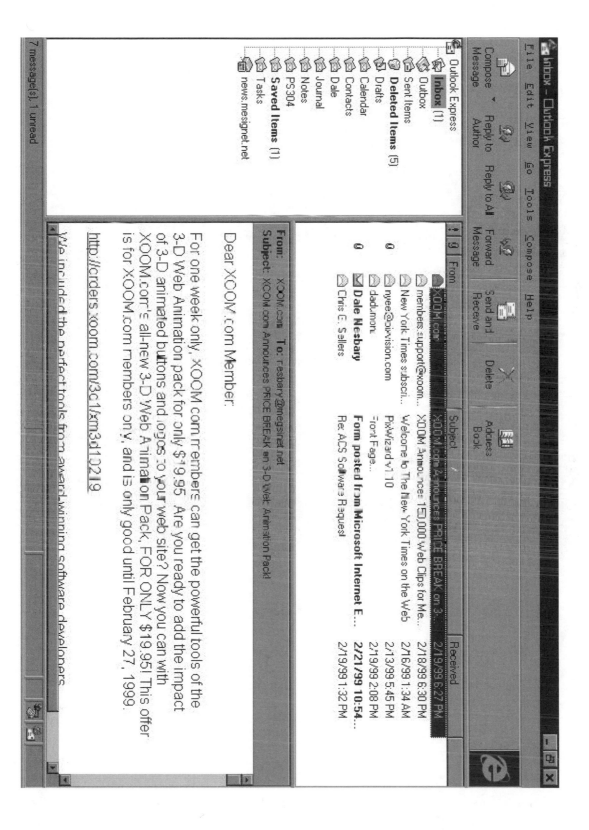

Figure 4.24: Microsoft Outlook Express

Step Six: Double-click the **attachment** icon (paper clip). A window opens with the attachment available for opening or saving. The file is named **postdata.att**. Right click on the postdata.att icon. Choose **Save As**. Save the file in a location that is easily accessible.

Step Seven: Open the **postata.att** file in a word processing program (Microsoft Word, WordPerfect). Ordinarily, the word processor will recognize the .att file extension as a word processing file. To ensure that you can find the postdata.att file using Microsoft Word, choose **File/Open** from the **Menu Bar**, then find the **Files of Type** text box at the bottom of the Open dialog box. Click the down arrow next to the Files of Type text box and choose **All Files**. All Files is the first choice on the drop down list, so you may have to scroll up a little bit. All Files allows you to see any file on your system, not just word processing files.

Step Eight: The postdata.att file opens. It is not a pretty sight (see Figure 4.25). The responses are organized in block style and separated by ampersands (&). This lack of formatting is the downside of not using FrontPage extensions. Select each ampersand and press the Enter key. Next, delete the (+) signs. These actions place each question on a separate line and remove the plus signs, making the responses more readable.

Figure 4.25 Postdata.att File Results

Response Before Formatting

```
QuestionOne=Strongly+Approve&QuestionTwo=Strongly+Approve&QuestionThree=Somewhat
+Disapprove&QuestionFour=Clinton&QuestionFive=Look+Around&QuestionSix=Democrats&
Congress=Regarding+fiscal+issues%2C+a+good+job.%0D%0ARegarding+social+issues%2C+
poor+job.&President=Regarding+fiscal+issue+a+good+job.%0D%0ARegarding+personal+i
ssues+a+poor+job.&RespondentName=Jane+Q.+Public&RespondentOrganization=Jamaica+P
lain+Seafood&Address=555+Roxbury+Drive&CSZ=Jamaica+Plain%2C+MA+02155&email=jane@
isp.com&T6=617-555-55555
```

Responses After Formatting

```
QuestionOne=Strongly Approve
QuestionTwo=Strongly Approve
QuestionThree=Somewhat Disapprove
QuestionFour=Clinton
QuestionFive=Look Around
QuestionSix=Democrats
Congress=Regarding fiscal issues%2C a good job.%0D%0ARegarding social issues%2C
poor job.
President=Regarding fiscal issue a good job.%0D%0ARegarding personal issues a
poor job.
RespondentName=Jane Q. Public
RespondentOrganization=Jamaica Plain Seafood
Address=555 Roxbury Drive
CSZ=Jamaica Plain%2C MA 02155
email=jane@isp.com
T6=617-555-55555
```

SENDING STANDARD SURVEYS VIA É-MAIL

Arguably the easiest method of distributing a survey is to create a standard text-based document and transmit it via e-mail attachment. Here is the short story:

- Create your survey instrument
- Save your survey as a text or word processing document
- Send your survey via e-mail attachment

After receiving the survey instrument via e-mail, the respondent must print it out and complete it, just like a regular mail survey. This means that your response time will likely be longer than that of a forms-based survey, but you do save time in the initial mailing. Additionally, the initial e-mail costs only the time it takes for you to send the e-mail.

Sending a Survey via e-mail

Step One: Create a survey instrument in a word processing or text-based format. Today most major word processors (Microsoft Word, WordPerfect, WordPro) recognize plain text (.txt) formatted documents, as well as each others' native formats. Using a plain text formatted survey instrument ensures that virtually any word processor will be able to read your survey. For this exercise, I have chosen a Microsoft Word (.doc) version of the State Law Enforcement survey discussed in Chapter Three.

Step Two: To send the survey, we will use a process similar to the one used when we read the results of our forms-based survey using an e-mail program. This time we will send the survey, rather than read the results. Again, here's the process to open your e-mail:

- **Double-click your e-mail program icon, or**
- **Click the e-mail button on the Microsoft Internet Explorer Toolbar (upper right corner). Select New Message from the menu, or**
- **Click the e-mail button on the Netscape Navigator Status Bar (lower left corner), or**
- **Click the appropriate e-mail button in other web browsers (e.g., AOL, Prodigy).**

Step Three: Microsoft Outlook Express New Message window opens (see Figure 4.23). In this window, we will compose an e-mail message describing the survey and how the respondent should open, complete and return it. For purposes of this exercise, address the e-mail to yourself. When your receive the e-mail, it will be proof that the attachment process works. The e-mail's subject should be the topic of your survey. Here is the text that I included in my e-mail message:

This survey is designed to assess web use by law enforcement agencies. Please take a few minutes to complete it. To open the survey, double click on the attachment (paper clip) icon, then double click on the survey icon (statxt.doc). It is in Microsoft Word format. Please return the completed survey by regular mail, e-mail or fax to:

Dale Nesbary, Ph.D.
Department of Political Science
Oakland University
Rochester MI 48309-4488
555-555-5555 phone
555-555-5555 fax
test@isp.com e-mail

You will receive a copy of the results of this survey after responses have been received (around June 1998). Thank you in advance for your cooperation.

Step Four: In this step, we will attach the survey to our e-mail. To do this, click the **Attachment** button on the toolbar. It looks like a paper clip. From here, navigate your computer until you find your survey document. When you find the survey, select it by clicking it once, and then click the **Attach** button at the bottom of the dialog box. You are now returned to the New Message window. Note that an icon representing the attached document now appears at the bottom of the New Window dialog box. This is exactly what the e-mail recipient will see, after he/she opens their e-mail.

Step Five: Click the **Send** button on the toolbar. Your e-mail and attachment are sent to the survey respondent. Your respondent may now open the e-mail attachment and complete the survey. (You may check your e-mail to be sure that the e-mail and attachment arrived.)

Figure 4.26: Microsoft Outlook Express New Message Window
E-mail Attachment Displayed

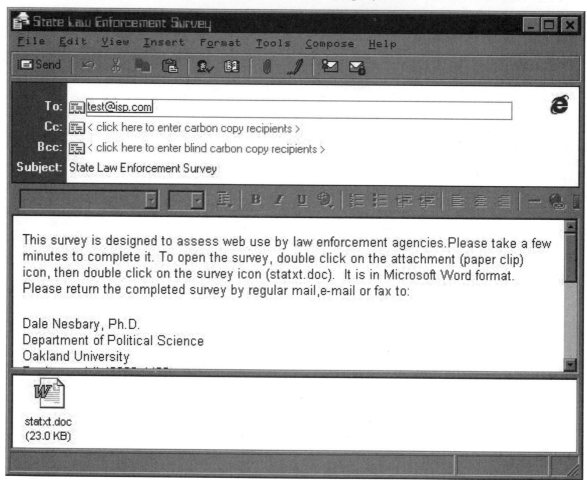

SUMMARY

When constructed and administered properly, web surveys are another useful and innovative tool in the researcher's bag of tricks. Web surveys have a number of strengths, including relative low cost, potential fast response time and response rate, as well as automatic coding of data. There are weaknesses as well. The relative lack of market penetration of the Web renders web surveys less useful than they will invariably be in the near future. This chapter demonstrated that web surveys can be constructed and administered with relatively little effort.

STUDY QUESTIONS AND EXERCISES

1) Obtain a short (one page or less survey instrument). Using what you learned in this chapter, convert the survey instrument into a forms-based survey using Microsoft FrontPage. Insert at least one radio button and one drop down list. Publish the survey using the FrontPage Publish command.

2) Take the same survey instrument and convert it to forms-based e-mail survey. Tip: Right-click the form and open the Form Properties dialog box.

3) Send at least three e-mails with attached files. The attachments do not necessarily have to be surveys. Tip: Remember to select the Attachment button on the toolbar to ensure the files you want to send along with your e-mail are actually attached.

FRONTPAGE DEVELOPMENT RESOURCES

<u>Beginner's Guide to Microsoft Image Composer.</u> Those of you interested in developing interesting images for your website should visit this site. It takes advantage of Image Composer, a free and well-developed add-in program that is available on the FrontPage install disk. URL=<u>http://erebus.bentley.edu/empl/c/rcrooks/toolbox/imagecom/</u>.

<u>FrontPage Resources.</u> Bill Burridge maintains an excellent list of FrontPage resources that is updated frequently. URL=<u>http://www2.essex.ac.uk/webauthoring/frontpage/links.html</u>.

<u>FrontPage Tip of the Week.</u> ZDNet provides a FrontPage Tip of the Week via e-mail free of charge. URL=<u>http://www.zdtips.com/mfp/zdt-f.htm</u>. ZDNet provides tips on many other software packages at <u>http:www.zdtips.com</u>.

<u>Links to Microsoft FrontPage</u> is a web directory of dozens of FrontPage related sites. Categories include Discussion Groups, FAQs, Software, Tips, Books and Manuals. URL=<u>http://www.cosy.sbg.ac.at/~ohaus/docs/frontpage.html</u>.

<u>Microsoft FrontPage Primary Website.</u> This is the official Microsoft FrontPage website, maintained by Microsoft Corporation. The site includes updated information, technical support, a FAQ (frequently asked questions) page and product ordering information. URL=<u>http://www.microsoft.com/frontpage/</u>.

SiteCrafters. <u>Microsoft FrontPage Support Resources</u> is arguably the most comprehensive FrontPage site outside of Microsoft Corporation. From my perspective, it is better organized than even Microsoft's site and is invaluable to anyone interested in Web development. It has extensive Web Bot support; those of us developing survey forms will find this site very useful. URL=<u>http://www.sitecrafters.com/support/fp98/index.htm</u>.

<u>The Complete Webmaster</u> includes a comprehensive set of tutorials on FrontPage, CGI Scripting, Active Server Page (ASP), development Java, and Java Script. This site is valuable, especially if you want to publish in a non-FrontPage Server Extension environment. URL=<u>http://www.abiglime.com/webmaster/</u>.

<u>The FrontPage Network</u> is another comprehensive Web directory of FrontPage resources. Of note, it includes reviews of FrontPage components and add-ins, as well as an online store. This site is also known as the FrontPage Web Ring. URL=<u>http://www.frontpagenetwork.com/</u>.

<u>The FrontPage User Group Website</u>, sponsored by Amazon.com provides a variety of FrontPage user forums, downloads and items for purchase. URL=<u>http://www.fpug.com/</u>.

Chapter Five: Web Search Exercises

A number of exercises in <u>Survey Research and the World Wide Web</u> call for the reader to search the Web for research-oriented information. Chapter Five comprises a series of exercises designed to help the novice Web-user become more familiar with web search tools and techniques. Specifically, this chapter includes a description of search engines followed by AltaVista and Yahoo exercises. In this chapter, you will do several different types of searches, including:

- Basic keyword
- Advanced keyword
- Refined keyword
- Web index
- Web directory

It is important to know how to conduct web searches because much data has already been collected and is available on the Web. You may be able to download this information and integrate it into your own research. Therefore, there may be no reason to prepare and administer a survey which may "reinvent the wheel." For more practice searching for Web data, use the Allyn & Bacon Quick Guide website. The Quick Guide website includes approximately 50 Web search exercises. The Quick Guide exercises are located at <u>http://www.nesbary.com/abacon</u>.

USING THE ADDRESS BAR TO FIND WEBSITES

Content on the Internet comprises a vast array of information. This information may be retrieved using several tools. The most basic and accurate method of retrieving information is by typing in the URL (uniform resource locator) in the Address bar in the web browser. For example, to open Nesbary's "Politics, Crime and Money" website, type: **http://www.nesbary.com/nesbary** in the Address Bar (See Figure 5.1). Without the URL, finding the Politics, Crime and Money website would be more difficult.

Figure 5.1: Internet Explorer Address Bar

USING SEARCH ENGINES

Search engines make finding websites and information on the Internet a fairly straightforward proposition. Search engines come in two types: web indexes and web directories. **Web indexes** are relatively fast and streamlined search tools designed to help the user find a webpage or other Internet-based document quickly. Web indexes include powerful search features such as Boolean operators, search refine and date parameters. Web indexes also include "spider" programs that seek out webpages and list them automatically on the web index. Alta Vista is an example of a web index.

Web directories are probably the most familiar search engines to students. If you have used an electronic card catalog at a library, you can use a web directory with no trouble. *PC Magazine* calls web indexes "massive, computer-generated databases containing structured information on millions of webpages or Usenet newsgroup articles." A good web directory provides the user with the ability to search for predefined topics along with user-defined query capability. Web directories also include many enhancements, such as electronic telephone books, road maps, news, weather reports and entertainment information. Web directories usually do not include spider programs, so the user must submit a website to the web directory for it to be listed. "Excite" and "Yahoo" are among the best of this category.

KEYWORD SEARCHES USING ALTA VISTA

Keyword searches are a primary method of finding information on the Web. Keyword searches are much more flexible and often less time-consuming than using web directories. With a keyword search, the researcher enters the specific words or plain English phrases to be found. These keywords are submitted and searched for, and all relevant webpages are then listed in order of relevance by the search engine (based on how often the keywords are found).

Web indexes are computer-generated databases containing structured information on web pages, Usenet newsgroup articles, and e-mail addresses. Web indexes may be searched by keyword, plain English phrases, and query operators (special characters used to restrict or expand the search). The keyword is typed into the text box that appears on the web index page. The user clicks the Search button. The web index searches for URLs and e-mail addresses and retrieves all relevant links.

"Alta Vista," "Hot Bot" and "Web Crawler" are examples of popular and fully-featured web indexes. The Alta Vista workspace includes a language selector, text box, Search button and Refine link. The Refine link is available only after an initial search has been conducted. The Alta Vista workspace may be seen in Figure 5.2:

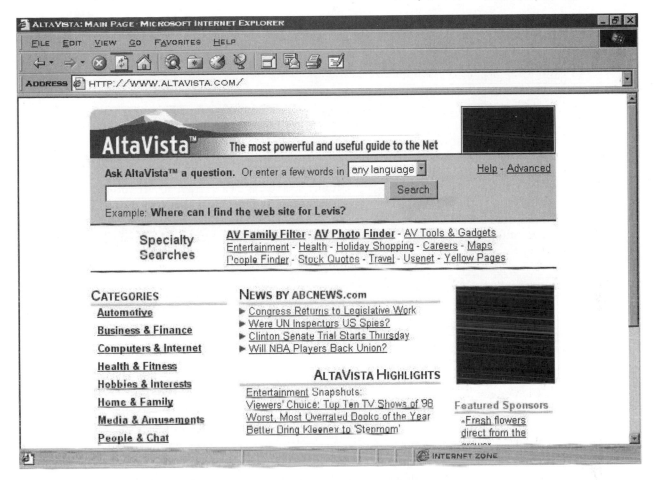

Figure 5.2: AltaVista Workspace

Please be aware that no matter how specific the search criteria, you still may not find the website or organization for which you are searching. Most times, the relevant website will appear among the first ten hits, but sometimes it will not. For example, in an Alta Vista search for the FBI homepage, our initial results will yield over 100,000 webpages, many of which may not be relevant. In Alta Vista, the first ten hits are listed. To find additional hits, scroll to the bottom of the search page and click on the next sequential number. However, many of the first ten hits will lead directly to the FBI homepage or may actually be a part of the FBI website, but not the homepage. Accordingly, tips on how to refine your search will be provided.

One method of restricting the number and enhancing relevance of keyword searches is with the use of Boolean Operators. The quote operator (") is one of the more useful tools in helping the user locate information. Be aware that the locations (URLs) of webpages change occasionally. Also, new pages are added and old ones deleted continually. As a result, each search may give different lists of websites. The following exercises cover basic and advanced keyword searches, refining searches and using operators in searches.

DEPARTMENT OF JUSTICE (DOJ)

Task: Locate DOJ website
Type: Basic keyword search with quote operator
Enter: DOJ web address in the address bar: **http://www.usdoj.gov** or search for the DOJ website using the Alta Vista search engine.
Step One: Open Alta Vista search engine. This is accomplished by typing **http://www.altavista.com** in the address bar or by clicking the **Search** button on the toolbar. Click on **Choose a Search Engine** from the search menu and then scroll down to find Alta Vista (in the right frame of your browser). Click the **Alta Vista** link.
Step Two: At the top of the Alta Vista screen is a text box followed by the Search Button. Type **"Department of Justice"** (with quotes) followed by a space and the word **website** (without quotes) in the Alta Vista search text box. By enclosing a phrase in quotes, Alta Vista searches for the phrase "Department of Justice" and not the individual words.
Step Three: Press the **Enter** key on your computer keyboard.
Step Four: Ten links appear including the phrase "Department of Justice" and the word website. You will have to scroll down to see all ten links.
Step Five: Examine each link for relevance.

Of the first ten hits, one is a search engine known as "Glimpse." Note that the Address Bar lists the server on which Glimpse is located as doj.gov, the primary Department of Justice website. To go to the DOJ homepage from here, erase ghindex.html from the Address Bar, then press **Enter** on your keyboard. You will then be transported to the Department of Justice homepage.

FEDERAL BUREAU OF INVESTIGATION

Task: Locate Federal Bureau of Investigation (FBI) website
Type: Using Refine to narrow our search. Basic keyword search with quote operators and separate search terms.
Enter: FBI web address in the address bar: **http://www.fbi.gov** or search for the FBI website using the Alta Vista search engine.
Step One: Open the Alta Vista search engine.
Step Two: Type **"Federal Bureau of Investigation"** (with quotes) followed by a space and the word **FBI** (without quotes) and the phrase **"Department of Justice"** (with quotes) in the Alta Vista search text box. The FBI is a bureau within the Department of Justice. By adding the Department of Justice phrase to our search, the likelihood is greater that we will find a page that is a part of the FBI website.
Step Three: Press the **Enter** key on your computer keyboard.
Step Four: Ten links appear including the phrase "Federal Bureau of Investigation."
Step Five: Examine each link for relevance.

Of the first ten links, none link directly to the FBI homepage, but several lead to FBI press releases. We will use the Refine feature of Alta Vista to generate a better list of links. Refine helps narrow the search parameters. Refine allows a user to Require or Exclude terms. A Required term must appear in a webpage for the page to be listed in a search. An Excluded term cannot appear in any page for which the user is searching. We will use both Require and Exclude in our search for the FBI website:

Step Six: Scroll to the top of the Alta Vista search window.
Step Seven: Click **Refine** in the upper right side of the Alta Vista search window. The Refine window opens.
Step Eight: Scroll down the Refine window. A series of terms are listed along the left margin. These terms are Required or Excluded by clicking the down arrow next to each term and selecting Require or Exclude. We will Require the terms "FBI" and "Criminals" and Exclude the terms "Security" and "Fraud."
Step Nine: Scroll up to the top of the Refine window and click **Search**. A new list of links appears.
Step Ten: Examine each link for relevance.

As a result of using Refine, several of the links are direct links to the FBI website. From these links, you may navigate to the FBI homepage or other FBI pages.

BUREAU OF JUSTICE ASSISTANCE - DOJ

Task: Locate Bureau of Justice Assistance website
Type: This is the third Department of Justice website for which we will search. Our strategy will be somewhat different. Besides entering the Bureau of Justice Assistance and Department of Justice as search criteria, we will also enter "Nancy Gist," the current BJA Director, as a search criterion. This often adds to the specificity of a search. Of course, the various bureaus within the Department of Justice are linked within the DOJ website. However, these search techniques may offer a more efficient search mechanism.
Enter: BJA web address in the address bar: **http://www.ojp.usdoj.gov/BJA/** or search for the BJA website using the Alta Vista search engine.
Step One: Open the Alta Vista search engine.
Step Two: Type **"Bureau of Justice Assistance"** (with quotes) followed by a space and the name **"Nancy Gist"** (with quotes) and the phrase **"Department of Justice"** (with quotes) in the Alta Vista search text box.
Step Three: Press the **Enter** key on your computer keyboard.
Step Four: Ten links appear including the phrase "Bureau of Justice Assistance."
Step Five: Examine each link for relevance.

Of the first ten links, none link directly to the BJA homepage, but several lead to BJA press releases. By selecting these links, one can navigate to the Bureau of Justice Assistance homepage.

CENSUS BUREAU, U.S. DEPARTMENT OF COMMERCE

Task: Locate U.S. Census Bureau website
Type: Advanced Search-Basic keyword search with quote operators and separate search terms
Enter: The Census Bureau web address in the address bar: **http://www.census.gov** or search for the Census Bureau website using the Alta Vista search engine.

Step One: Open the Alta Vista search engine and Click the **Advanced Search** link in the upper right of the Alta Vista window.

Step Two: Type **"U.S. Census Bureau"** (with quotes) followed by a space and the term **demographics** (without quotes) and the term **STF** (without quotes) in the Alta Vista search text box. STF is a special file format often used by the Census Bureau, which will help narrow the search.

Step Three: Locate the Date text boxes in the Advanced Search window. You may enter a beginning and ending date. Since a search for U.S. Census Bureau webpages will yield thousands of hits, restricting our search is advisable.

Step Four: Enter **01/01/97** in the From text box and **01/07/98** in the To text box. This restricts our search to pages created between the dates January 1, 1997 and July 1, 1998, inclusive.

Step Five: Press the **Enter** key on your computer keyboard.

Step Six: Ten links appear with the phrase "U.S. Census Bureau."

Step Seven: Examine each link for relevance.

Many of the hits link directly to a Census Bureau website or to an organization with a link to the Census Bureau.

SOURCEBOOK OF CRIMINAL JUSTICE STATISTICS

Task: Locate Sourcebook of Criminal Justice Statistics website

Type: Basic keyword search with multiple search criteria

Enter: Sourcebook web address in the address bar: **http://www.albany.edu/sourcebook** or search for the Sourcebook website using the Alta Vista search engine.

Step One: Open the Alta Vista search engine.

Step Two: Type **"Sourcebook of Criminal Justice Statistics"** (with quotes) followed by a space and the word **albany.edu** (without quotes) and the term **"crime statistics"** (with quotes) in the Alta Vista search text box. The address albany.edu is the server on which the Sourcebook website is located. It will help narrow the search.

Step Three: Press the **Enter** key on your computer keyboard.

Step Four: Ten links appear with the phrase "Sourcebook of Criminal Justice Statistics."

Step Five: Examine each link for relevance.

Each of the first 10 hits includes links to the Sourcebook website. To quickly find the Sourcebook link on a page a) select one of the first ten hits, b) select **Edit**, then **Find** from the Menu Bar, 3) type **Sourcebook** into the Find Text Box, then press **Enter**. The Find function will search the webpage until the term Sourcebook is found.

CENTRAL INTELLIGENCE AGENCY

Task: Locate Central Intelligence Agency website

Type: Basic keyword search with multiple search criteria

Enter: The CIA web address in the address bar: **http://www.odci.gov/cia/index.html** or search for the CIA website using the Alta Vista search engine.

Step One: Open the Alta Vista search engine.

Step Two: Type **CIA** (without quotes) followed by a space and the phrase **"Central Intelligence Agency"** (with quotes) and the word **website** (without quotes) in the Alta Vista search text box.

Step Three: Press the **Enter** key on your computer keyboard.
Step Four: Ten links appear including the phrase "Central Intelligence Agency."
Step Five: Examine each link for relevance.

Each of the first 10 hits includes links to the CIA website. Select any hit and find the CIA link. If the CIA link is not visible, use the **Edit Find** menu item from the menu bar.

MICHIGAN STATE POLICE

Task: Locate Michigan State Police website
Type: Basic keyword search. The agency is located on multiple web servers.
Enter: The Michigan State Police web address: **http://www.voyager.net/msp/** or search for the Michigan State Police website using the Alta Vista search engine.
Step One: Open the Alta Vista search engine.
Step Two: Type **"Michigan State Police"** (with quotes) followed by a space and the phrase **"Department of State Police"** (with quotes) in the Alta Vista search text box. Enter Department of State Police, because this is the legal name of the Department. The commonly used name is Michigan State Police.
Step Three: Press the **Enter** key on your computer keyboard.
Step Four: Ten links appear with the phrase "Michigan State Police."
Step Five: Examine each link for relevance.

Several of the first 10 hits include links to the Michigan State Police website. Notice that the homepage of the Michigan State Police is on a Voyager (voyager.net) net server, while the remainder of the website is located on the State of Michigan server (state.mi.us). Many websites begin their life as a creation of a knowledgeable staff person and later are transferred to an "official" server. The Michigan State Police have chosen to keep their homepage on the original server. This site was originally created by a MSP captain as a way to communicate the mission of his division.

TEXAS DEPARTMENT OF PUBLIC SAFETY

Task: Locate Texas Department of Public Safety website
Type: Basic keyword search with quote operators and separate search terms
Enter: The Texas Department of Public Safety web address in the address bar:
http://www.txdps.state.tx.us/ or search for the Texas Department of Public Safety website using the Alta Vista search engine.
Step One: Open the Alta Vista search engine.
Step Two: Type **"Texas Department of Public Safety"** (with quotes) followed by a space and the word **website** (without quotes) in the Alta Vista search text box.
Step Three: Press the **Enter** key on your computer keyboard.
Step Four: Ten links appear with the phrase "Texas Department of Public Safety."
Step Five: Examine each link for relevance.

Two of the first three hits are direct links to the Texas Department of Public Safety homepage.

VANCOUVER (BRITISH COLUMBIA) POLICE DEPARTMENT

Task: Locate Vancouver Police Department website
Type: Basic keyword search. Website has recently moved.
Enter: The Vancouver Police Department web address in the address bar:
http://www.city.vancouver.bc.ca/police/ or search for the Vancouver Police Department website using the Alta Vista search engine.
Step One: Open the Alta Vista search engine.
Step Two: Type **"Vancouver Police Department"** (with quotes) in the Alta Vista search text box.
Step Three: Press the **Enter** key on your computer keyboard.
Step Four: Ten links appear including the phrase "Vancouver Police Department."
Step Five: Examine each link for relevance.

Among the hits are several direct links to the Vancouver Police Department homepage. There is less of a likelihood of finding local law enforcement websites, because local websites are relatively new. It may take search engines up to a month to find a newly created website, so there are likely to be fewer hits on new websites than to those that are older and more established. There are also fewer links to local law enforcement agencies than to state or federal agencies.

ATLANTA (GEORGIA) POLICE DEPARTMENT

Task: Locate Atlanta Police Department website
Type: Basic keyword search
Enter: Atlanta Police Department web address in the address bar: **http://www.atlantapd.org** or search for the Atlanta Police Department website using the Alta Vista search engine.
Step One: Open the Alta Vista search engine.
Step Two: Type **"Atlanta Police Department"** (with quotes) in the Alta Vista search text box.
Step Three: Press the **Enter** key on your computer keyboard.
Step Four: Ten links appear including the phrase "Atlanta Police Department."
Step Five: Examine each link for relevance.

Among the hits are several direct links to the Atlanta Police Department homepage, as well as other pages on the Atlanta Police Department Website. Again, our luck is worse with local law enforcement agencies, because of the relative newness of the site and the lack of links to the site from other websites.

WEB DIRECTORY EXERCISES USING YAHOO

Web directories are hierarchically organized lists of websites, Usenet newsgroup articles, and e-mail addresses. They may be searched in exactly the same way as web indexes, by clicking on predefined lists of topics. Many users find this technique easier than a keyword search. Most web directories look like a library computer card catalogue. Linked websites are arranged by topic and are searchable in the same way.

Yahoo, as a web directory, provides two primary methods of searching for websites. The methods are 1) using the Yahoo hierarchical menu structure or 2) using Yahoo Quick Search. Yahoo is organized in 12 primary categories including:

Business and Economy	Recreation & Sports
Computers and Internet	Reference
Education	Regional
Entertainment	Science
Government	Social Science
Health	Society and Culture

Each of these categories includes thousands of websites. Usually a website may be found by selecting four or five subcategories. However, the recommended method of searching Yahoo is through Quick Search. To use Yahoo Quick Search, type the search criteria in the search text box. It looks like this:

Figure 5.3: Yahoo Workspace

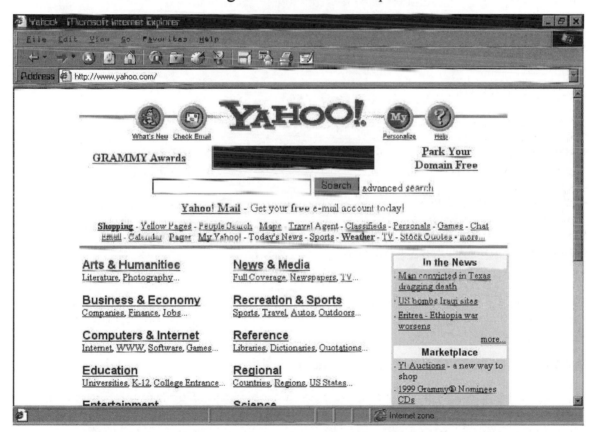

A Yahoo Quick Search will typically result in one or more listed hits. When using Yahoo, one must be aware that Yahoo includes only those links submitted by users and approved by Yahoo. Consequently, while Yahoo may have many thousands of validated websites, Yahoo searches are much more limited than a full web search using a web index like Alta Vista. However, Yahoo (and most web directory) results tend to be more precise than search engine results. While most Yahoo searches will yield less than 10 results, the results are likely to be accurate hits. Be aware, however, that not all websites are registered with Yahoo. If Yahoo does not yield a hit, use a search engine like Alta Vista to improve your hit rate.

The following exercise involves searching "Yahoo," finding the Federal Bureau of Prisons website, and downloading a file from the site. This exercise is indicative of the exercises found on the Quick Guide website. The Quick Guide website has links to Yahoo and several other web directories and search engines. I suggest that the novice web user try the Quick Guide website to access Yahoo and other search engines initially. After a little practice, going directly to the search engine is the preferred method of searching the web. To open the Quick Guide website, type **http://www.nesbary.com/abacon**. Click on the **Quick Guide Exercises** button at the top of the page. Finally, click on the **Web Directory Exercises** link.

If you choose to do the exercises without the benefit of this book, it is suggested that you open a new web browser. A new web browser gives the user two sessions of Internet Explorer running simultaneously. The user can do exercises in one browser and have the Quick Guide website instructions open in the other browser. The second web browser is opened by clicking on **File** from the menu bar, then selecting **New** followed by **Window** from the menu list. At this point, two exact duplicates of the Quick Guide Website exercise page are open. Use one browser to reference exercise instructions and use the other to do the exercise itself.

To find the Bureau of Prisons website, do the following:

Step One: Click on the "Yahoo" icon in the exercise, or click on the **Search** button, scroll down, and then click on "Yahoo" from the list of search engines.

Step Two: Click on the following links in sequential order. About halfway down on the first page, click on **Government**. Another page will appear. Find and click on **Law**. Follow the same procedure for the next three links: **Criminal Law and Justice**, **Criminal Justice**, and **Federal Bureau of Prisons**. In some cases you may have to scroll down to find the correct link.

Step Three: Click on the **Documents** link found on the Federal Bureau of Prisons page. Next, find the **Civil Rights of Institutionalized Persons Act** link and click on it. If this file is not available, click on any other available file at that address.

Step Four: Download the file. To do this, click on **File** on the menu bar, then **Save As** from the menu list. A prompt (computer instruction) will appear to save the file. Save the file in the directory on your hard drive where your working files ordinarily are saved. This file may be opened from the hard drive using any word processing program, such as Microsoft Word.

Congratulations! You have downloaded and saved your first file from the Web. Several other web directory exercises now follow.

U.S. DRUG ENFORCEMENT ADMINISTRATION

Task: Locate the U.S. Drug Enforcement Administration website
Type: Basic keyword search using Yahoo quick search
Enter: The Drug Enforcement Administration web address in the address bar:
http://www.usdoj.gov/dea or search for the Drug Enforcement Administration website using the Yahoo web directory.
Step One: Open the Yahoo web directory. This is accomplished by typing:
http://www.Yahoo.com in the address bar or by clicking the **Search** button on the toolbar, click **Choose a Search Engine** from the search menu and then scroll down to find Yahoo (in the right frame of your browser). Click the **Yahoo** link.

Step Two: Type **Drug Enforcement Administration** (without quotes) in the Yahoo search text box.
Step Three: Press the **Enter** key on your computer keyboard.
Step Four: Two links appear including the phrase "Drug Enforcement Administration."
Step Five: Examine each link for relevance.

Notice that only two hits are generated from this search. One of the hits is the homepage for the Drug Enforcement Administration.

Iowa Department of Public Safety

Task: Locate the State of Iowa Department of Public Safety website
Type: Agency has not yet registered their website with Yahoo. Yahoo web directory search.
Enter: The Iowa Department of Public Safety web address in the address bar:
http://www.state.ia.us/government/dps/index.html or search for the Iowa Department of Public Safety website using the Yahoo web directory.
Step One: Open the Yahoo web directory.
Step Two: Type **Iowa Department of Public Safety** (without quotes) in the Yahoo search text box.
Step Three: Press the **Enter** key on your computer keyboard.
Step Four: Two links appear including the phrase "Iowa Department of Public Safety."
Step Five: Examine each link for relevance.

Notice that only two hits are generated from this search. These links lead to the Department of Public Safety at Iowa State University. As of July 1998, the State of Iowa Department of Public Safety website was not registered with Yahoo. An alternative does exist using Yahoo. By searching Yahoo's menu structure, the Iowa Department of Public Safety may be found. Follow this example:

Step One: Open the Yahoo web directory.
Step Two: Select the Government link in the Yahoo web directory.
Step Three: Scroll down and select the U.S. Government link.
Step Four: Scroll down and select the U.S. States link.
Step Five: Select the State of Iowa link. The State of Iowa website opens.
Step Six: Select the Government button on the right side of the page.
Step Seven: Scroll down and select the Public Safety link. The Iowa Department of Public Safety website opens.

This is a much longer process than using the search text box. But remember the Iowa Department of Public Safety was not registered with Yahoo. However, the State of Iowa website was registered with Yahoo. After finding the State of Iowa, it was a relatively simple search to find the Iowa Department of Public Safety website.

NEW ORLEANS POLICE DEPARTMENT

Task: Locate the New Orleans Police Department website
Type: Web directory search, save an html file to disk.
Enter: The New Orleans Police Department web address in the address bar:
http://www.acadiacom.net/nopd/index.htm or search for the New Orleans Department of Public Safety website using the Yahoo web directory.
Step One: Open the Yahoo web directory.
Step Two: Type **New Orleans Police Department** (without quotes) in the Yahoo search text box.
Step Three: Press the **Enter** key on your computer keyboard.
Step Four: Three links appear including the phrase "New Orleans Police Department."
Step Five: Examine each link for relevance.
Step Six: Click the first New Orleans Police Department Link. The New Orleans Police Department website opens.
Step Seven: Click **File/Save As** on the Menu Bar. This action allows you to save a copy of the homepage of the New Orleans Police Department on your hard disk. This same action (File/Save As) can be used with any file on the Internet.

SUMMARY

Chapter Five introduced several methods of searching for criminal justice information on the Web. Web directories provide a structured method of finding information. Keyword searches allow the user to customize a search. By entering plain English instructions or query-based commands, needed information may be found quickly.

Appendix A: Survey and Web Definitions

This section defines common Internet-related terms. Although all are not included in <u>Survey Research and the World Wide Web</u>, they are all important for persons conducting research on the Web.

Anonymous FTP (File Transfer Protocol)
A service provided to make files available to Internet users. The user's identity remains anonymous throughout the file transfer process.

ANSI
The American National Standards Institute sets standards for certain computer technologies, including file format.

Archie
A service that provides searches for Internet files from anonymous FTP sites.

ARPA
The original Internet system that served as the basis for early networking research, as well as a central backbone during the development of the Internet. The term ARPA was derived from the U.S. federal government agency that managed its creation, the Department of Defense Advanced Research Projects Agency.

Backbone
A high-speed connection within a network that connects shorter, slower circuits. International telephone companies and cable television providers maintain most Internet backbone connections.

Bandwidth
The capacity of a medium to transmit a signal. It represents how much information may be transmitted at one time. Standard modems are slow, compared to Ethernet connections, so modems are said to have "narrow bandwidth."

Cache, disk
An area of hard disk storage reserved by a web browser to store files on a long-term basis. Instead of having to download a file from a remote computer, the web browser retrieves the file from the disk cache. This process speeds up processing significantly.

Cache, memory
An area of random access memory reserved by a web browser to store files and pages currently in use. Instead of having to download a file from a remote computer, the web browser retrieves the file from the memory cache. This significantly speeds up processing.

Client
The user of a network service. It also refers to a computer that relies upon another for some or all of its resources.

Client software
Client software allows the Internet user to access data from remote computers. Netscape and Internet Explorer are examples of client software programs. Client software typically resides on personal computers.

Content
Content consists of the vast array of information available on the Internet. Content may be accessed in the form of graphics, video, audio, and text.

Domain
Domain is a part of the Internet site location naming structure. A domain name consists of a series of words separated by dots.

Element
Individuals selected from the population comprising the sample.

E-mail
Electronic mail, an easy way to send messages via the Internet to other individual users or groups. An e-mail address usually includes the username followed by the domain name (e.g., nesbary@oakland.edu). In this example, nesbary is the username and oakland.edu is the domain or computer server name.

FTP (File Transfer Protocol)
The Internet standard high-level protocol for transferring files from one computer to another.

Hits
A list of links generated as a result of a search engine or web directory search.

Home page
The web page designated to be the first page seen upon entering a website.

HTML (hypertext markup language)
The programming language that is used to create World Wide Web pages, allowing a user to mix multimedia objects with text, change the appearance of text, and create hypertext documents.

HTTP (hypertext transfer protocol)
The Internet command for connecting to the World Wide Web.

Hypertext
Web browser text that transmits the user to another website by means of clicking the highlighted text. Hypertext provides access to graphics, photographs, sounds, or video clips.

Internet
A global array of computers connected by a network. Internet also refers to the technologies facilitating transmission of data across the network.

Intranet
A method of connecting multiple computer systems over a relatively small area using Internet technologies. An Intranet can be as small as two computers in one room to 1,000 or more computers on a university campus.

Local area network (LAN)
A method of connecting multiple computer systems over a relatively small area. A LAN can be as small as two computers in one room to 1,000 or more computers on a university campus.

Link
A location on a webpage that a user can click on to access another webpage having related material. Links are in the form of underlined words or phrases in special colors, pictures or graphical icons.

Mail gateway
A machine that connects to two or more electronic mail systems and transfers mail messages among them.

Measurement units (data storage)
Computer memory and hard disk storage is measured in bytes. One byte is equivalent to one character (number, letter, or symbol). Approximate storage units are:

One kilobyte (KB) = One thousand bytes or one typewritten page
One megabyte = One million bytes or one thousand typewritten pages
One gigabyte = One billion bytes or one million typewritten pages
One terabyte = One trillion bytes or one billion typewritten pages

Medium
The material used to support data transmission. This can be copper wire, coaxial cable, optical fiber, or electromagnetic wave (as in microwave).

Netiquette
Proper conduct on the Internet is called etiquette (as in etiquette for the Net). E-mail users or newsgroup posters should exhibit good netiquette, treating other Internet users with respect.

Network
A group of computers connected to transmit information among any or all computers. Two kinds of networks exist: local-area networks and wide-area networks.

Node
A computer attached to a network.

Parameter
A characteristic of the entire population is called a parameter. Examples: The number of residents driving on Empire Avenue on a given day; the number of female residents in the population; or the number of United States citizens living in Westlawn.

Population
The group or phenomenon under study is the population. Example: The 100,000 residents of Westlawn.

Protocols
A formal description of computer message formats and the rules two computers must follow to exchange those messages.

Sample
A subset of a population selected to reflect the characteristics of a population. Examples: A subset of residents driving on Empire Avenue on a given day; a subset of female residents in the population; or a subset of United States citizens living in Westlawn.

Sampling Error
A measure of how much a statistic varies from a parameter. A sampling error of 5 tells us that the actual parameter could fall in a range of 5 percent above or 5 percent below a statistic, yielding a range (confidence interval) of 10 percent.

Sampling Frame
The actual list of all of the individuals comprising the population. The sample is selected from the sampling frame. Example: A database comprising all students at Westlawn.

Search Engine
Internet-based search and retrieval software programs. They may be hierarchical lists organized by category (web directories) or computer-generated lists of webpages and Internet files.

Server
A computer that shares its resources, such as printers and files, with other computers on the network is called a server. Internet servers provide mail, news, and web-based content to client computers.

Server Software
Server software allows Internet providers to transmit files and other information across the Internet. Java, Novell NetWare and Windows NT are examples of server software. Netscape

and Internet Explorer have Internet-specific server software available. Server software usually resides on powerful personal computers, workstations, mini and mainframe computers.

TCP/IP (Transmission Control Protocol/Internet Protocol)
A set of protocols used by the Internet to support services such as hypertext transfer, remote login (telnet), file transfer (FTP) and mail (SMTP).

SMTP (simple mail transfer protocol)
The Internet standard protocol for transferring electronic mail messages from one computer to another. SMTP specifies how two mail systems interact and which format of control messages they exchange to transfer mail.

Statistic
A characteristic of a sample is a statistic. Examples: The estimated percent of residents driving on Empire Avenue on a given day; the estimated percent of female residents in the population; or the estimated percent of United States citizens living in Westlawn.

Telnet
The Internet standard protocol for remote terminal connection service. Telnet allows a user at one site to interact with a remote timesharing system at another site as if the user's terminal were connected directly to the remote computer. Many libraries use Telnet to allow remote users to connect.

URL (uniform resource locator)
The primary naming convention for Internet files and servers. URLs appear in the location bar in web browsers.

Variable
A set of mutually exclusive attributes is called a variable. Examples: Gender, age, employment status, or level of education. Social researchers describe the distribution of attributes exhibiting variation in a population. Therefore, a researcher may describe the gender distribution of a population by presenting a frequency distribution of gender in the population.

WAN (wide area network)
A network spanning a wide geographic area is called a WAN. A network could cover one city or the entire world.

Web Browser
A program that displays text, graphics, audio and visual information is a web browser. This information is accessible by clicking on a hypertext link.

Webpage
Any document capable of being displayed in a web browser is a webpage.

Website
Any location on the Internet capable of storing web pages or hypertext information.

137

Workstation

A workstation is a networked personal computing device with more power than a standard personal computer. Typically, a workstation has an operating system capable of running several tasks at the same time. Workstations have multiple megabytes of memory and a large, high-resolution display.

World Wide Web

The portion of the Internet structured for use with a web browser. The Web is a subset of the Internet.

Index

Hundreds, tens and units

Here are 100 cubes.

Here are 10 cubes.

Write how many cubes in each set.

1

	1	3	2
1.			

2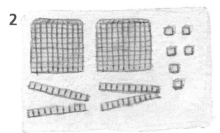

3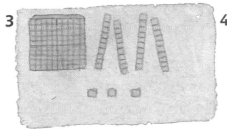

4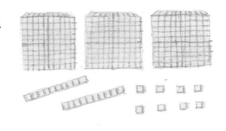

5

6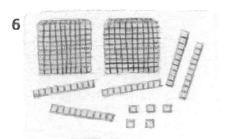

7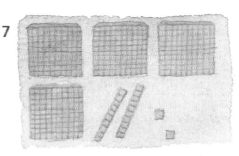

8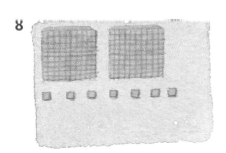

9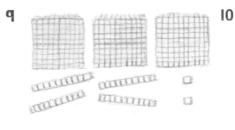

10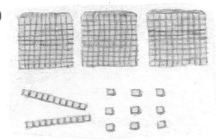

Explore

You need six £1 coins, six 10p coins and six 1p coins.

Choose any five coins (use at least one £1 coin).
Write how much you have.
Do this again.

How many different amounts can you make?

Hundreds, tens and units

Draw coins to match the prices.

1
242p

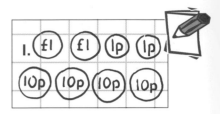
1. £1 £1 1p 1p
10p 10p 10p 10p

2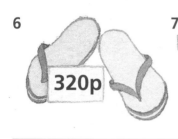
421p

3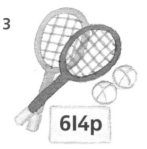
614p

4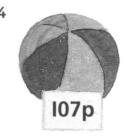
107p

5
123p

6
320p

7
515p

8
365p

9
FRISBEE 222p

Write the totals.

10 $400 + 30 + 5$

10. 4 3 5

11 $800 + 60 + 5$

12 $700 + 10 + 8$

13 $500 + 40 + 9$

14 $100 + 70 + 3$

15 $400 + 7$

16 $500 + 30$

17 $300 + 40 + 2$

18 $700 + 1$

19 $600 + 90$

Explore

Use number cards 9, 6, 4, 0.

How many different 3-digit numbers can you make?

Which is the smallest number you can make?

Which is the largest?

9 4 6

6 0 4

Hundreds, tens and units

Write each number in hundreds, tens and units.

1  327

1. $300 + 20 + 7$

2  532

3  645

4  258

5  823

6  419

7  764

8  246

9  354

10  938

11  434

12  909

13 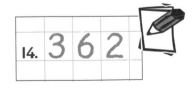 660

Write the matching number for each number name.

14 Three hundred and sixty-two

14. 362

15 Four hundred and fifty-three

16 Eight hundred and seventy-two

17 Nine hundred and ninety-nine

18 Six hundred and forty-seven

19 One hundred and six

20 Two hundred and ten

21 Three hundred and sixteen

22 Seven hundred and nine

7

Write these numbers in order, from smallest to largest.

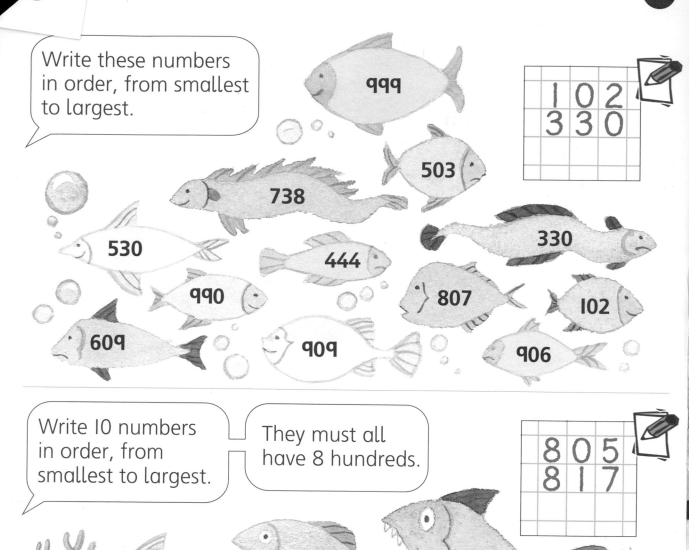

| 1 | 0 | 2 |
| 3 | 3 | 0 |

Write 10 numbers in order, from smallest to largest.

They must all have 8 hundreds.

| 8 | 0 | 5 |
| 8 | 1 | 7 |

Write 6 numbers in order, from smallest to largest.

They must all have 5 tens.

| 3 | 5 | 0 |
| 4 | 5 | 2 |

8

Hundreds, tens and units

Throw 3 dice and write a 3-digit number.

3 dice

Make 10 more numbers and write them.

Write your numbers in order, from smallest to largest.

3 4 1

Write 2 numbers between these.

They must be in order, from smallest to largest.

1. | 4 2 3 | 4 3 0 | 4 3 5 | 4 3 6 |

1. | 423 | | | 436 |

2. | 528 | | | 542 |

3. | 660 | | | 680 |

4. | 900 | | | 910 |

5. | 104 | | | 114 |

6. | 208 | | | 218 |

7. | 333 | | | 346 |

8. | 487 | | | 495 |

9. | 796 | | | 803 |

10. | 856 | | | 859 |

9

Write the missing numbers.

1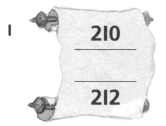
210
___
212

1.

2	1	0
2	1	1
2	1	2

2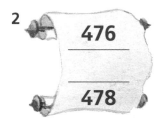
476
___
478

3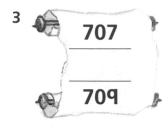
707
___
709

4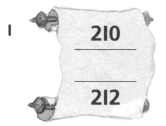
816
___
818

5
978
___
980

6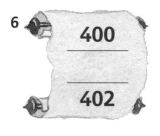
400
___
402

7
399
___
401

8
200
___
202

9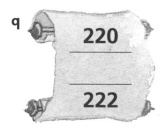
220
___
222

10
829
___
831

11
561
___
563

12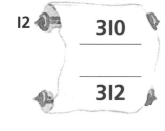
310
___
312

13
701
___
703

Explore

In between 100 and 200, how many numbers have a 9?

Write them in order.

119

199

109

191

196

10

Adding to 10

There are 10 cherries in each group.

How many are in each bag?

1

1. 7

2

3

4

5

6

7

8

9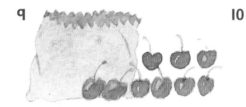

10

Write the missing numbers.

11 $6 + $ 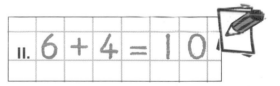 $ = 10$

11. $6 + 4 = 10$

12 $5 + $ = 10

13 $4 + $ = 10

14 $3 + $ = 10

15 $8 + $ = 10

16 $1 + $ = 10

17 $2 + $ = 10

18 $7 + $ = 10

19 $0 + $ = 10

20 $10 + $ = 10

Adding to 10

Each strip has 10 cubes.

Write how many are hidden.

1.

1. 7

2.

3.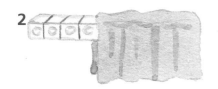

4.

5.

6.

7.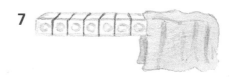

8.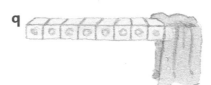

9.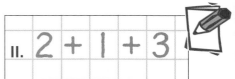

10.

Each rocket splits into 3.

Write 3 numbers for each rocket.

11.

11. 2 + 1 + 3

12.
8

13.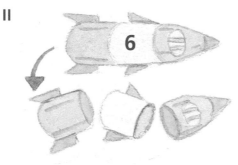
10

14.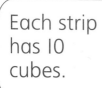
9

15.
7

16.
11

17.
5

Adding to I0

Each badge costs I0p.

Write how much more you need to buy each one.

I
5p Ip Ip

I. 3p

2
5p

3
Ip Ip Ip

4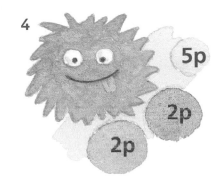
5p 2p 2p

5
Ip

6
5p 2p Ip

7
2p

At Home

Shuffle a pack of cards (with Kings and Jacks removed). Spread them out face down.

Take turns to reveal 2 cards. If they add to I0 keep them (Queen = 0, so Queen + I0 = I0). Otherwise replace them.

When all the cards are taken, who has the most pairs?

Adding to 10

Each log is split in 2.

Write different pairs of numbers for each log.

1
6

3 **3**

1. $3 + 3 = 6$

2
5

3
7

4
5

5
6

6
8

7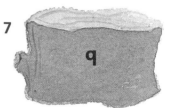
q

8
7

q
6

10
5

Explore

Use cubes.

How many different ways can you find to make 7?

| + | + | + | + | + | + | = 7

4 + 3 = 7

14

Nearest ten

Write the nearest ten to each number.

1 476

1. 4 8 0

2 234

3 149

4 501

5 698

6 714

7 409

8 98

9 358

10 836

11 108

12 22

13 927

Write 2 numbers that have each of these as their nearest ten.

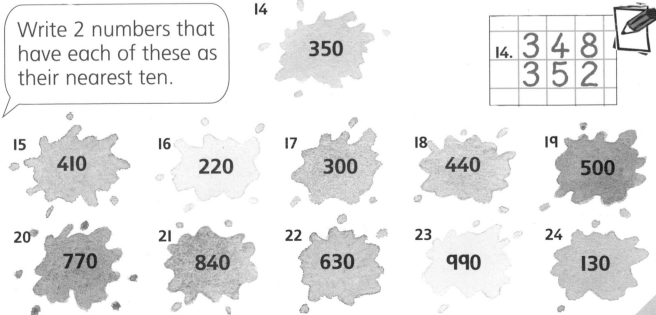

14 350

14. 3 4 8
    3 5 2

15 410

16 220

17 300

18 440

19 500

20 770

21 840

22 630

23 990

24 130

Nearest ten

Write the number to match each set of coins.

Round the number to its nearest ten.

1

1.	3	4	2	p
	3	4	0	p

2

3

4

5

6

7

8

9

Draw a grid like this. Write 480 in the middle.

Write 8 numbers that have 480 as their nearest ten.

Do the same for the other numbers.

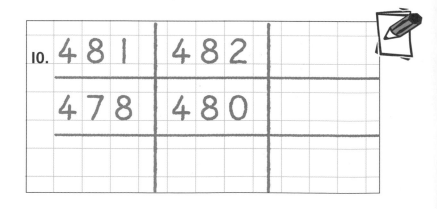

10.	481	482	
	478	480	

10 480   **11** 610   **12** 980

13 200   **14** 340   **15** 520

16

Nearest ten

Write which cars have the blue garage number as their nearest ten.

Do the same for the pink, red and yellow garages.

Blue 5 0 8

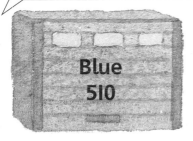
Blue 510

497

Pink 570

534

502

525

495

573

569

565

508

516

Red 530

505

528

Yellow 500

Explore

How many numbers have 500 as their nearest ten?

As their nearest hundred?

17

Counting on

15 16 17 18 19 20 21 22 23 24 25 26 27 28 29 30 31 32 33

Copy and complete.

Use the number track and your fingers to help.

1 16 + 5 = 21

1. 16 + 5 = 21

2 17 + 4 = 21

3 18 + 6 =

4 15 + 6 =

5 20 + 4 =

6 23 + 5 =

7 19 + 6 =

8 19 + 8 =

9 22 + 7 =

10 24 + 9 =

11 16 + 8 =

Each child scores 5 more.

Write the new scores.

12

Score 19

12. 19 + 5 = 24

13

Score 24

14

Score 26

15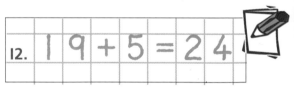

Score 18

16

Score 23

17

Score 21

18

Score 17

18

Adding to 20

Write how many more cubes you need to make 20.

1

I. $13 + 7 = 20$

2

3

4

5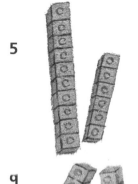

6

7

8

9

| 0 + 10 | 1 + 9 | 2 + 8 | 3 + 7 | 4 + 6 | 5 + 5 | = 10 |

Write the missing numbers.

10 $3 +$ $= 20$

10. $3 + 17 = 20$

11 $1 +$ = 20

12 $4 +$ = 20

13 $6 +$ = 20

14 $2 +$ = 20

15 $5 +$ = 20

16 $7 +$ = 20

Use the number facts to help you.

17 $10 +$ = 20

18 $8 +$ = 20

19

Adding to 20

Addition N5

There are 20 rabbits in each group.

Write how many are in the burrow.

1

I. $3 + 17 = 20$

2

3

4

5

6

7

8

9

10

Write how many beads you need to make 20.

11

II. $14 + 6 = 20$

12

13

14

15

16

17

20

Adding to 20

Write the numbers to make 20.

1

1. $18 + 2 = 20$

2  10

3  15

4 12

5 13

6 8

7 7

8 1

9 4

10 1 ... 17

10. $1 + 2 + 17 = 20$

11 2 ... 5

12 4 ... 10

13 7 ... 3

14 6 ... 2

15 0 ... 10

16 1 ... 11

17 3 ... 3

18 13 ... 4

19 15 ... 4

Explore

Use number cards 0 to 20.

Make pairs which add to 20.
How many can you find?

Make pairs that add to other numbers: 15, 18, …

7 13 11 9

Adding several numbers

> Copy and complete.

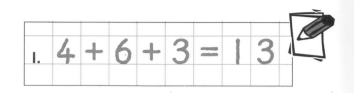

I. $4 + 6 + 3 = 13$

> Look for
> tens first.

1 $4 + 6 + 3 =$ 2 $7 + 8 + 3 =$

3 $5 + 6 + 5 =$ 4 $8 + 8 + 2 =$

5 $9 + 7 + 1 =$ 6 $10 + 10 + 5 =$ 7 $5 + 8 + 2 =$

8 $6 + 6 + 4 =$ 9 $1 + 9 + 1 =$ 10 $3 + 3 + 7 =$

> Copy and complete
> the table.

11

+	5	7	3	12	9	8	10	4	6	11
9	14	16								

> Add 9 by adding 10
> and taking 1 away.

> Copy and
> complete.

12 $24 + 9 =$

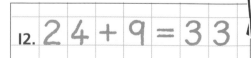

12. $24 + 9 = 33$

13 $14 + 9 =$ 14 $15 + 9 =$ 15 $17 + 9 =$

16 $28 + 9 =$ 17 $29 + 9 =$ 18 $36 + 9 =$

19 $18 + 9 =$ 20 $25 + 9 =$ 21 $21 + 9 =$

Adding several numbers

> Choose any 3 chains and write their lengths.

> Add them and write the total.

> Write 6 different additions.

←— 3 cm —→

$$6\,cm + 4\,cm + 5\,cm = 15\,cm$$

← 1 cm ►

←— 4 cm —→

←————— 7 cm —————→

←——— 5 cm ———→

← 2 cm ►

←——— 6 cm ———→

←——— 9 cm ———→

←——— 8 cm ———→

At Home

Try this trick on a friend.
Ask them to think of a number between 1 and 20 (not telling you what it is).

Point to each star, in turn, asking them if their number is in that star.

Add the centre numbers of all the stars that contain your friend's number.
The total is their number!

Adding several numbers

> Copy and complete.

1　$6 + 8 + 4 =$

 1. $6 + 8 + 4 = 18$

2　$17 + 9 + 5 =$　　3　$9 + 1 + 9 =$

> Look for tens first.

4　$6 + 7 + 2 + 3 =$　　5　$7 + 6 + 4 =$

6　$12 + 9 + 2 =$　　7　$13 + 9 + 6 =$

8　$2 + 9 + 8 =$　　9　$9 + 2 + 6 + 1 =$

> Add 9 by adding 10 and taking 1 away.

10　$4 + 1 + 6 + 9 =$　　11　$9 + 3 + 7 =$

> Choose 1 monster of each colour and write their prices.

> Add them and write the total.

> Write 6 different additions.

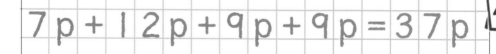 $7p + 12p + 9p + 9p = 37p$

7p

12p

11p

9p

8p

12p

9p

6p

4p

2p

9p

3p

Adding several numbers

Choose any 3 items and write their prices.

$8p + 9p + 6p = 23p$

Add them and write the total.

Write 10 different additions.

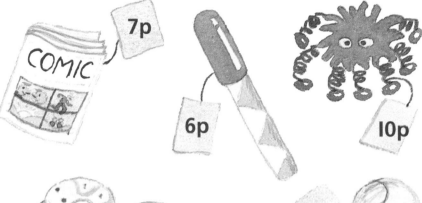

7p

COMIC

6p

10p

14p

5p

4p

9p

9p

13p

COMIC

9p

7p

8p

COMIC

Explore

Add all the numbers from 1 to 10.
Guess first.

2   5   6   10   8   9   3   7   4   1

Write how many cubes.

1

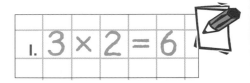
1. $3 \times 2 = 6$

2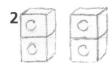

3

4

5

6

7

8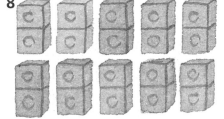

9

10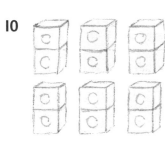

Copy and continue the lines of numbers.

2, 4, 6, 8,

2 4 6 14 20

10 12 18 30

Twos

Copy and complete.   1 × 2 =

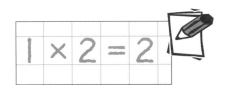

2 × 2 =   3 × 2 =   4 × 2 =

5 × 2 =   6 × 2 =   7 × 2 =

8 × 2 =   9 × 2 =   10 × 2 =

Write how many eyes in each picture.

1

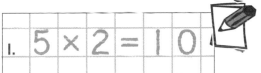

2

3

4

5

6

7

8

9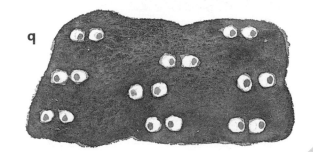

Twos

Write how many socks in each box.

1
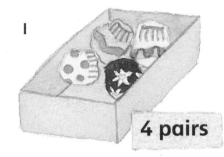

4 pairs

I. $4 \times 2 = 8$

2
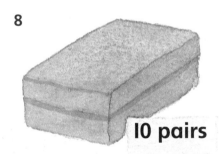

3 pairs

3
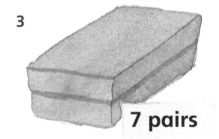

7 pairs

4

6 pairs

5
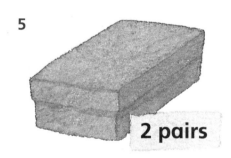

2 pairs

6
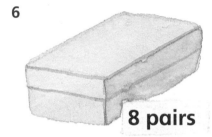

8 pairs

7
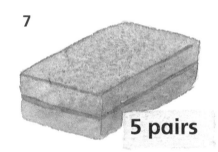

5 pairs

8

10 pairs

9
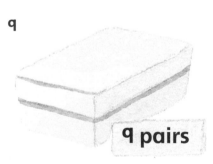

9 pairs

10
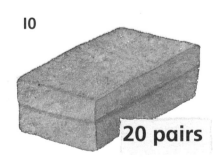

20 pairs

Explore

Copy and complete these grids.

Colour the numbers in the ×2 table (2, 4, 6, …).

Describe the patterns.

1	2	3	4
5	6	7	

1	2	3	4	5
	6	7		

Twos

Helen and Amit collect cans.

They get 2p for each can.

Write how much they get for each group.

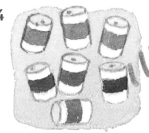

1. $4 \times 2p = 8p$

2.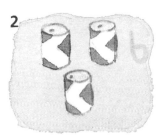

3.

4.

5.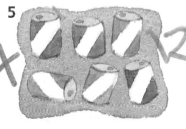

6.

7.

8.

9.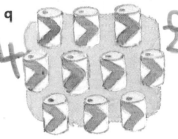

Amit spends his money on stickers.

Each sticker costs 2p.

Write how much he spends.

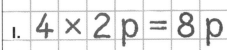

10. $3 \times 2p = 6p$

10	3 stickers		
11	6 stickers	12	4 stickers
13	7 stickers	14	2 stickers
15	10 stickers	16	5 stickers
17	9 stickers	18	8 stickers

Doubling

Darts in the green ring count double.

Write the score for each board.

I

Double 4 is the same as 4 × 2.

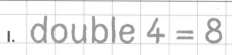

I. double 4 = 8

2

3

4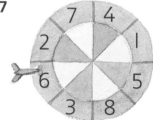

5

6

7

Copy and complete the table.

in	6	3	5
out	2		

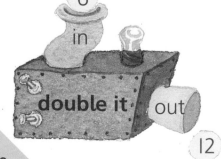

in	6	3	5	11	7	10	8	2	9	12	20
out											

Tens

> Copy and complete.

$1 \times 10 =$

$1 \times 10 = 10$

$2 \times 10 =$ $3 \times 10 =$ $4 \times 10 =$

$5 \times 10 =$ $6 \times 10 =$ $7 \times 10 =$

$8 \times 10 =$ $9 \times 10 =$ $10 \times 10 =$

> Score 10 points for each skittle knocked down.

1.

1. $6 \times 10 = 60$

2.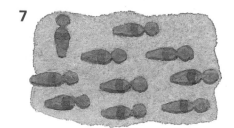

3.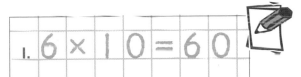

4.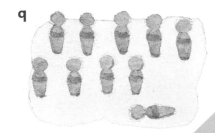

5.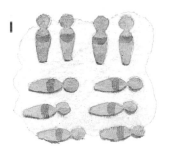

6.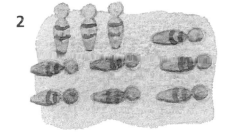

7.

8.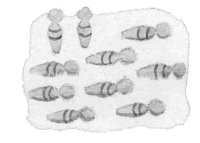

9.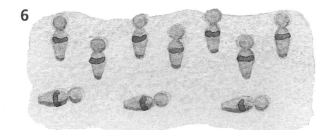

Fives

 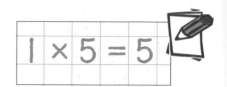

Copy and complete.

$1 \times 5 =$

$$1 \times 5 = 5$$

$2 \times 5 =$ $3 \times 5 =$ $4 \times 5 =$

$5 \times 5 =$ $6 \times 5 =$ $7 \times 5 =$

$8 \times 5 =$ $9 \times 5 =$ $10 \times 5 =$

Write how many fingers are on each set of hands.

1

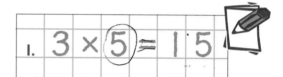
1. $3 \times 5 = 15$

2

3

4

5

6

7

8

9

Fives and tens

Score 10 for every red alien and 5 for every blue alien.

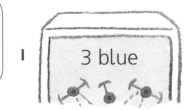

1 — 3 blue

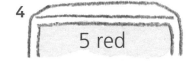

1. $3 \times 5 = 15$

2 — 7 red

3 — 8 blue

4 — 5 red

5 — 9 red

6 — 6 blue

7 — 5 blue

8 — 7 blue

9 — 9 blue

10 — 8 red

Explore

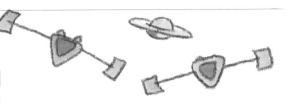

Yellow aliens are worth 2.
How many yellows do you need to match each red score above?

At Home

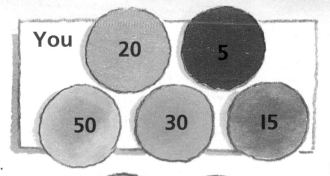

You 20, 5, 50, 30, 15

Take turns to throw a dice. Each spot on the dice is worth 5 or 10 (you choose).

So a throw of 3 is worth 15 or 30. If the score matches one of your circles, cover it with a counter (or coin).

The winner is the first to cover all their circles.

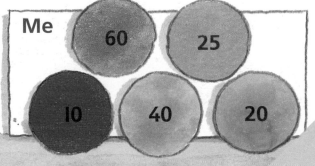

Me 60, 25, 10, 40, 20

33

Multiplying

Write how many stamps in each set.

1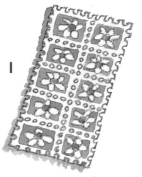

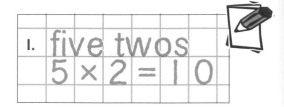
1. five twos
$5 \times 2 = 10$

2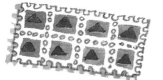

3

4

5

6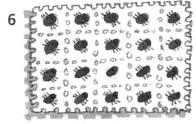

7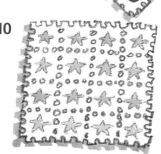

8

9

10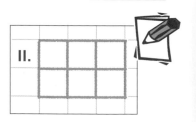

Draw sets of stamps for these.

11   2×3

II.

12   3×6 13 4×5 14 2×6 15 1×8

16   5×3 17 2×4 18 7×2 19 5×6

34

Multiplying

Write how many pegs are in each board.

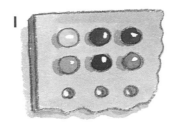

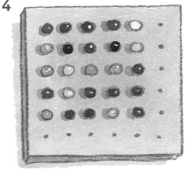

1. two threes
   $2 \times 3 = 6$

2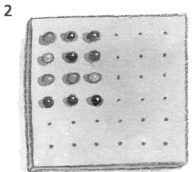

3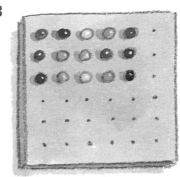

4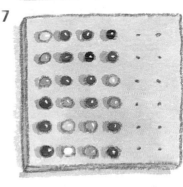

5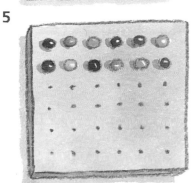

6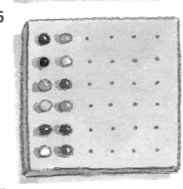

7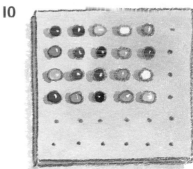

8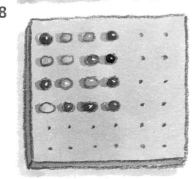

9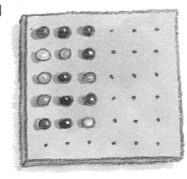

10

 **Explore**

For each peg board above write 2 multiplications.

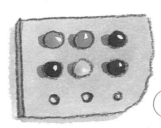

Two rows of three
$2 \times 3 = 6$

Three columns of two
$3 \times 2 = 6$

Multiplying

Copy and complete the multiplication table.

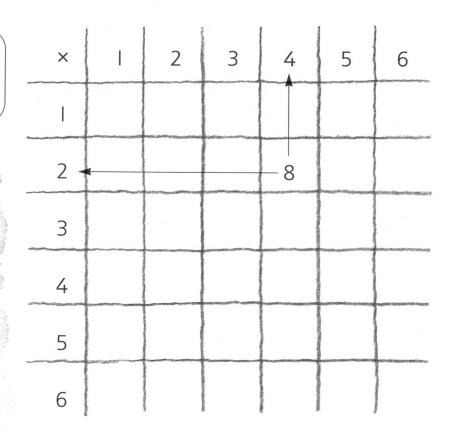

×	1	2	3	4	5	6
1						
2				8		
3						
4						
5						
6						

Use counters to help you.

$2 \times 4 = 8$

Explore

How many times does each number appear in the table?

Which numbers appear most?
Which numbers up to 36 don't appear?

Copy and complete.

×	3	4	5	6
1				
2				
3				
4				

×	5	2	6	3
1				
3				
4				
6				

Multiplying

wash window 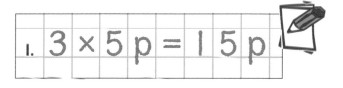 5p	feed cat 3p
wash car 10p	empty bin 2p
walk dog 6p	

Annie and Jo do lots of jobs.

Write how much they earn.

I wash 3 windows

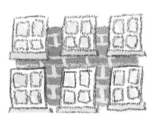

I. $3 \times 5p = 15p$

2 wash 4 cars

3 wash 4 windows

4 feed 3 cats

5 walk 6 dogs

6 empty 10 bins

7 wash 7 cars

8 wash 6 windows

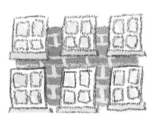

9 empty 3 bins

Explore

Use squared paper.
Cut out different rectangles,
each with 12 squares.

The next ten

Add to each red number to make the next ten.

1	1	2	3	4	5	**6**	7	8	9	10
2	11	12	13	14	15	16	17	18	**19**	20
3	21	22	23	24	25	26	27	**28**	29	30
4	31	32	**33**	34	35	36	37	38	39	40
5	41	**42**	43	44	45	46	47	48	49	50
6	51	52	53	54	55	**56**	57	58	59	60
7	61	62	63	**64**	65	66	67	68	69	70
8	**71**	72	73	74	75	76	77	78	79	80
9	81	82	83	84	85	86	**87**	88	89	90
10	91	92	93	94	**95**	96	97	98	99	100

1. $6 + 4 = 10$

2. $19 + 1 = 20$

Add to each number to make the next ten.

11.

$$10 \quad 16 \quad 20 \quad 30$$

11. $16 + 4 = 20$

12.

$$0 \quad 7 \quad 10 \quad 14 \quad 20$$

13.

$$10 \quad 14 \quad 20 \quad 26 \quad 30$$

14.

$$30 \quad 32 \quad 40 \quad 47 \quad 50$$

15.

$$40 \quad 45 \quad 50 \quad 58 \quad 60$$

16.

$$60 \quad 70 \quad 80$$

17.

$$20 \quad 30 \quad 40$$

The next ten

> Add to each pile to make the next 10p.

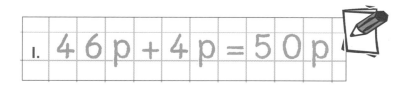

1. $46p + 4p = 50p$

1

2

3

4

5

6

7

8

9

> How many more pages to the next ten?

10

10. $27 + 3 = 30$

11

12

13

14

15

16

39

Change

> Write how much change you will have.

I. $24p + 6p = 30p$

6p   change

1 24p 10p

2 33p 10p

> Use coins to help you.

3 46p 10p

4 19p 10p

5 35p 10p

6 24p 10p

7 28p 10p

8 52p 10p

Explore

Use number cards 4, 7, 3, 8.

Make different
2-digit numbers.
Add to each to
make the next ten.

$38 + 2 = 40$

3 8
4
7

The next ten

How many more kilometres to the next ten?

I. $35\ km + 5\ km = 40\ km$

5 km

1
35 km

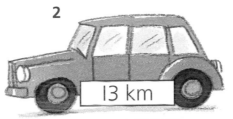
2
13 km

3
52 km

4
28 km

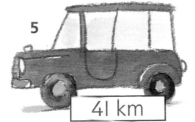
5
41 km

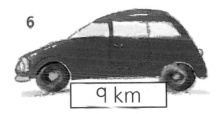
6
9 km

7
85 km

8
107 km

9
79 km

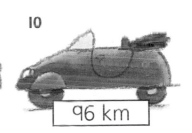
10
96 km

Write the missing numbers.

11  $+ 4 = 20$

II. $16 + 4 = 20$

12  $+ 3 = 20$

13  $+ 8 = 20$

14  $+ 5 = 10$

15 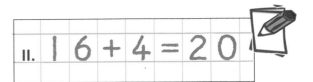 $+ 4 = 100$

16 $+ 6 = 40$

17 $+ 2 = 30$

Which numbers add together to make 10?

Copy and continue the lines of numbers.

Add 10 each time.

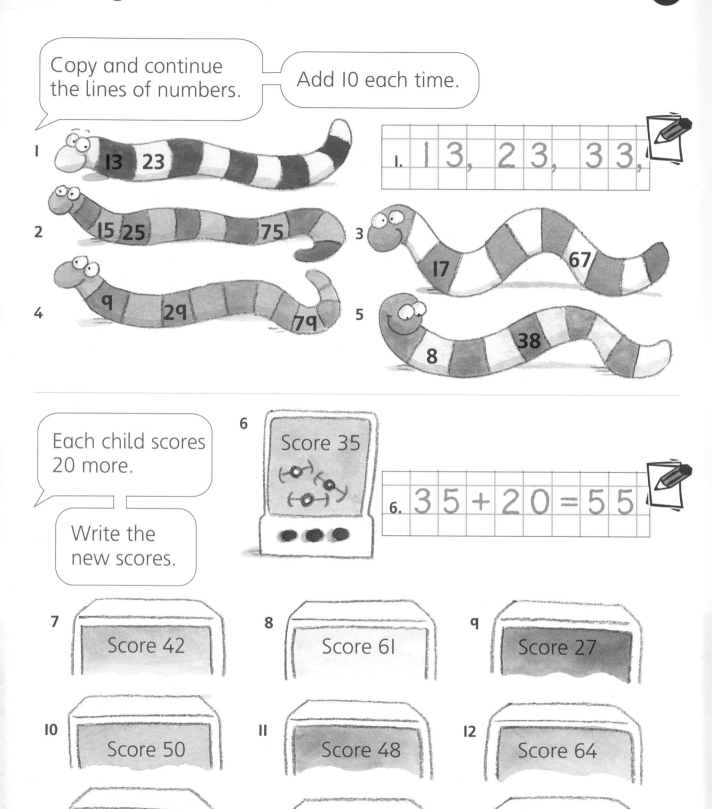

1. **13 23**

1. 13, 23, 33,

2. **15 25 75**

3. **17 67**

4. **9 29 79**

5. **8 38**

Each child scores 20 more.

Write the new scores.

6. Score 35

6. 35 + 20 = 55

7. Score 42

8. Score 61

9. Score 27

10. Score 50

11. Score 48

12. Score 64

13. Score 22

14. Score 53

15. Score 36

Each item has gone up by 30p.

Write the new prices.

1. $61p + 30p = 91p$

1

61p

2 29p

3 7p
Choco

4 18p

5 Juice
Juice 56p

6 CRISPS 42p

7 Biscuits 35p

8 Soup 28p

9 Pasta 93p

At Home

You need four 10p coins, a cup, a dice, paper and pencil. Each throw the dice and write your number.

Take turns to tip 4 coins out of the cup. Count how many are tails. Add that number of tens to your dice number.

Continue until someone goes over 100. Play 3 times. Who wins overall?

Adding 10, 20, 30, …

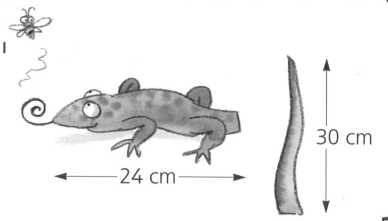

The lizards have lost their tails.

Each tail was 30 cm.

Write the length of each lizard before it lost its tail.

1. $24 \text{ cm} + 30 \text{ cm} = 54 \text{ cm}$

2. 32 cm

3. 36 cm

4. 29 cm

5. 45 cm

6. 40 cm

7. 34 cm

Explore

Throw 2 dice to make a 2-digit number.

Add 10, 20, 30 or 40 to make the nearest number you can to 60.

Make 10 numbers.

$54 + 10 = 64$
$42 + 20 = 62$
$26 + 30 = 56$

Adding 10, 20, 30, …

Write each score.

1.

2.

3.

4.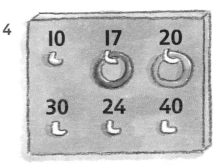

5.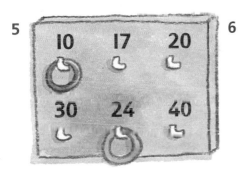

6.

7.

Each balloon goes up 40 metres.

Write the new heights.

8. $41m + 40m = 81m$

8. 41 m

9. 56 m

10. 20 m

11. 63 m

12. 70 m

13. 38 m

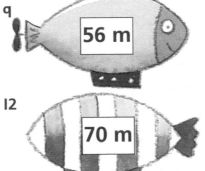

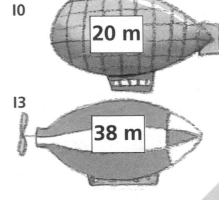

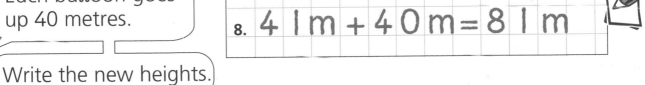

45

Adding 11, 12, 13, …

Continue adding 10 to each line.

Stop when you go over 100.

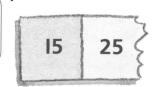

1

1. 15, 25, 35,

2 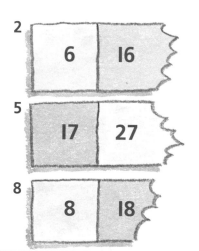 6 | 16

3 1 | 11

4 9 | 19

5 17 | 27

6 2 | 12

7 26 | 36

8 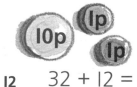 8 | 18

9 3 | 13

10 14 | 24

Copy and complete.

11 25 + 14 =

II. 25 + 14 = 39

12 32 + 12 =

13 46 + 11 =

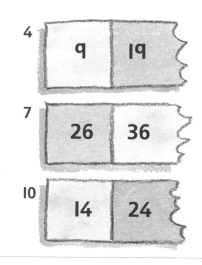

14 43 + 15 =

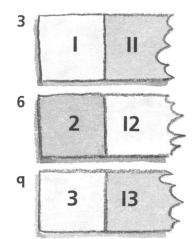

15 32 + 16 =

16 28 + 11 =

17 25 + 14 =

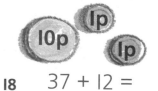

18 37 + 12 =

19 36 + 13 =

20 55 + 14 =

Adding 11, 12, 13, ...

All these items have gone up by 12p. Write the new prices.

1. $36p + 12p = 48p$

1 36p

2 43p

3 48p

4 35p

5 28p

6 62p

7 37p

8 49p

15p is added to each purse. Write the new totals.

9 10p 1p 1p 1p 1p 1p

10 1p 1p 1p 1p

11 10p 10p 1p 10p 10p 1p 1p 1p

12 10p 10p 1p 1p 1p 1p

13 10p 10p 10p 10p 1p 10p 1p

14 1p 1p 10p 10p

15 10p 10p 1p 10p 1p 1p 1p 1p

16 1p 10p 1p 1p

Adding two numbers

 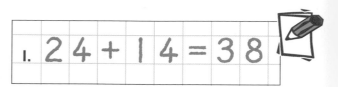

Copy and complete.

1 24 + 14 =

1. $24 + 14 = 38$

2 32 + 16 =

3 35 + 12 =

Use your fingers or coins to help you.

4 43 + 15 =

5 62 + 17 =

6 25 + 15 =

7 31 + 18 =

8 44 + 15 =

9 50 + 19 =

10 53 + 13 =

11 47 + 11 =

Add each circle to each square.

Write 12 additions.

$34 + 12 = 46$

12   26   34   14   45   13   53

Explore

You need a set of dominoes.

Use the dominoes as 2-digit numbers. Add two together.

Make different additions.

$61 + 13 = 74$

48

Adding two numbers

Use these 4 numbers to make additions.

One number should always begin with I.

Write all the additions.

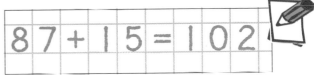

$$87 + 15 = 102$$

 **Explore**

Here is an addition triangle.

The total goes in the middle.

This is always a 2-digit number.

This is always 10.

This is always a 1-digit number.

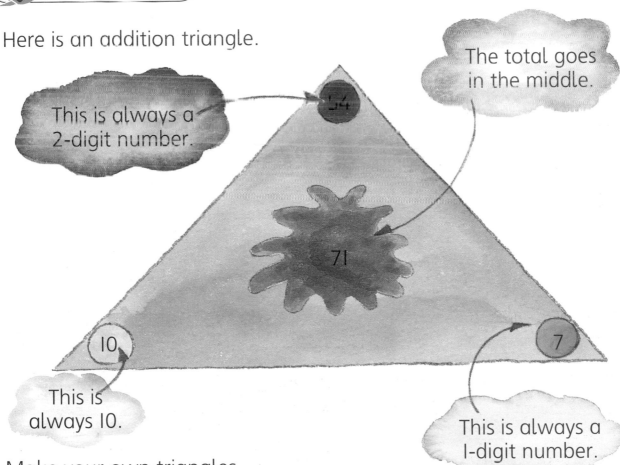

Make your own triangles.
Can you get a total of exactly 100?

Differences

Write the difference between each set of cubes.

1

1. d = 1 1

2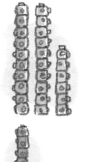

3

4

5

6

7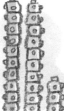

Write the difference between each pair of numbers.

8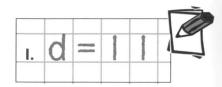

10 16 20 24 30

8. d = 8

9

0 5 10 16 20

10

0 10 11 17 20

11

10 18 20 26 30

12

10 12 20 28 30

13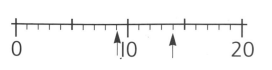

0 10 20

14

10 20 30

15

10 20 30

16

0 10 20

50

Differences

Anup
28p

Andrew
13p

Jan
9p

Mike
16p

Ruth
21p

Write the difference between each pair's pocket money.

1 Anup Ruth

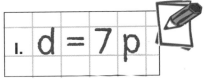
1. d = 7 p

2 Anup Andrew

3 Andrew Jan

4 Ruth Andrew

5 Mike Anup

6 Jan Mike

7 Anup Jan

8 Mike Ruth

9 Ruth Jan

10 Andrew Mike

Explore

Draw 4 stamps, each a different colour.

Write a different price on each.
Write the differences between pairs.

Differences

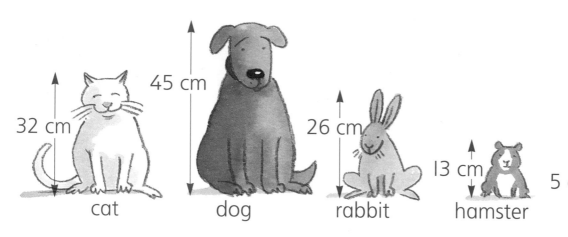

32 cm — cat

45 cm — dog

26 cm — rabbit

13 cm — hamster

5 cm — mouse

Write the difference in height between each pair.

1

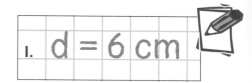
1. d = 6 cm

2

3

4

5

6

7

8

q

Explore

Measure the heights of 5 objects in centimetres.

Write the differences between pairs.

Differences

> Copy the difference tables.

> Write the difference between each pair of red and blue numbers.

	5	6	7	8	
5			2		
6	1				

	5	6	7	8	9
5					
6					
7					
8					
9					

	5	11	17	23
7				
13				
19				
25				

> How many times does each number appear in each table?

At Home

You will need some paper and about 20 coins.
Cut the paper into 20 small 'cards'.
Number the cards from 11 to 30.

Shuffle them and spread them out face down.
Choose to be 'even' or 'odd'.
Take one card each, and find the difference
between the two numbers.

If it is even, you collect a coin. If it is
odd your partner collects a coin.

Continue until someone
has 8 coins.

Counting back

| 15 | 16 | 17 | 18 | 19 | 20 | 21 | 22 | 23 | 24 | 25 | 26 | 27 | 28 | 29 | 30 |

Copy and complete.

1 $19 - 4 =$

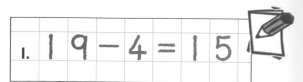
I. $19 - 4 = 15$

Use the number track and your fingers to help.

2 $23 - 4 =$

3 $25 - 6 =$

4 $28 - 3 =$

5 $29 - 7 =$

6 $30 - 5 =$

7 $25 - 4 =$

8 $24 - 8 =$

9 $26 - 7 =$

10 $30 - 2 =$

6p is spent from each purse.

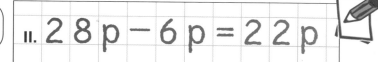
II. $28p - 6p = 22p$

Write how much is left.

11

12

13

14

15

16

54

Counting back in tens

> Count back in tens from each red number.

	11	
	21	
	31	

1. **31, 21, 11, 1**

	1	2	3	4	5	6	7	8	9	10
	1	2	3	4	5	6	7	8	9	10
	11	12	13	14	15	16	17	18	19	20
	21	22	23	24	25	26	27	28	29	30
	31	32	33	34	35	36	37	38	39	40
	41	42	43	44	45	46	47	48	49	50
	51	52	53	54	55	56	57	58	59	60
	61	62	63	64	65	66	67	68	69	70
	71	72	73	74	75	76	77	78	79	80
	81	82	83	84	85	86	87	88	89	90
	91	92	93	94	95	96	97	98	99	100

> Enter each number on a calculator.

> Press $-$ 1 0 $=$. Write the number.

> Continue taking away 10 until you reach a 1-digit number.

11. **23**

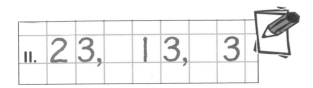

11. 23, 13, 3

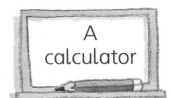

A calculator

12. **37**　13. **52**　14. **75**　15. **68**　16. **49**

Count back 4 tens from each number.

1
46

1. 36,   26,

2
58

3
67

4
54

5
93

6
61

7
87

8
75

9
49

Count the fingers. Count back that many tens.

10

10. 75,   65

11

12

13

14

15

16

17

18

19

Counting back in tens

Count back in tens along each train.

Write the hidden numbers.

1
67 · · · 37 27

I. 5 7, 4 7

2
67 57 · · · 27 17

3
76 66 · · · 26 16

4
83 73 · · · 43 33

5
92 82 · · · 42

6
95 85 75 · · · 15

7
88 78 · · · 18

8
84 74 64 · · · 14

Explore

Make up 5 of your own trains with hidden numbers.

Taking away 10, 20, 30

> Write how many cubes are left in each group.

1
take away 20

I. $42 - 20 = 22$

2
take away 10

3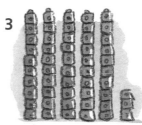
take away 30

4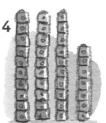
take away 20

5
take away 30

6
take away 10

7
take away 20

> Copy and complete.

8 $87 - 40 =$

8. $87 - 40 = 47$

9 $63 - 30 =$

10 $29 - 10 =$

11 $44 - 40 =$

12 $95 - 40 =$

13 $65 - 20 =$

14 $51 - 30 =$

15 $32 - 20 =$

16 $58 - 20 =$

17 $76 - 30 =$

Write the new prices.

1.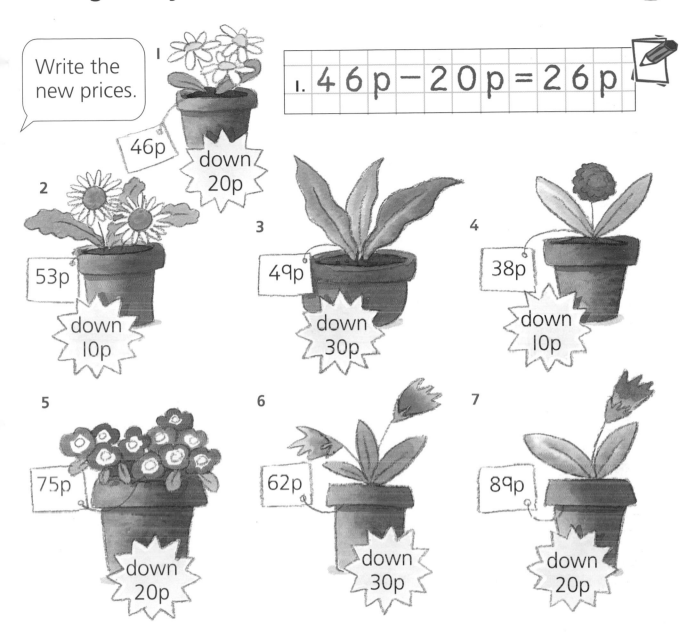

1. $46p - 20p = 26p$

46p

down 20p

2. 53p — down 10p

3. 49p — down 30p

4. 38p — down 10p

5. 75p — down 20p

6. 62p — down 30p

7. 89p — down 20p

At Home

Find the prices of 10 items.

Reduce each price by 10p, 20p or 30p, and write the new price.

Put the items in order from cheapest to dearest.

Write each clock time 20 minutes ago.

1

1. 3:28 → 3:08

2

3

4

5

6

7

8

9

10

11

12

13

Copy and complete the table.

in	42	57	73	
out	12			

take away 30

in	42	57	73	95	39	64	87	66
out								

Taking away 10, 20, 30

Take away:
10 seconds from the blue times.
20 seconds from the red times.
30 seconds from the yellow times.

1  `47s`

1. $47s - 10s = 37s$

2  `32s` **3**  `53s` **4**  `64s` **5**  `78s`

6 `57s` **7** `91s` **8** `24s` **9** `46s`

Write the missing numbers.

10 $- 20 = 42$

10. $62 - 20 = 42$

11  $- 10 = 31$ **12** $- 10 = 45$

13  $- 30 = 58$ **14** $- 30 = 67$

What leaves 42 when you take away 20? Try adding $42 + 20$.

15 $- 20 = 16$ **16** $- 10 = 74$

Odd and even

Count the balls in each set. Write odd or even.

1

1. 3 → odd

2

3

4

5

6

7

Write the next 5 even numbers.

8  40 42

8. 40, 42, 44, 46,

9 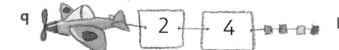 2 4

10 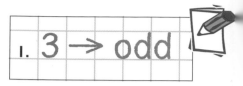 14 16

11  36 38

12 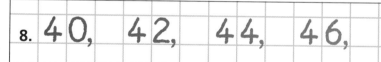 28 30

Write the next 5 odd numbers.

13 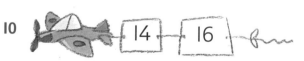 5 7

14  31 33

15  57 59

Odd and even

 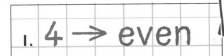

Count the sides
on each shape.
Write odd or even.

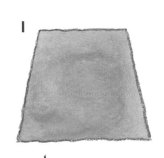

1. $4 \rightarrow$ even

1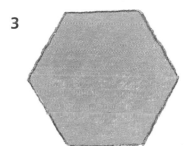

2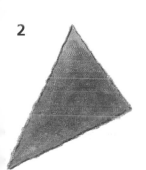

3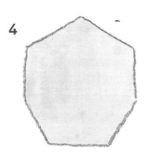

4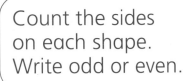

5

6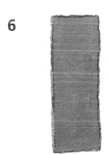

7

8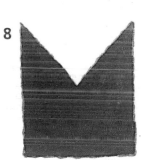

9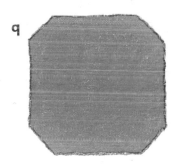

Explore

These numbers are in the × 3 table: 3, 6, 9, 12, ...
The pattern is: odd, even, odd, even, ...

Write more numbers in the × 3 table.
How does the pattern continue?

Explore odd and even patterns
in other times tables.

3   odd
6   even
9   odd
12   even
15

Odd and even

1

Write odd or even for each bus number.

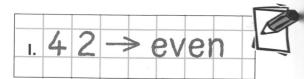

1. $42 \rightarrow$ even

2  16

3 57

4 130

5 459

6 2001

7 996

8 371

9 95

Write odd or even.

10 $3 + 7$

10. $3 + 7 = 10 \rightarrow$ even

11 $5 + 4$

12 $7 - 2$

13 $18 + 7$

14 3×2

15 $9 - 5$

16 $61 + 8$

17 3×4

18 $23 - 10$

19 2×5

20 $2 + 4 + 1$

Explore

Use number cards 3, 5, 2.
Make different 2-digit numbers.

How many are odd? How many are even?

Repeat with different cards.
Can you see any patterns?

Contents

How to use this book

Each page has a title telling you what it is about.

Instructions look like this. Always read these carefully before starting.

Sometimes you need materials to help you with the activity.

Sometimes there is a 'Hint' to help you.

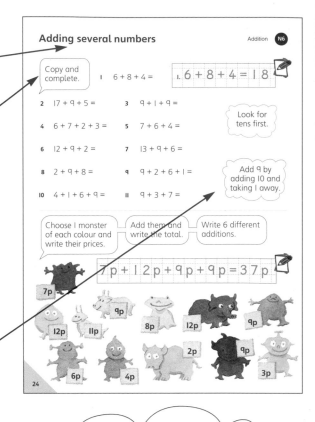

This shows you how to set out your work. The first question is usually done for you.

This shows that the activity is an 'Explore'. Work with a friend.

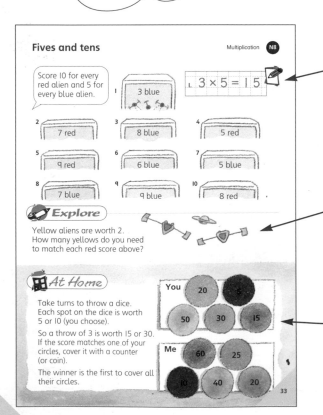

Some activities are meant to be taken home. Your teacher will tell you about these.

Tens and units

Write how much in each purse.

1

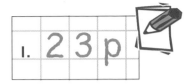
1. 2 3 p

2

3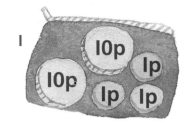

4

5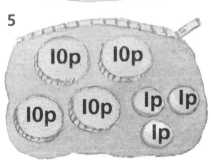

6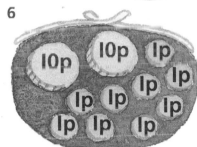

7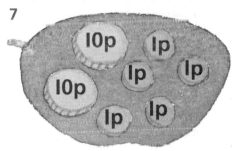

Add each pair of cards.

8 50   q

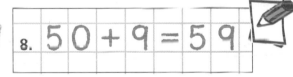
8. 5 0 + q = 5 q

q 60   8

10 70   3

11 30   4

12 10   2

13 20   2

14 40   1

15 80   q

16 q0   3

17 10   1

18 30   0

19 q0   q

20 50   5

3

Hundreds, tens and units

Write how many pence in each set.

1

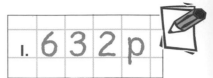

1. 6 3 2 p

2

3

4
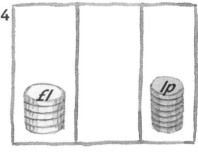

5

6

7
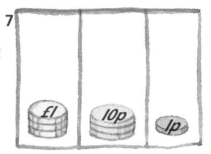

Write how many pence in each bank.

8

8. 2 3 4 p

9

10

11
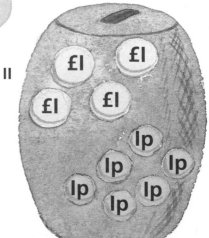

4